MISSING GIRLS

A totally gripping British crime mystery

BRIAN BATTISON

Detective Jim Ashworth Book 7

Originally published as
Jeopardy's Child

JOFFE BOOKS

Revised edition 2021
Joffe Books, London
www.joffebooks.com

First published by Constable in Great Britain in 1997
as *Jeopardy's Child*

Cover art by Nick Castle

ISBN: 978-1-78931-868-5

For Miles Huddleston
with much gratitude

PROLOGUE

'We need to go deeper,' the man rasped, in an agitated whisper. 'At least six feet . . . make sure nobody finds her.'

His companion merely grunted and once more stabbed the spade into the damp, cloying earth. Clouds scuttling across the moon's face suddenly thinned and an eerie glow cast their shadows to the far reaches of the huge field.

They laboured diligently, tossing the loose soil into a huge mound at the side of the makeshift grave. And all the while an owl hooted and noises of tiny nocturnal creatures scrambling busily along the hedgerows rang out loudly in the quiet of the night. Occasionally the diggers paused and strained their ears for human sounds while their protesting lungs hungrily pulled in air. But that ever-present fear of discovery determined that the length of their rest periods became increasingly shorter until the shovelling of the earth was almost frenzied.

Finally, their spades grated upon large fragments of rock and, satisfied with the depth of the hole, they heaved themselves out of it, staggering slightly as they stood at its rim and viewed the void that they had created. There was no need for discussion; both knew what had to be done. They snaked their way towards the gate, unperturbed by the fact that their shoes were sinking into the soft earth, leaving clean imprints of the soles. The operation had been meticulously planned and they were well aware that tomorrow the field would be tilled and left fallow for the winter. All evidence of the disturbed soil, all tell-tale signs of their presence would be destroyed by the churning blades of the plough.

In the quiet lane beyond the gate no vehicles passed while they hurried towards their car. It had been left in a small lay-by a hundred yards away, out of sight to any passers-by, a lifeless body in its boot.

The chill night air had already dried the sweat that caked their faces and bodies and it fogged their breath as they opened up the boot of the car. In the moon's pale glow, pleasure showed clearly on their faces when they lifted out the body encased in an old grey blanket. Ever vigilant for the sounds of approaching cars and the orange glare of headlights they hastened along the lane with their macabre bundle, but the field was reached without incident and the body deposited beside its newly dug grave.

They touched the body repeatedly with a tender reverence; the way one does when saying that final goodbye to a cherished loved one.

'Poor Nicky, she so wanted to please us and could never wait to be punished.'

'Yes, she was a good girl, but now she's gone we'll have to find someone else to play our games with.'

'We'd better be careful, though. I mean, we've buried three here in two years—'

'You worry too much. Remember, Nicky was the only one who lived locally. The police are still looking for her, aren't they? What's the problem?'

'Okay, so we'll take the next one from Birmingham, or London, maybe—'

'No.'

The word was spat out, and tenderness was now forgotten as the man callously kicked the pitiful body along the ground until it toppled into its final resting place, landing with limbs askew.

'But, where then?'

'There's a girl here that I want. She studies at St Giles's School, and I see her at Sunday school. She can never take her eyes off me. She wants me. She's the one.'

CHAPTER 1

Jan Morrison was driving home from the Maternity hospital after visiting her daughter. A grandmother at last. She was delighted, but even so her joy was marred for the happy event had brought home to her quite sharply the truth that she was now fifty-six years old. The fact that she only *felt* about thirty mattered little when a grandchild was forever there to remind her otherwise. The baby was beautiful, though, and it was the thought of his tiny, wrinkled face that kept a smile to her lips as she drove on.

Taking a short cut along the winding lanes on the outskirts of Bridgetown, with the barren fields of Anderson's Farm on her left, Jan slowed to take a bend and it was then that she caught sight of a man in the arc of her headlights. He was perhaps a hundred yards away and was in the act of climbing a gate when the lights swept over him. He froze at first with one leg straddling the top bar, his mouth falling open in surprise, and then a shadowy figure pulled him back into the field and the two shapes vanished behind the hedgerows.

Jan increased her speed, anxious to get past the spot, but she soon relaxed after checking the rear-view mirror and finding no strange creatures of the night or axe-wielding maniacs following in pursuit.

'A couple of poachers after pheasants,' she muttered. 'Or a courting couple, perhaps.'

Always an avid fan of *Crimewatch*, Jan wondered what she could do if it came to light that something terrible had happened in that field. What could she tell the police? Or better still, what could she relate to that dishy Nick Ross? Not much had stayed in her mind, but she was certain that the man climbing the gate was wearing a black jersey over a white shirt. He was caked in mud, carrying what looked like a spade, and he definitely looked shifty. Perhaps she should phone the police. Yes, why not? As soon as she got home.

* * *

Next morning, the thoughts of Chief Inspector Jim Ashworth were centred on the disappearance of eight-year-old Nicky Waldon as he drove past the field where she was buried. A dawn start by the ploughman had already covered all traces of the freshly dug grave, but of course Ashworth was totally unaware of that as he waved cheerily at the innocent partner in crime.

The chief inspector was a large man, six foot two and thirteen stone, but exercise and a careful diet had kept him fitter in his mid-fifties than most men half his age. In fact, the grey that was beginning to pepper his thick black hair was all that betrayed his years.

He handled his Ford Scorpio with a great deal of skill in the narrow winding lanes which soon gave way to the outer fringes of Bridgetown; and a frown creased his brow as he viewed the modern housing estates all around. That frown remained firmly fixed until he reached the town centre with its old cottages that had made up the original village and that were now tastefully converted into shops and banks.

His mind was still on Nicky Waldon. The girl had literally disappeared into thin air three months ago. Extensive searches of the surrounding countryside made by the police and hundreds of members of the public produced nothing.

The television appeals by Nicky's distraught parents provoked not one response. Canals, lakes and rivers had all been scoured by police frogmen, but to no avail. Nicky, it seemed, had vanished without trace.

The case was still open and on file, as all unsolved cases were, but for Ashworth at least it was not locked away in some metal filing cabinet, it was forever at the corner of his mind.

Deep in his heart, he knew that the child was dead. A scowl darkened his face at the thought and it deepened instantly as his gaze fell upon the police station building; his loathing for that glass monstrosity was well known and often voiced. With a resigned sigh, Ashworth parked the car and bounded up the station steps.

* * *

Amy Byron was a pretty girl and as precocious as any other eight-year-old. With nothing on her mind but that afternoon's hockey match, she pulled on the grey large-brimmed hat which matched the rest of her school uniform and gazed into the hall mirror to check her appearance.

Her parents had saved hard and had forgone many luxuries to put Amy through private school, but already their sacrifices were beginning to pay dividends. She was a bright girl who excelled at everything and was invariably top of her class in most subjects.

Her mother bustled into the hall and grabbed her car keys from the table. 'Are you ready, darling? If the traffic's bad, we'll be late.'

'All ready, Mum,' Amy replied cheerfully.

Outside, in the drive, Jilly Byron let her daughter into their ten-year-old Metro and set off in the direction of the school, quite unmindful of a small light grey car which immediately pulled in behind them. It had been following the Metro for over a week but Mrs Byron had never noticed. She hated driving in the heavy traffic and was always quite stressed when they reached the school a little over two miles away.

The bells were ringing out and the teachers were already shepherding the children into the school building when they approached. As always, the main road had cars parked on either side and was heavily congested with traffic, forcing Mrs Byron to pull into a vacant space quite a way from the school's main entrance. Ever since the disappearance of Nicky Waldon she had made a point of walking Amy to the school grounds, but the worry was beginning to fade with time — and she had so much shopping to do, bills to pay, the evening meal to prepare . . .

'Be careful, darling,' she said, kissing her daughter's cheek. 'I'll pick you up at four.'

Amy rewarded her with a broad grin then scrambled out of her seat with youthful enthusiasm, hoisted her satchel over her shoulder and skipped away. Just then a car horn blared out and made Mrs Byron jump. She swivelled around nervously to find a Ford Granada parked alongside.

'Are you pulling out?' the male driver mouthed.

She nodded and slipped the car into first gear while the Granada reversed, ready to pull into the space. When she glanced back she saw that a car had stopped at the kerb fifty yards away, and that the driver had opened the passenger door and was leaning over and talking to her daughter.

'No, Amy, no,' Mrs Byron yelled.

The engine stalled as she took her foot off the clutch and reached for the door handle. Amy was moving closer to the car. Only her head and feet were visible now; the rest of her body was hidden by the open passenger door.

Mrs Byron bolted from the Metro, screaming, 'Amy, don't get into the car.' But her voice was drowned out by the traffic noise as she hurtled towards her daughter. Then she stumbled and fell heavily, but quickly regained her footing.

'Don't get into the car,' she bellowed at the top of her voice as she kept on running and stumbling and pushing startled on-lookers out of her path.

CHAPTER 2

Detective Sergeant Holly Bedford took the call. With the receiver trapped between her ear and shoulder, distorting her features somewhat, she scribbled urgently on her notepad. But even that awkward pose could not disguise the fact that Holly was indeed a good-looking woman.

She was twenty-eight, with huge green eyes and short dark hair, and her expert make-up lent her an almost angelic appearance which was wholly deceptive. Holly was in fact rather promiscuous, rapidly moving from one lover to the next and always declaring that the latest would most definitely be the last. Her curvaceous body was perfectly proportioned for her five feet ten inches, and not only could it attract men but it could very quickly repulse them if necessary, for Holly was highly trained in the martial arts.

'Okay, Gordon, thanks for letting me know, we'll handle it,' she said into the mouthpiece. The receiver was dropped into its cradle. 'That was central control. It seems a man tried to pick up a young girl outside the church school.'

Detective Constable Josh Abraham glanced up from the computer screen.

'What stopped him, then?'

'The girl's mother got to the car in time and he drove off.'

'Did she get the registration number?'

'No,' Holly said, tapping her pen thoughtfully on the desktop. 'She said the plate was covered in mud, but the car was a light grey colour.'

Josh gave a sarcastic snort. 'Well, that shouldn't be too hard to find, then.'

'Oh, come on, Josh, you know damn well that lots of parents out there are very nervous since Nicky Waldon disappeared.'

'I know,' he muttered, turning back to the computer. 'But how many reports have we had like this one in the past few months? And they've all turned out to be false alarms.'

Holly studied his broad back and smiled fondly. Josh was tall, well built, and exceptionally good-looking. Since working at the station he had broken many female hearts, his homosexuality making him unattainable. He was blessed with a calm, down-to-earth approach to life which effectively counterbalanced the volatile natures of both Holly and his chief inspector.

'Jan Morrison's been on to central control again,' she said, her smile easing into a grin.

'Oh God, what's she reported this time?'

Before she could reply, Ashworth bustled into the office.

'Morning,' he said gruffly.

'Morning, guv,' they replied in unison.

'You've heard, I take it?' he said, settling at his desk.

'About the attempted abduction outside St Giles's School?' Holly queried.

'Yes, the signals we're getting are rather confused at the moment. So, I want you and Josh to go and see the head teacher, while I visit the girl and her parents. It could be another case of over-reaction, but at the same time there could be a tie-in with the disappearance of the other girl.'

Holly hid a mischievous grin. 'Your supergrass has made contact again, guv.'

'I know,' Ashworth muttered with a sigh. 'And before you start, I don't think for one minute that she fancies me.

Jan Morrison is just very public-spirited, that's all.' His tone was abrupt, but his eyes twinkled with good humour nevertheless. She was driving past Anderson's Farm last night, apparently, when she spotted a man, his clothes covered in mud, climbing over a gate. She thinks there was another man behind him and they were both carrying spades. Anyway, they ran back into the field when they saw her car and Mrs Morrison claims they both looked guilty. 'And,' he added, after a long-suffering pause, 'the man climbing the gate was wearing a high-necked dark jersey and a white shirt.'

Holly and Josh exchanged a glance, and both suppressed a laugh.

'Well, we shouldn't have any difficulty picking him up with that description,' Holly cut in.

'Don't mock,' Ashworth said gently. 'She said she spent a sleepless night, talking it over with her husband, trying to remember anything that might be of use to us.'

'She'll remember something, guv, it'll give her a chance to talk to you again.'

'Now, cut that out, Holly.' He shot her a baleful glare. 'But exactly what would these two men be doing in a field, covered in mud and carrying spades?'

'Don't plumb the depraved depths of her mind,' Josh said, glancing at his watch. 'It's only been an hour since I had breakfast.'

Holly pulled a face as they laughed and collected her shoulder bag *en route* to Josh's desk.

'Come on, lover,' she said, running her fingernails across the nape of his neck. 'Take me to meet the head teacher.'

Ashworth watched the inviting sway of her hips, which were neatly packaged in a well-tailored navy blue suit, as she left the office.

'That should be a meeting of great moralities,' he mused, when the door had closed behind them.

* * *

The Byrons' home was a large semi-detached on one of the estates surrounding Bridgetown, and when Ashworth stepped into the hall, he immediately sensed the love and security of a close-knit family unit.

Jilly Byron's face was pale and her hands were visibly shaking when she showed him into the comfortable lounge.

'This is my husband, Larry,' she said, returning straight away to her daughter. 'And this is Amy.'

Larry Byron rose from the settee. 'Thank you for coming, Chief Inspector, although undoubtedly you think we're wasting your time.'

'I think no such thing, sir,' Ashworth was quick to assure him. 'Recent events suggest that we should all be vigilant.'

'Please, sit down,' Mrs Byron fussed.

Ashworth lowered his bulk into an armchair, all the while smiling encouragingly at the little girl and beckoning for her to come to him.

'Now, Amy, would you like to tell me what happened, in your own words?'

She nodded, her nose wrinkled and her brow furrowed as she concentrated her thoughts. 'Well,' she finally said, 'the car door opened just as I was passing, and the man smiled at me.'

'Did he say anything?'

'He asked me if I went to St Giles's School, and I said yes. Then he said his daughter did, too, and he wondered if I'd give her some sandwiches she'd left in the car.'

'I was running towards Amy by that time,' her mother interjected. 'I was frantic because it looked as if she was about to get into the car.'

'Were you, Amy?' Ashworth asked.

The girl gave a firm shake of the head. 'I wasn't going to get in, but the man was holding the sandwiches and when I reached for them he sort of grabbed my arm. That's when Mum got to me.'

'I snatched her back pretty quick, Chief Inspector, and the man said he was sorry, he was only talking to her and hadn't meant to frighten me. He'd got the car engine running and seemed in a great hurry to close the door and drive off.'

'I see,' Ashworth murmured. 'Amy, can you tell me what the man looked like?'

She nodded enthusiastically. 'He was really old.' Realising that from a child's viewpoint such a description could fit anyone over the age of twenty-five, Ashworth smiled and glanced inquiringly at her mother.

'Mrs Byron, can you think of anything that might help us?'

'I don't know,' she said, her hands constantly fidgeting. 'He was wearing a cap . . . that's all that registered, really. All I could think about was getting Amy away from him.'

'I can understand that, of course. Now, can you remember anything about the car?'

'Nothing . . . I'm sorry,' she said, with a hopeless shrug.

'It's all right, don't worry.' He turned his attention back to Amy. 'I can see you're a very friendly little girl.'

She gave another spirited nod and favoured him with a beaming smile.

'But you must remember that nowadays you have to be very careful. I know it's difficult, but you must stay away from strangers.'

'That's what Mum and Dad are always telling me.'

'And you must listen to them. Unless you know somebody really well, don't trust them.'

He leant forward and touched her cheek, and his heart went out to the little girl when she wrapped her small fingers around his thumb.

'I don't know you,' she said, 'but I trust you.'

'Don't even trust a chief inspector in the police force,' he warned with mock severity.

Amy giggled. 'I like you, you're nice.'

'Thank you, but don't tell anybody,' he whispered, 'or you'll ruin my reputation.'

'If that's all,' Mrs Byron said, 'I'll take Amy into the kitchen and make her a milkshake.'

'Yes, I won't take up any more of your time,' Ashworth replied, getting to his feet. 'It's been nice meeting you, Amy.'

The girl repeatedly turned to grin at him as she followed her mother, and Ashworth felt an immense liking for the child.

'It's so difficult,' her father said, when they were at last alone. 'I mean, she's such a friendly, trusting kid, and it's a very narrow line between teaching her to be careful and making her frightened of everybody she meets.'

'Yes, I know, sir, but for the time being I'd rather she was frightened out of her wits, because the alternative doesn't bear thinking about.'

'Do you really think she was in danger this morning?'

'I shouldn't think so,' he lied, 'but for the moment we'll be watching all schools and advising parents to be extra vigilant where their children are concerned.'

Larry Byron visibly relaxed and gave Ashworth a relieved smile. 'Thank you for coming, Chief Inspector. I'll show you out.'

CHAPTER 3

Sergeant Dutton was manning reception back at the station and, as soon as Ashworth stepped through the doors, he signalled for him to come to the desk.

'Sorry, Jim, but He On High has been asking for you,' he said, pointing towards the ceiling.

Ashworth's sigh was deep and heartfelt. 'He'll just have to wait, Martin. Don't let on you've seen me.'

He On High was Superintendent John Newton, a stern disciplinarian who had recently taken over the helm at Bridgetown Police Station. Ashworth and the superintendent had crossed swords from day one, and although an uneasy peace had developed between them, Newton was still smarting from his apparent inability to make the chief inspector kowtow as all other officers did.

'Anything in the report about the attempted abduction?' Dutton asked, his bald head shining pink beneath the harsh fluorescent lighting.

'I think there might be, Martin.'

'That's a pity.'

A door banged loudly at the rear of the desk and Bobby Adams emerged, loaded down with files. The young constable had recently finished a short stint in CID and was eager to get back there. He smiled warmly at the sight of the chief inspector.

'Hello, guv. Oh, sorry, I suppose now I'm back in uniform I should be calling you sir.'

'Don't worry about it, Bobby.'

'There's no chance of a recall into CID, is there?' he asked hopefully.

Ashworth shook his head. 'Not at the moment, son. For the present I'm more interested in having as many uniforms as possible outside schools when the children come and go.'

'That's what Newton wants to see you about,' Dutton told him in a hushed tone. 'He thinks you're over-reacting to this morning's incident. He keeps muttering on about resources.'

'He would, wouldn't he?' Ashworth said, heading for the stairs. 'You haven't seen me — all right?'

* * *

He strode into CID to be met by a low sun streaming in through the glass walls. Shielding his eyes, he shook his head ruefully and sank into his chair.

Holly looked up. 'Guv, that story the man told Amy about his daughter going to the school doesn't hold water. The head teacher asked all the girls at assembly, and it seems none of their fathers dropped them off at school this morning.'

'I already knew it wasn't true, Holly. He'd have known by her uniform that she went to the school, so why ask if she did? No, that was just a ploy to start a conversation with her.' He paused for thought. 'Do you two think I'm over-reacting about this?'

'No, guv,' Josh said, picking up a file from beside the computer. 'When Nicky Waldon vanished, her abductor could have been a lorry driver just passing through, anybody like that. But if other kids are starting to be approached, that points to somebody living locally.'

'Yes, but it's only one child at the moment, hence the charge of over-reacting. Have we got the file on Nicky Waldon?'

'Here in my hand, guv,' Josh said, passing it across.

The chief inspector had no need to open it up in order to bring the facts to mind, but looking at the typed pages helped to put the events into chronological order. Even so, anger brought a tightness to his throat with every page he turned.

Nicky had vanished on Saturday 15 June. A young innocent girl popping out to the corner shop to buy an ice cream on a hot stuffy evening, never to be seen again. All those with a history of sexual assaults, especially to do with children, had been interviewed, but the inquiry had led them nowhere. However, two men in particular stayed in Ashworth's mind: Tom Gardiner and Gilbert Randall.

Gardiner was around sixty and lived with his wife in a rundown cottage on the edge of town. He had a string of convictions for minor assaults on young girls and it was suspected, but never proven, that Mrs Gardiner had taken part. Both were totally illiterate and undoubtedly evil but, if they chose, could come across as friendly and utterly harmless, especially to children.

Ashworth had speculated at the time that maybe Gardiner had snatched Nicky and then realised that letting her go would surely mean prison again and this time for a very long stretch. So, unable to face such a prospect, he and his wife had decided that the easiest way out would be to kill the girl and dispose of her body in the acres of farmland that surrounded their ramshackle home.

He had said as much to Superintendent Newton who smugly pointed out, after studying the man's form, that Gardiner's last conviction was over twenty years ago and abduction had never been part of his method. Ashworth had to concede both points, and it did seem that Gardiner was steering clear of trouble, vigorously so; nevertheless, the chief inspector found he could not wholly disregard the man.

Was his intuition pointing him in the right direction, yet again, or was Gardiner simply a convenient hook on which to hang a conviction? Ashworth had asked that question of himself countless times and was still in need of an answer. He shook his head as if to clear it.

Gilbert Randall, his other likely suspect, had one conviction for being in possession of a pornographic video featuring child sex and torture. Ashworth could see him clearly in his mind's eye. A small slight man in his forties, Randall had ginger hair and a hatchet face with a mouth that was permanently turned down at the corners. He was, in contrast to Gardiner, well-educated and articulate. He worked as head clerk in Bridgetown's largest bank and, although not sociable after hours, he did seem to mix well with his colleagues.

Randall had always claimed that the video came into his possession by mistake. He never denied that he knew it was pornographic but insisted in court that its title, *Young Girls*, was misleading; and he swore to the judge that he only became aware of its content on playing the tape.

The man's earnest tone and impeccable background almost entirely swayed the judge and Ashworth could still remember that awful sinking feeling in his stomach when sentence was read out. Twelve months' imprisonment suspended for two years. He felt a very strong dislike for Gilbert Randall and would take a perverse pleasure in turning up on his doorstep for further questioning.

He glanced up from the file to find Holly watching him closely, a pessimistic look in her eyes.

'Oh no, guv,' she said, shaking her head. 'Not the Gardiners.'

'Yes, I'm afraid so,' he said, chuckling. 'If you and Josh take Tom and his beloved wife, I'll take Mr Randall.'

* * *

Holly's rash driving style reflected her fiery temperament. Indeed, Josh always claimed that wherever he travelled in her car, he was always glad to arrive. But when Holly's Micra came to a screeching stop outside the Gardiners' homestead, he was ready to eat his words.

The cottage was set back behind a huge front garden filled with old cars and countless black rubbish sacks that had evidently found their permanent home given the thick creeping weeds growing over them. Adjacent to the cottage was a tumble-down barn with most of the slates missing from its roof. It would seem that Gardiner had little interest in home repairs.

As soon as they left the car four huge mongrel dogs came hurtling through the open kitchen door, barking and growling fiercely.

'Bloody hell,' Holly muttered as she locked the car. 'This is all I need.'

'Shut up, and get back in here,' Gardiner shouted to the dogs from within the cottage.

And then he appeared in the doorway, an old army greatcoat dwarfing his hunched frame and filthy khaki trousers tied around his knees with pieces of twine. His thin straggly grey hair was plastered over his head in a vain attempt to conceal the obvious fact that he was bald.

A furtiveness stole across his features when his gaze rested on the two detectives. But then his face broke into a sunny smile and he ambled down the rickety path towards the double gates shouting, 'Get in here,' to the growling dogs. He herded them back inside the house and moments later, with the vicious sounds muffled, Gardiner was once again on the threshold.

'Come on in,' he called. 'I've put them in the other room.'

'Let me do the talking,' Josh muttered as he opened the gates.

'Gladly,' Holly huffed.

Tom Gardiner offered them an expansive welcome when they stepped into his kitchen, a poky room which stank of dogs and stale cooking. Mrs Gardiner was washing up in the cracked enamel sink. She was a large woman, and her long unkempt grey hair and heavily lined face seemed to match perfectly her creased grey dress. She paused and viewed the detectives with distaste before allowing herself a smile.

'Look who's come to see us, Rose,' Gardiner said as he set about clearing two scruffy armchairs of old yellowing newspapers.

She gave a suspicious sniff. 'And what might they want?'

'They'll tell us in their own good time,' he said, laughing a little too loudly. 'We've got nothing to be scared of because we haven't done anything.' He indicated the armchairs.

'No thanks, Tom, I'll stand,' Josh said quickly. 'Sorry to disturb you, but we just wondered what you were doing with yourself these days.'

'I'm scrapping cars, Mr Abraham. Turning an honest penny, as they say. The enterprise economy, Europe and all that.'

Holly, who couldn't stomach the smell, had stayed by the door, and she turned to look at the cars littering the garden.

'That's great, Tom,' Josh said. 'Now, listen, we're really here because this morning somebody tried to abduct a young girl from outside the church school . . .'

Rose dropped the plate she was drying and it smashed on impact with the quarry-tiled floor. The unexpected noise set off the dogs in the next room and Holly's skin prickled at the sounds of savage barking and long vicious claws scratching roughly at the door.

'I told you, Tom,' Rose whined, as she stooped to pick up the pieces. 'The police will never leave you alone. They sit in that station plotting how to get you.'

'Don't go on, Rose,' Gardiner said. And then he aimed a hefty kick at the living room door. Noise from the dogs subsided instantly and there was a smile on his face when he turned back to Josh. 'Don't mind Rose, Mr Abraham, she thinks you've got it in for me.'

'They have, Tom, they'll never leave you alone.'

'Don't go on,' he snarled at the woman. 'What'll these officers think of us? They're only here because I did some daft things years ago and they have to eliminate me from their inquiries. Isn't that right, Mr Abraham?'

'Spot on, Tom. So, can you tell us where you were at around nine this morning?'

Gardiner flattened the grey hair across his head as he stood mulling over the question.

'Nine a.m.? I reckon I'd just started work about that time.'

'Can anybody vouch for that?' Holly asked.

'Rose can. She'd be clearing the breakfast things and she'd see me in the garden.

'That's right, Tom,' Rose said, her expression adamant. 'You'd just started work, I remember.'

'But no one else saw you? No other person saw you here at that time?' Holly persisted.

Gardiner's grin revealed a row of surprisingly clean teeth. 'I don't need anybody else to, do I, Miss Bedford?'

'Not for now,' Josh interjected. 'By the way, what car are you driving at the moment?'

'Whichever one comes in with an MOT and some tax on it,' he said, chuckling.

'And which one's that at the moment?' Holly snapped.

'Go easy,' Gardiner said. 'I reckon you got out the wrong side of the bed this morning. I know my rights, you know. I'm only helping you with your inquiries.'

Josh shot a withering look in Holly's direction, and said, 'It's all right, Tom, nobody's going to infringe your rights. Just tell us what car you're driving and the colour.'

'A Ford Capri, Mr Abraham. A white Ford Capri.'

'Great. Okay, do you mind if we take a look around? Just to make sure everything's in order?'

'No, of course I don't,' he said, leading them to the door. 'You don't need one of those search warrants with me, I've got nothing to hide.'

Outside Gardiner made a great show of pointing out the car to Josh, sidling up to him, being over-helpful, while Holly wandered off to look inside the barn. Rusting hinges grated as she pushed on the door and pigeons disturbed by the noise flew from the rafters, the flapping of their wings sounding strangely ominous in the quiet of the countryside. And there in the gloom stood a small grey Vauxhall Nova.

'Josh,' she called. 'Over here, quickly.'

Gardiner followed him across the garden, his long coat gaping open and billowing behind as he struggled to keep in step.

'Look,' Holly said, pointing to the car.

'Well, well, Tom, what have we got here?' Josh murmured, walking around the vehicle as Gardiner looked on nervously. 'How long have you had it?'

'About a week, I reckon. Why, there's nothing wrong with it, is there? It isn't stolen, or anything like that?'

'Does it go, Tom?'

'Well, I drove it here, but I reckon the battery'll be flat by now. Hold on, I've got the keys here somewhere.' He dug into the deep pockets of his coat and produced about twenty keys which he proceeded to sort through. 'I have to draw the shapes of the cars on the labels because I don't read too well. Ah, here you are, Mr Abraham, this is the one.'

Josh took the key and opened the driver's door. Holly waited long enough to hear that the battery was indeed flat and then wandered off towards the rear of the barn.

Gardiner seemed about to follow when Josh said, 'Lift the bonnet up, Tom, I'd like to look at the engine.'

Holly pushed open a door at the far end of the barn and found herself in a small room which at one time must have been the outside lavatory; another door to her right hid steps leading down to a small cellar. She glanced up to find the roof still intact but the walls black with damp.

'Thanks, Tom,' she heard Josh say. 'You've been a great help.'

'I'm always willing to cooperate with the police, Mr Abraham. Now I'd better find your mate before she gets lost. You'd never think a slip of a girl like that'd be in the police.'

Holly chose that moment to stroll back into the barn.

'Oh, there you are,' Gardiner said, clearly relieved. 'I was a bit concerned about you, Miss Bedford. There's a lot of rubbish back there, and I wouldn't want you to have an accident.'

'I'll bet,' she said, making no attempt to hide a sneer.

Tom Gardiner fawned and grovelled all the way to the gate, and by the time they were safely installed inside the Micra the dogs were loose in the garden again, growling and yapping as they followed the scents of the two strangers.

'Bloody dogs,' Holly exclaimed.

'Calm down,' Josh said, struggling into his seat belt. 'I think you offended old Tom in there.'

She glanced with disdain towards the cottage. 'They give me the creeps, Josh, the pair of them.'

'Neither of them is over-intelligent, Hol.'

'Oh, come on, they're both really cunning. That's all an act, Josh, that yes Mr Abraham, no Mr Abraham, whatever you say Mr Abraham. Try remembering that string of convictions Tom has for assaults on kids.'

'They were only minor, Hol. Tom and his old lady have the minds of children and those offences were harmless, like being at school — you show me yours and I'll show you mine.'

Holly grinned. 'Okay, I'll take you up on that. We'll pull into somewhere quiet on the way back and I'll convert you.'

Josh pulled a face which suggested that the prospect was hardly exciting, and Holly's grin turned into a raucous laugh.

* * *

Tom Gardiner stood at the kitchen window and watched until the car had pulled away.

'They've gone,' he told Rose. 'I wonder what they were talking about all that time.'

'They'll catch you, Tom. All those things we did years ago, they don't forget. You'll go inside for twenty years this time.'

'No, I won't, my little darling,' he said, smiling. 'They won't find anything out. I'm too clever for that lot.'

CHAPTER 4

'Oh God, no. What the hell do you want?'

Gilbert Randall was clearly far from overjoyed to find Ashworth installed on his front step.

'Good afternoon, Mr Randall,' he said cheerily. 'I wonder if I might come in and have a word?'

The man looked appalled and cast hasty glances up and down the road to check that none of his neighbours had witnessed the chief inspector's arrival.

'I suppose you'd better,' he said, his annoyance thinly disguised.

Ashworth stepped into the hall mouthing a silent protest at the ear-shattering blare of a television set coming from the room on his left.

'In there,' Randall muttered, nodding towards that very room as he closed the front door.

Ashworth viewed his surroundings with a critical eye. The room was long and narrow, with a large stone fireplace dominating one entire wall. The furnishings were tasteful and the carpet thick-piled and expensive. The huge television was installed in one corner and Ashworth almost winced at its volume.

'What do you want, then?' Randall demanded.

'I'm checking your whereabouts at around nine a.m. this morning, sir.'

The man made no attempt to turn off the television; indeed, he seemed impervious to its sound.

'For what reason?' he asked.

'Someone attempted to abduct a young girl at that time,' Ashworth said, his voice raised to compete with the inane laughter induced by an American sitcom.

'Jesus Christ,' Randall spat. 'When are you people ever going to leave me alone?'

'Just making inquiries, sir,' Ashworth said easily, as his ears picked up the slamming of the front door.

'In here, Gerald,' Randall called.

Ashworth turned to see a young man standing in the lounge doorway. He had blond hair and a mocking light in his clear blue eyes. He leant casually against the door surround, hands dug deep into the pockets of his blue jeans. Ashworth was quick to note that he wore a navy blue sweater over a white shirt.

'Sorry, Gilbert,' he said, a sly grin on his lips. 'I didn't know you had company.'

'This is definitely not company. He's the local fuzz.'

The man's eyes sparkled with humour. 'Ah, I see. The news is all over town that a young child was almost kidnapped—'

'And you find that amusing, do you?' Ashworth snapped.

'No, of course he doesn't,' Randall retorted. 'What's amusing Gerald is the fact that I had one lousy tape — by mistake, as you'll remember — and because of it you lot are going to hound me for the rest of my life.'

'You're running out of places to go,' his friend taunted. 'Even Russia and South Africa are far too civilised nowadays.'

Ashworth bristled. 'And who might you be?'

'He's Gerald Clark,' Randall informed him. 'A colleague from the bank. We're taking a week off to chill out.'

'Chill out?' Ashworth echoed.

Clark laughed. 'As in stay cool, relax, that sort of thing.'

'I see. Now, are you going to tell me where you were at nine this morning, Mr Randall?'

'Why not?' he replied easily. 'I was here with Gerald, and now I've answered your question I would like you to leave my property.'

'It'll be a pleasure, sir,' Ashworth said, already heading for the door. 'I'll see myself out.'

On the pavement, he turned back to look at the house. It was an ex-council detached with a small front garden. He could see the television flickering through the net curtain and could still hear it, even above the roar of traffic thundering along the expressway which snaked past the side of the house at first-floor level.

He kept his gaze fixed on the building for several moments, muttering under his breath while his thoughts raced. The distance between the television set and the outside wall seemed too wide — a good two feet, at least.

'No,' he murmured, shaking his head. 'These houses were well built, but no wall's that thick.'

* * *

Young Shannon Dixon lived on a large estate with a rough reputation to the north of Bridgetown. Many of the families living there were decent and law abiding, but the area contained the only housing available to the council and therefore it attracted more than its fair share of problem tenants.

The police did all they could to keep the crime level down but it was still a tough place, where a trouble-free life was guaranteed more by keeping in with the handful of villains than by any number of panda cars making their presence felt on the streets.

Shannon was only eight years old but had already learnt that it was far wiser to be one of the gang, for outsiders were savagely bullied. When Nicky Waldon disappeared the local kids thought up a new game called 'Chicken'. This involved crossing the deserted recreation ground, after dark and alone;

and those children who bottled out had their lives made a misery. Tonight it was Shannon's turn.

With Nicky's disappearance so far in the past she hadn't felt too worried about it, but throughout the day news of Amy's near abduction had spread by word of mouth across the estate, and now Shannon was frightened. Especially as Ryan Volkes, who lived four doors down, had said that anybody crossing the Rec with a nutter on the loose taking girls' knickers down would need a lot of bottle and then some.

Bravado, and that need to be accepted, ensured that Shannon was at the gates to the Rec at the required time. Most of the local kids were already there and the betting was that she wouldn't show. When they cheered and catcalled as she edged nervously into the arc of light created by the street lamps, a glow immediately settled upon the girl and helped to dispel her fears. All she had to do was get across the Rec and then she would be the star of the estate.

Urged on by the others, she walked those first few faltering steps. It would take her about twenty minutes to reach the other side where the rest of the gang would be waiting to make sure she completed the journey. The iron gates were behind her now and all that went through her mind was her mother's repeated warning. You be careful, she had said throughout the day, because there's a bloody pervert running about.

Shannon stopped and glanced back. The street lights were a long way off. Her stomach rolled and she swallowed hard as she carried on walking. Up ahead, huge trees with gnarled branches looked black and menacing against the night sky, and all around bushes rustled. She was totally engulfed by darkness now, and as she quickened her step Shannon began to tremble.

* * *

Ashworth and his wife, Sarah, walked their dog, a Jack Russell terrier called Peanuts, along the quiet country lanes close by their large four-bedroom detached house. It was a ritual they followed most evenings, during which they would tell each other about their day and generally relax.

Sarah was a handsome woman in her fifties who made no attempt to disguise the grey creeping into her hair, and had a liking for twin sets, tweed skirts and flat sensible shoes. This particular evening she was puzzled by her husband's brooding silence.

'Penny for them, Jim,' she said, as the dog stopped to sniff the grass verge.

Ashworth gazed down at her and smiled. 'Oh, I don't know, Sarah, we both learnt years ago that being a copper wasn't easy, but I can understand most of the crimes I have to deal with — stealing, crimes of passion, even things people get up to under the influence of drink and drugs. However despicable the acts, I can always find a reason for them . . .'

The dog finally finished her meticulous examination of every blade of grass and allowed them to continue their walk.

'So what's the problem now?' Sarah asked gently.

He sighed. 'I suppose I'm saying I can see a solution to all of those things. But there are two types of criminal who're completely beyond my comprehension: the terrorists who plant bombs that kill and maim the innocent, and by doing so think they're winning in some way; and the men who get their sexual thrills from abusing a child. I've never had to deal with people like that, but if I did I wouldn't be able to find an excuse for their behaviour and I don't know how I'd react.'

Sarah was probably the only person in the world who knew how deeply her husband felt about issues important to him. She took his hand and squeezed it lovingly.

'You're worried about that little girl who was nearly taken today, aren't you?'

'Amy, yes,' he replied, a trace of a smile on his lips. 'She went back to school this afternoon to take part in a hockey match, and I was waiting there when she came out. Her mother was parked some yards away from the school gates and I'd already told her that I'd walk Amy to the car.'

He let out a soft chuckle. 'I told that young lady this morning that she was not to trust any stranger, not even a chief inspector. Anyway, as we walked along she took my hand and told me to stop treating her like a child. She said she'd checked with her dad and he told her that I'd been in the force for thirty years, that you went to church every Sunday, things like that. And she explained that she'd decided I could be trusted because she'd checked me out. I couldn't believe I was talking with an eight-year-old child.'

'She sounds delightful,' Sarah said, grinning.

'She is . . . and I can't stop worrying about her. Oh, come on, let's turn for home.'

He was eager now to indulge in his other ritual that was rarely missed: that of enjoying a few measures of malt whisky before bedtime.

* * *

Shannon could feel the sweat running down her spine; a single drop traced its way along the line of her backbone, sliding over her smooth, oh so cold skin. Her step had become hesitant as fear gripped and cramped the pit of her stomach. She must be half-way across, she reasoned, viewing the familiar silhouettes of the slides and toddlers' swings.

Loath to take any other route but the shortest she crossed the sandpit, her feet sinking ankle deep into the damp clinging sand which immediately worked inside her shoes. Hobbling slightly and wishing that she had put on socks, Shannon picked a path underneath the slides, hurried past the swings and, with determined pace, carried on towards the park keeper's hut which stood on top of a small hill. From that vantage point she could see the distant glow of street lamps on the other side of the Rec, but as she slipped and slithered down the slope their comforting gleam vanished and she was once more plunged into almost total blackness.

The sand in her shoes was rubbing the soles of her feet but she dared not stop to shake it out. Soon she reached the path and walking was far easier, but the hard tarmac only made her gritty feet more uncomfortable.

Her steps rang out loudly as she walked along the tree-lined avenue where the branches of giant horse chestnuts almost met overhead, adding to the darkness and deepening her sense of isolation. Their gnarled trunks took on the appearance of hideous gargoyles about to pounce as the gloom continually played tricks with her eyes and fuelled her alarm. Then someone coughed, and white teeth flashed only yards away to her left.

CHAPTER 5

John and Iris Waldon were restless within their neat semi-detached house on the edge of the council estate. David Thorne, the vicar of St Giles's Church, had not long left, and although he had been a welcome visitor immediately after Nicky's disappearance, bringing as he did hope and support, three months on his visits only intensified their feelings of pain and loss.

Somehow they had both managed to carry on with their daily lives, John never missing a day from his job as a garage mechanic, and Iris only occasionally taking time off from hers as counter assistant in a snack bar.

They knew in their hearts that Nicky was dead, although neither had dared to voice the fact for the realisation brought with it so much pain. They knew too that the vicar was trying to prepare them for the worst, with his talk of everlasting life and finding strength to bear the grief and pain through prayer. At first John had wanted to hit out at just about anybody, to cause someone else pain in the hope of alleviating his own. But that phase was over and a numbing acceptance had taken its place. He strolled from room to room amid sounds of crockery clinking in the bowl as his wife washed the tea things used for the softly spoken vicar. From the window of the main bedroom John could see the dark expanse of the recreation ground and as he gazed out over it he offered up a silent prayer for his beloved daughter's soul.

His feet felt like lead as he forced himself to take those few steps along the landing to Nicky's bedroom and open up its door. He turned on the light, and in a few stark seconds his mind absorbed every single detail of the room: the bed with its pink pillow and duvet cover; the teddy bear that was bought on the day Nicky was born; the countless dolls. Memories cascaded over him as he crossed to the bed and ran a hand along its length: the longed-for puppy that he had brought in hidden under his coat; Christmas lights and party hats; and laughter, lots of laughter. Then, for the first time, he was aware of his wife standing in the doorway.

'Nicky's gone, hasn't she?' Iris whispered.

He gave a grim nod. 'I think so, love. I think she's dead.'

'Oh, John, what are we going to do?'

He darted forward as she crumpled before him and held her tightly to his chest, conscious of her hot tears soaking through his shirt.

'We'll try to carry on as best we can. We'll . . .'

But then his voice broke and for the first time since that dreadful day when Nicky vanished, he started to sob.

* * *

Shannon was running as fast as she could, breaking to her right, all thoughts of reaching the other side of the Rec driven from her mind. She was taking the shortest way out now, and her shoes pounded on the grass as she bolted for the side entrance.

Menacing footfalls and the sounds of laboured breath were so close behind and, although her own lungs were heaving, she dared not slow for a second. Once or twice she stumbled and almost fell but blind panic kept her upright. Soon her youthfulness began to triumph and the fearsome sounds started to fade as she outran her pursuer.

Close to exhaustion now, Shannon kept her head bowed and concentrated on the grass flashing by between her feet, willing herself to go on. But her chest felt as if it were about to burst and, with an anguished cry, she collapsed on to all fours, her ears pricked for any sounds that might betray the man.

An eerie breeze rustled the leaves as Shannon, still listening earnestly, crawled to the relative safety of a clump of dense bushes to her right. There, she quickly took off her shoes and tossed them to one side at the very moment that footsteps, slow and steady, reached her ears. She peered out, and the breath caught in her throat when she saw the man's silhouette against the night sky.

Without thinking she broke cover, her bare feet slapping on the grass as she darted for the exit, and her heart pounded painfully when she heard the man behind start to run. Then the gates of the Rec came into view and immediately renewed her strength, yet even as she dashed towards them she knew that he was gaining ground.

She risked slowing slightly and glanced back; he was about fifty yards behind but bearing down on her. The gates were a hundred yards away, and then ninety, eighty. Shannon's aching legs threatened to give way, but the man's heaving breath and angry curses kept her going.

The gates were fifty yards in front, their iron structure bathed in the dim glow of the street lights. Shannon reached them, terror rising in her young chest, for once out of the Rec there was nothing but a maze of deserted side streets. Leather-soled shoes beat an ominous path behind her and she could almost feel the presence of the man; he was virtually close enough to reach out and grab her.

Catching sight of a parked car to her left, she dashed towards it and skidded to a halt, beating her clenched fists against its windows.

'Let me in,' she screamed. 'There's a man chasing me.'

The car door swung open.

* * *

Andrew Webb was celebrating the result of his application to excavate a site on the now deserted Aldridge Farm. At long last, he and his team had been granted permission to organise a dig in the corner of a field where a large number of Roman coins had been unearthed by a metal detector enthusiast.

Webb, a forty-year-old archaeologist, was certain that Bridgetown had been the site of a major Roman town around the time of Christ's birth and if he could only prove it, he would put the town and himself on the map.

In his rented room above the Bull and Butcher public house he found the undulating walls most disconcerting, but despite that he staggered drunkenly to his backpack and opened another can of beer.

* * *

Shannon scrambled into the car, not caring that she was on the back seat. The engine started even before she could close the door and she welcomed its comforting throb which sent soothing vibrations throughout her weary body. The driver turned and smiled, and then Shannon was screaming because the man who had chased her was calmly climbing on to the back seat. In an instant his huge hand was clamped across her mouth and she was wrestled to the floor beside his feet. She landed in a heap, her eyes pleading with his, but the man simply snarled and aimed a punch at her face.

'I said we'd find one on the council Rec, didn't I?'

All sound and all feelings grew distant then, and their voices seemed to be coming from a long way off. A hand tore at her skirt and felt between her legs, its touch rough and brutal enough to bring a whimper of pain from her lips even in her semi-conscious state. Their voices swam all around her but, thankfully, Shannon could not hear the words.

CHAPTER 6

Chief Inspector Ashworth took a detour on his way to the police station the next morning. He had decided to go to Anderson's Farm. Jed Anderson was an old friend of his and he wanted to check if the farmer had noticed anything unusual in the field where Jan Morrison had reported seeing those two men.

Although most of the officers at the station regarded the woman as a joke, Ashworth did not. He could see little point in asking the public for their help and then making them feel like nuisances when they offered it.

As he steered the car along a lengthy winding path to the farmhouse, he pondered that he would like to have been a man of the soil. He felt extremely comfortable in open spaces, not hemmed in by bricks and mortar, or worse still, glass.

The farmer, a large man of Ashworth's age with a ruddy complexion, was working on the engine of a tractor when the Scorpio glided to a silent halt.

'Hello, Jim,' he called out heartily. 'I must say, you're looking as fit as ever.'

'I only wish I felt it,' Ashworth replied with a wry grin. 'Listen, Jed, you ploughed Water Field the other day, I believe, and I was wondering whether you noticed anything odd about it.'

Anderson tossed aside his spanner and wiped his hands thoughtfully on an oily rag. 'Funny you should mention that. Young Sean did the job, and he was wittering on about something.' He chuckled. 'I think he fancies himself in your job. Mind you, I must admit he very rarely misses much.'

'There are days when he could have my job, Jed. Is he about?'

The farmer winked, and humour bubbled in his voice as he shouted, 'Sean, the police are here. I told you to get that car taxed and insured.'

The man strolling out of the barn was not in the least perturbed. Indeed, his thick blond hair framed a cheerful and clearly honest face.

'This is Chief Inspector Ashworth,' Anderson told him. 'He wants to know if you spotted anything unusual when you ploughed Water Field.'

'Oh, yeh, Chief Inspector, I did, as a matter of fact,' he said, leaning against the tractor. 'I was telling Mr Anderson, there were a lot of footprints about — I mean, a real lot. I know people walk their dogs in the fields and do their courting there, but these prints weren't like that. They went backwards and forwards to the gate, backwards and forwards.'

'That's interesting,' Ashworth mused. 'Can you remember anything else?'

'Yeh, a lot of long grass had been ripped up from the edge of the field and sort of spread about. It's probably nothing, but it just looked strange, that's all.'

'Could somebody have been trying to conceal something, do you think?'

'Yeh, could have been. Mind you, I didn't see anything that shouldn't have been there while I was ploughing.'

'Could you show me the exact spot, if you had to, Sean?'

'I don't know,' he said, frowning. 'Not the exact spot, but somewhere round about it, I suppose.'

* * *

Ashworth got to work an hour late, and as soon as he pulled into the car park he knew that something was amiss. Uniformed officers were pouring out of the building, and through the glass swing doors he could see Superintendent Newton pacing reception. Ashworth sighed heavily as he approached the station; Newton was the last person he wanted to see. He was hardly inside the door before the superintendent pounced.

'Ah, Chief Inspector, you've arrived at last.'

'Yes, sir,' Ashworth replied, attempting as usual to hide his dislike for the man. 'I had some inquiries to make.'

'Really?' Newton said, glancing pointedly at his watch. 'Well, another little girl has gone missing from the council estate. In your absence I ordered DS Bedford and DC Abraham to look into it. They've just radioed in for uniformed back-up. Maybe you'd like to find out exactly what's going on and report back to me.'

'Yes, sir.'

Ashworth stood glaring at the superintendent. Everything about the man irritated him, his prissy manner, his too immaculate appearance, but more especially his lack of respect for anyone of lower rank in a time of crisis.

'Get to it then, Chief Inspector,' he said, striding towards the stairs.

'I'm going to thump him one of these days,' Ashworth vowed under his breath as he hastened across to the reception desk.

'I heard that.' Dutton grinned. 'He's not improving with age, is he?'

'That he's not,' Ashworth agreed. 'Martin, your lads are still keeping an eye on the schools, I hope?'

'Of course, Jim, but I think we're closing the stable door after the horse has bolted.'

'Hmm, I do, too.' Ashworth leant heavily on the desk. 'Do we know who the missing girl is?'

'Shannon Dixon, eight years old, from the council estate.' He stopped to consult some papers on his desk. 'Her mother reported her missing at eight-thirty this morning and Holly and Josh are attending. That's all I know.'

* * *

Holly viewed the several acres that made up the recreation ground with a sinking sensation in the pit of her stomach. Uniformed officers were fanned out in a long line, searching the whole area, and Josh seemed to be reading her thoughts as they ambled along behind the procession of blue uniforms.

'Not much hope, is there?'

'I don't think there is, Josh, no. We're either going to find nothing, or one very dead little girl. Can you believe a mother going out to an all-night party and leaving an eight-year-old alone?'

A mood of depression had settled upon the two detectives when they discovered that the last sighting of the girl had been around 9 p.m. the previous evening. They had visited Shannon's school where it took them some time to uncover the story of the 'Chicken' run across the Rec. Apparently, when she failed to show at the other end the gang assumed that she had bottled out and left the Rec by the shortest possible route.

'Over here, I've found something.'

The shout came from their left, and they turned to see a uniformed officer gesticulating wildly as he crouched alongside a clump of bushes.

'Here we go, lover,' Holly said with a weary sigh, as they hurried in the direction of the arm-waving constable.

'It's a pair of kid's shoes — girl's,' PC Dickens announced when they arrived at his side.

Holly peered through the foliage. 'Right, we'd better get Forensic on to this, Josh, and when they've finished we'll have to get a positive ID on the shoes.'

'On it now,' he said, already calling through to central control.

'Oh, Jesus Christ,' Holly muttered loudly. 'What the hell's the vicar hanging about for? He pissed me off on the Nicky Waldon case.'

'Hol, do you mind?' Josh said, indicating the radio. 'I'm having a job to hear, as it is.'

She fell silent but continued to glare at the clergyman who was standing on the perimeter of the recreation ground.

'Forensic's coming in now,' Josh announced.

'Good.' She returned her gaze to the shoes, all the while biting anxiously on her lower lip. 'Why should the kid take her shoes off here?'

'So she could run faster?' he suggested.

'And where the bloody hell's the guv'nor?' she snapped.

* * *

It was two hours before Ashworth turned up, and by that time Forensic had finished their work. He marched across to Holly and Josh who were deep in discussion by her Micra on the road outside the iron gates.

'Well, what have we got?' he demanded.

Holly straight away consulted her notebook. 'No sign of the girl, guv, but we found her shoes in some bushes. They've been positively identified by her mother. Forensic say there's traces of sand on them and they've managed to follow her progress. She must have come through the sandpit which is back there . . .' She pointed in the general direction. 'It looks as if she hid in the bushes and, for whatever reason, took off her shoes.'

'She couldn't have been attacked there?' Ashworth queried.

'No, guv, there's no sign of a struggle, and she definitely walked or ran out of those bushes. She still had sand on the soles of her feet, and Forensic found traces of it a good ten yards away. She was heading for the side exit.'

'And into the road, if she made it that far,' Ashworth muttered.

'We've carried out house-to-house inquiries, but nobody saw anything. Mind you, that's not unusual on this estate, is it?'

'But surely with a child abducted . . . ?'

'Anyway, where have you been, guv?' she asked tartly. 'It's been over three hours.'

'I don't have to answer to you, Holly,' he bristled.

'Hey, hey,' Josh said, pushing between the two. 'Look, none of us like this case, so shall we avoid taking it out on each other?'

Ashworth and his sergeant stood with eyes locked. Holly was the first to look away.

'Okay,' she said, 'but I just think that on a case like this we should have a full team.'

'We have a full team,' Ashworth informed her tersely. 'If you must know I've been checking at Anderson's Farm about Jan Morrison's two men, and I also got on to the council.'

'Why the council?' Josh asked.

'It could be something or nothing, but the one bright spot in all this is the fact that we haven't yet found Nicky Waldon's body, which means that at this moment in time the girl could still be alive. Now, the way I figure it, if someone's keeping a child captive they must either live in a very secluded spot, or there's somewhere in the house — a hidden room, perhaps — that's not easily seen from inside. Anyway,' he said, 'I've put in an inquiry about Gilbert Randall's house. They said they'd deal with it as soon as possible.'

Without waiting for a response, he turned on his heel and headed back to the car.

Josh frowned. 'What was all that about?'

'Search me,' Holly said morosely.

'What's the matter with you, Hol, aren't you getting enough sex these days?'

'Do me a favour, Josh,' she said, rounding on him. 'Don't give me any of your aren't-you-getting-enough jokes, because I'm not in the mood. Okay?'

She left him standing open-mouthed and returned to the bushes where the shoes had been found.

'Sorry, Hol, I didn't mean anything . . .'

'I don't know if I can cope with this,' she told him quietly, her eyes fixed on the bushes. 'I've never been on a paedophile case before.'

'You'll just have to stay detached—'

'But that's the point, I can't stay bloody detached. Christ, Josh, an eight-year-old kid's going through God knows what right now, just because she had to prove she'd got the guts to walk across the Rec. What kind of arseholes are we dealing with here?'

'I don't like it any more than you do,' he said, placing a comforting hand on her shoulder.

'Sorry, Josh, but I'm going to be a real pain until this case is over.'

'You're always a pain, I'm used to it,' he said lightly. 'Come on, let me buy you a cup of tea.'

She gave him a weak smile 'All right, then.'

* * *

Ashworth was experiencing the same revulsion that was shortening Holly's temper so drastically, but his many years in the police force had taught him how to conceal it. A volatile anger slowly built inside him as images of the child's predicament repeatedly flashed through his mind; but when Reverend Thorne approached him at his car, Ashworth afforded him a genial smile.

'What can I do for you, vicar?'

'I just wanted to know if there was any news yet.'

'None, I'm afraid, but we're doing all we can.'

'Oh, I'm sure you are,' Thorne said, his expression earnest. 'Absolutely dreadful business. I've been to see the mother, but she was very distraught and a touch unpleasant, I'm afraid.' He gave a helpless shrug. 'Not all people turn to God in times of trouble.'

Ashworth felt irritated by the clergyman, but was at a loss to know why. He was quite an ordinary man, tall and very thin with a slight stoop. His hair was rust-coloured and matched his bushy eyebrows perfectly. He had a habit of clasping his hands as if in permanent prayer; perhaps it was that mannerism which rankled the chief inspector.

'I wonder if you could pay me a visit at the vicarage?' Thorne asked hesitantly. 'I really would like to discuss what we can do about the safety of children. It's such a responsibility — the choir boys, the Sunday school . . .' His voice trailed off.

'Yes, of course I'll come,' Ashworth said, relenting slightly. 'I'll call round at two p.m. this afternoon if that's convenient?'

'Perfectly, Chief Inspector, I shall look forward to it.'

Ashworth's mouth was once more set in a grim line as he watched the tall figure hurry away.

CHAPTER 7

The dig at Aldridge Farm got off to a promising start. Andrew Webb and his team of twenty student archaeologists had already unearthed a number of coins and some nice fragments of pottery. Nothing really exciting, but it was encouraging.

As he sifted through the earth, Webb's gaze kept straying to a slight mound he had noticed in the adjoining field. If his guess was correct and this was the site of a Roman village then that mound could well be a burial ground. Countless graves, all destroyed by time, could lie in that field, and all so rich in artefacts.

A coin jangled in his sifter and the mound was temporarily forgotten. Webb looked down, his excitement rising, but then he laughed. It was an old English penny, dating back to 1963.

* * *

Ashworth pulled up outside the vicarage and studied the building for a few moments. It was most striking, double-fronted with a deep porch, and every inch of its brick and timber facade was adorned with variegated ivy in the act of encroaching ever further upon the attractive leaded windows.

The carved oak door was opened by Reverend Thorne himself, a few seconds after Ashworth pushed the bell.

'Please, do come in, Chief Inspector,' he said graciously, stepping back. 'Perhaps you'd like to follow me into the drawing room. I've already made us some tea.'

'Surely,' Ashworth said, glancing around.

The drawing room was comfortable and obviously well used, and Ashworth was very taken with an antique mahogany bookcase which completely concealed one wall. Without delay, he was ushered into an old-fashioned winged armchair while the vicar sat at his desk and poured the tea.

'I haven't seen you in church, Chief Inspector, and yet Mrs Ashworth attends regularly.' He flashed a pleasant smile. 'We haven't offended you, have we?'

'Well, yes, you have, as a matter of fact.'

The vicar's eyebrows rose. 'Sugar?'

'Three, please,' Ashworth said, settling back. 'Yes, it seems that some areas of the church are now casting doubt on the validity of the Old and New Testaments. And from what I've read, some men of the cloth are even questioning whether God exists at all.'

'And that bothers you?' Thorne asked, handing Ashworth his tea in a delicate cup and saucer.

'Thank you,' he said, taking a sip. 'Yes, it does. I happen to have my own concept of God, and I do try to live by His teachings, to fit them into the modern world.'

'But you don't feel the need to worship with others?'

'You're pushing me on this one, vicar,' he said, with a challenging smile. 'How can I put this? The truth is, I'd find it very difficult to sit there listening to someone, who quite possibly doesn't believe there is a greater power, telling me how to live my life. I'd go as far as saying that, to my mind, there are some clergymen who seem to have assumed the role of God for themselves, and that's not acceptable to me.'

'You're very blunt, Chief Inspector.'

'When asked a direct question, I try to make my answer unambiguous — it often avoids misunderstandings later on.'

Thorne drained his teacup and appraised Ashworth with piercing eyes.

'Well, I do believe in God,' he said, looking away to set his cup on its saucer.

Ashworth grinned. 'That's a good start in your line of business.'

'Now, about the reason for your visit,' the vicar said, glad to be changing the subject. 'We have so many church functions now, and all are well attended by the local youngsters. I really am concerned for their safety in light of what's happening.'

'If they're very young children, you could always ask their parents to come and collect them,' Ashworth suggested.

'I already do, but not all parents respond. The smaller children are ferried home as much as possible, of course, but some of the youngsters from the estates resent any suggestion that they should be protected. In fact, many of the older ones are quite affronted by it.' He spread his hands in a gesture of despair.

'You say you have a lot of functions that are attended by the youngsters in the community?'

'Countless, and the number is still rising. I have a helper, Noel Harper, he's a youth leader and a dynamo of a chap. He's young, in his thirties, has a ponytail and plays the guitar — you know, the very type youngsters nowadays can relate to. He and his wife are marvellous with the kids, and they in turn respond splendidly. Noel organises discos, hot gospel sessions, that sort of thing, and he's livened up the Sunday school no end. He's bringing youngsters into the church who would normally give it a wide berth.'

'It all sounds very encouraging,' Ashworth remarked, 'but if the parents aren't willing to do their bit then the only advice I can give is that the children keep to well-lit public places and avoid areas such as the recreation ground and the parks, especially after dark. Sorry to state the obvious, vicar, but as we can't have uniformed officers on every street corner there's a limit to what we can do.'

'I understand that,' Thorne said, sighing deeply. 'It's all very worrying.'

'But I do share your concern and, in spite of our limited resources, we'll be keeping a strong police presence on the streets.' He placed his empty cup on the floor. 'Now, if you'll excuse me . . .'

'Of course,' the vicar said, leaving his seat. 'Thank you for coming by, and perhaps you'll give my regards to your wife.'

'Surely.' Ashworth got to his feet and allowed himself to be ushered towards the front door. 'I must say, the vicarage is very impressive.'

'It is,' Thorne agreed. 'I don't quite know when it dates back to—'

'To the time of Henry VIII.' The vicar looked impressed, and Ashworth added, 'Local history is a bit of a hobby of mine.'

'Really? So you'll know that this house and the large cottage further along the lane, which Noel and his wife occupy, were part of a huge estate. Both houses apparently have priest holes hidden away in their structures. But do you think I can find them . . . ?'

Ashworth stepped out into the weak sunshine and turned back to the vicar with a smile. 'Well, around that time in history, if a priest hole had been easy to locate, it wouldn't have been much use, would it?'

'No, I suppose not,' the vicar said, chuckling.

* * *

Shannon Dixon was locked away in a place that was cold and damp, alone in the pitch black. During her hours of captivity she had crawled around and, by sense of touch, had established that her prison was long and narrow, its floor uneven and icy.

Her jailers visited that confined space regularly, always with balaclavas covering their features. They allowed her to use the lavatory and gave her food and drink in what she assumed was the kitchen, each time applying a blindfold to her frozen face before leading her out.

Hope rose up in Shannon whenever she was led away from that room, but it died in her chest every time she was pushed back there. Now, wrapped in two blankets, she lay shivering on the floor, bewildered and frightened. Suddenly the door creaked open and a shaft of light cut through the air as two figures slipped inside.

'I'm so cold,' she whimpered.

'Cold, cold,' they cooed. 'Shannon's cold.'

A match burst into flame in the shadows, allowing her a brief glimpse of their faces, but then it was blown out and all that remained was the red glow of two lighted cigarettes. In the total darkness those twin spots of crimson bore down on her . . .

CHAPTER 8

Jan Morrison was walking her dog, a brown and white cross-breed called Patch, so named because of the black around his left eye which lent him the air of a pirate.

She was at last coming to terms with her new role as grandmother and was also getting used to living in Bridgetown. The area was very quiet compared with Leeds, where she and her husband had lived until twelve weeks ago. They had upped sticks to be near to their daughter and son-in-law and, in all truth, Jan was doubting the wisdom of the move within the first week.

In Leeds she had run a Neighbourhood Watch scheme and had encountered considerable difficulties while doing so. Jan took everything she did very seriously and therefore insisted on reporting every incident to the police, however insignificant. To start with they had seemed pleased with her diligence, but after a time it was obvious that she was being viewed as a positive nuisance.

Her thoughts turned to Chief Inspector Ashworth and she let out a girlish giggle while Patch sniffed in the gutter. That handsome man had been good to her so far, highly patient and utterly charming. But even the lovely chief inspector had failed to act on any of the information she had supplied. So could he too be seeing her as a silly woman, dominated by the menopause and therefore prone to flights of fancy?

She sighed and passed under the bridge of the expressway, its walls and support pillars covered with irritating graffiti and telephone numbers one could supposedly ring for any number of sexual favours. The roar of heavy goods vehicles overhead reminded her of Leeds and she felt a fleeting pang of homesickness but that was swiftly forgotten when, emerging from beneath the bridge, Patch cocked his ears and growled at some unseen danger.

'What is it, boy?' she murmured, casting urgent glances into each shadowy corner.

The dog continued to growl and whine in the empty street, and Jan listened carefully. Yes, there *was* a noise. But what was it? It came again, louder this time. A scream, followed by another, and then the sounds of muffled sobbing.

Jan studied the house in front of her. Were the noises coming from there? It was a nice house, different from the others. They were all semis, whereas this one was detached, and she thought it a shame that the expressway should pass so close to its side bedroom window.

Those faint screams came again. It sounded to Jan as if someone inside the house — number nine — was in agony. She turned on her heel and started to walk back, noting the street name as she went. Lime Street. Number nine Lime Street. She would tell the police that loud screams were coming from that house. There were two telephone boxes at the end of the road; she would report it from there.

The first telephone was out of order, and her resolve weakened slightly in the face of that irritating hold-up. Indeed, doubts were already surfacing in her mind as she ducked into the adjoining booth. After all, she could hear sounds from other houses — laughter, raised voices, all filtering through double-glazed windows set on night vents. What if those at number nine were having a domestic dispute? Unpleasant, yes, but not against the law. Her hand hovered over the receiver.

Yet what if the screams were coming from the mouth of that little girl who had gone missing? It was her duty to make the call. She lifted the receiver and dialled nine . . .

* * *

Shannon found she could scream no longer; all that came out of her mouth was a hoarse choking sound. Every inch of her body hurt and their violent kicks, which even now were being aimed at her ribs, thrust her to the very brink of oblivion.

'Stop now, or we'll kill her too soon,' a voice said, grabbing Shannon's fragile attention. 'She won't last the week if we carry on with this.'

'I don't care, she's not the one I wanted.'

'Well, I care. I don't want to kill her too soon.'

Their angry voices continued to come to Shannon for a long time but, thankfully, the kicking stopped.

* * *

Jan hesitated again after dialling the second nine. What if she'd been mistaken? The police were sure to ask if she had seen anything, and she would have to say no. She would hear doubt in the policeman's voice. Right madam, so you think you heard screaming. But I *did* hear screaming, she would insist, and as this is a 999 call you're duty bound to respond. And could I have your name, madam? Yes, Morrison, Jan Morrison. That familiar oh-it's-you tone would creep into his voice then.

With a decisive huff, she replaced the receiver.

'Come on, Patch,' she said, 'let's go home.'

* * *

The days were dragging by and still no progress was being made on the case of Shannon's abduction. Her mother had made an emotional television appeal, but nothing had come of it so far. Likewise, extensive police inquiries had unearthed nothing untoward.

Every possible advance put forward by Ashworth was fiercely blocked by Superintendent Newton, which made for a very strained atmosphere in CID. Josh, as always, was keeping his own counsel, but Holly had definitely lost her bounce and sparkle and had started to smoke heavily.

It was Wednesday morning and Ashworth was at his desk, mulling over reports of burglaries, muggings and car thefts cleared up by CID during the past two weeks.

'I've had the answers from the council that I've been waiting for,' he said, tossing aside the last of the reports. 'As I said they relate to number nine Lime Street, home of Gilbert Randall, that man of child pornography fame.'

'Is this to do with Shannon?' Holly asked.

'It could well be. When I was there making inquiries on the day that Amy Byron was almost taken, I noticed that the outside of the house didn't match the interior . . .'

'Come again, guv,' Holly said, shooting a puzzled glance at Josh as she lit a cigarette.

Ashworth rose from his seat and pointedly opened a window, all the time watching cigarette smoke spiralling towards the ceiling.

'I was standing on the pavement and I could see his television set against the lounge wall,' he said, returning to his desk. 'Now, most outside walls are nine-inch cavities, but number nine Lime Street's outside wall looked a good three feet away from the back of the television. Even before Victorian times, no houses were built with walls that thick, so I decided to look into it and the council have just provided me with the answer.'

He picked up a sheet of paper. 'Now, the expressway was constructed some twenty years ago, and it cut straight through Lime Street. At the time number nine was a semi, just like all the other houses in the street, but number seven had to be demolished to make way for the road.'

'This is leading somewhere, I presume?' Holly said irritably as she demolished her cigarette in an already overflowing ashtray.

Ashworth glowered at her for some moments, and then returned his gaze to the council's reply.

'They've gone so far as to admit that number nine should also have been demolished but, because it was council-owned, they were loath to lose the rent from two houses. So, when number seven was pulled down they knew they'd have to build an outer wall for the side of number nine. That's when they hit upon the idea of preserving at least two feet of the demolished property and building the outer wall on to that. Which means there's a cavity of that depth between the wall of number nine and the outer wall, to insulate it against noise from the expressway.'

Holly took some time to digest all of that. Finally, she said, 'Are you saying that when you stand in the lounge of Randall's house, there's a secret compartment between the inner wall and the outer wall?'

Ashworth nodded. 'To be precise, there's a cavity at least two feet wide.'

'Large enough for a small child to be kept in,' Josh ventured.

'Exactly,' Holly said. 'Okay, then, guv, what do we do about it?'

'Nothing,' he said, shrugging. 'Newton says we've got no reason to go storming in there, asking questions, and we most certainly wouldn't get a search warrant.'

'So, we do nothing,' she muttered, with a cutting edge to her voice.

'That's right, Holly, the same as we do nothing about Mrs Morrison's report of two men with spades in a field at Anderson's Farm. Again Newton says we haven't enough evidence to act on and I must admit, however reluctantly, that I agree with him on that one.'

'This is really beginning to piss me off,' Holly moaned as she grabbed her shoulder bag and stormed out of the office.

'That girl's language is getting worse,' Ashworth remarked calmly when the door slammed shut. 'What's wrong with her?'

'She's taken Shannon's disappearance to heart,' Josh told him. 'It's really bugging her. I think she's getting involved on too personal a level. She's even been to visit the girl's mother.'

Ashworth shook his head. 'She's a copper, she ought to stay detached from the case. If she becomes emotionally involved, Josh, she's likely to do something foolish. Can't you have a word with her?'

'Guv, there are two things in life I know I can't do, and one of them is talking sense into Holly when she's got the bit between her teeth.'

'Hmm, I'd have to agree with you there. She can be a bit much at times.'

Ashworth set about shuffling together the papers on his desk while Josh returned to his computer work. Suddenly, he looked up.

'You said there were two things you can't do, Josh. What's the other?'

The detective turned in his chair, a resigned look on his face. 'The other thing, guv, is trying to talk sense into you when you've got the bit between your teeth.'

'Nonsense,' Ashworth scoffed, genuinely offended. 'There's no one more level-headed or capable of detaching themselves from a case than I am.'

'Yes, guv,' Josh mumbled.

CHAPTER 9

Andrew Webb's excitement was growing with each moment that passed. The odd Roman coin and sliver of pottery was giving way to combs carved from bone, tiny figures worked in bronze and, even more important, drinking vessels and arrowheads. With each new discovery Webb would hoist his arms above his head in a victory salute.

He sank to his knees and almost embraced the dry earth. Down there, he thought, maybe another six feet down, might be the remains of a tiled floor on which a Roman soldier and his family had stood two thousand years ago.

He glanced feverishly towards the small mound in the next field and pondered on what might lie beneath that. The skeleton of a child? Its death caused by disease or accident, or even some hostile action by forces opposed to the Roman occupation?

Yes, he decided, that was definitely the grave of a child.

* * *

Tom Gardiner could not have looked more furtive if he'd tried, despite the fact that he was doing his level best to appear nonchalant. He was trudging across the garden to his large barn, the four dogs snapping at his heels and growling at each sharp kick from Gardiner's boot.

At the barn door he cast surreptitious glances towards the lane before entering and then let out a loud curse when, in the gathering gloom, his shin met with the bumper of the grey Nova. Looking around to make sure he was not being watched, he unlocked the door to the little room at the back and stepped inside. Immediately the smell of damp was in his nostrils.

'I'd better keep this door locked all the time,' he muttered. 'Don't want that DS Bedford nosing about in the cellar.' He gave a sudden throaty chuckle. 'Lucky you weren't in here yesterday when she looked.'

* * *

The church hall was throbbing with the sounds of an Oasis record. Children with ages ranging from six to early teens were swaying and gyrating to the music while strobe lighting flashed.

Noel Harper, the youth leader, was standing with his wife, Beth, at the side of the hall, tapping his foot in time with the beat and keeping a close eye on the youngsters. The record came to an end, and the room was filled with loud groans when the main hall lights came on. With a broad smile on his face, Harper pushed back stray hair that had escaped from his ponytail and vaulted on to the stage.

'That's all, people,' he announced to even louder moans. 'Now, come on, it's nine p.m. and there're a lot of parents outside waiting to take you rabble home.' He stuffed his hands into the pockets of his blue jeans and waited for the protests to die down. 'Okay, anybody who hasn't got a lift hold up your hand.'

About a dozen arms were held aloft and Harper made a great show of counting them.

'That's great, Beth and I will take you home as usual but it'll mean two trips. So I want those who have to wait to stay in the hall with Reverend Thorne.'

It was when his gaze fell on his wife that Harper noticed a man standing by the main doors of the hall.

'Yes, can I help you?' he asked, scrambling from the stage and quickly making his way through the children.

'I'm Chief Inspector Ashworth,' he said, producing his warrant card.

Harper studied it closely. 'I'm sorry, I should have known.'

'No reason why you should,' Ashworth said, smiling. 'I don't attend many discos these days.'

Harper laughed. 'One has to be so careful.'

Amy Byron, who was picking a path through her friends, overheard the remark and straight away put the wrong interpretation to it.

Rather bossily, she said, 'Relax, Noel, the chief inspector's all right, I know him.'

Harper just about managed to keep a straight face and decided to go along with the girl.

'Are you sure, Amy?' he asked anxiously. She nodded. 'Okay, then, if you say so. I supposed I was being over-cautious.'

'You can't be over-cautious, really,' she said. 'Not with the things that are happening nowadays.'

Ashworth supposed that those were her father's words and tried hard to suppress a laugh, but he could not stop an amused smile coming to his lips.

He said to Harper, 'I just called in to see if I could be of any assistance. I was talking to the vicar earlier, and he was telling me that you sometimes have problems running the children home. So, as I was passing I thought I'd offer my services.'

'Are you saying you'll give some of them a lift?' he asked hopefully.

'Yes, my wife's outside in the car. We could take about four.'

'That's great,' he enthused. 'Okay, if you take Amy and her friends, we can handle the rest.'

Amy seemed wholly in favour of a lift from the nice chief inspector and hurried off in search of her friends.

'She's a lovely girl,' Harper remarked.

'That she is,' Ashworth agreed.

They were joined then by an attractive blonde whose clear blue eyes sparkled prettily within an exceptionally friendly face.

'This is my wife, Beth,' Harper said. 'Beth, this is Chief Inspector Ashworth. He's kindly offered to take some of the kids home for us.'

'Oh, that's really good of you,' she said, with a stunning smile. 'Having so many of them to look after is very worrying sometimes.'

* * *

Amy chattered constantly throughout the fifteen-minute journey and it soon became apparent that she was very much the leader of the group, continually directing and dominating the others like a miniature mother. She was the last of the children to be dropped off, and Sarah accompanied her and Ashworth to the front door.

'Don't bother to ring,' the child said, when Ashworth reached for the bell. 'I've got my own key.'

'That's as maybe, but I think we'd just better let your parents know what's going on,' Ashworth said lightly.

'Fine,' she said, wrapping her hand around his large thumb.

Larry Byron had a worried frown on his face when he opened the door, but he relaxed the minute he saw his daughter.

'You gave me quite a turn there, Chief Inspector. I could only see you through the door, and I thought . . .'

'My wife and I were passing St Giles's hall, so we thought we'd give some of the children a lift.'

Amy released his hand and stood by her father's side, beaming up at them.

'It's been nice meeting you, Mrs Ashworth,' she said, 'and I'd like to thank you and the chief inspector for the lift.'

'It was a pleasure,' she said, smiling, as the girl bounced into the house.

Her father grinned widely. 'I'm sorry,' he whispered. 'She can be a shade bossy, and she tries too hard to be grown up.'

'She's a lovely girl,' Ashworth replied. 'You must be very proud.'

They said their goodbyes and strolled back to the car.

'I think that child's taken to you,' Sarah remarked.

'Understandable,' Ashworth quipped. 'I wonder if our kids were ever like that? I mean, after a quarter of an hour with Amy we now know that her parents enjoy a drink and that's why they didn't pick her up.'

She gave a wry laugh. 'By the way, Jim, what did you think of that youth leader and his wife?'

'A little too whiter than white for my liking, as is the vicar.'

Sarah's eyes widened. 'You're joking, surely? You don't think they'd, well . . . ?'

'Read the papers, Sarah, and watch the news. Vicars, priests, even bishops can get up to some very funny things.'

He skirted around the car and opened up the passenger door. Sarah settled into the seat and was mulling over his words while Ashworth climbed into the driver's side.

'There are no new leads in the abduction case, then?'

'No,' he said heavily. 'It's very difficult because, although we know what the motive is, it's nearly always impossible to link it to the people involved. These kids are picked at random, and all we have to fall back on is the list of those with convictions for sex crimes against children.'

'You were joking about David Thorne and that young chap, Harper?' she said, shooting him a sideways glance.

'Only half joking, Sarah. The person or persons we're looking for don't come across in everyday life as they really are. If they did, they wouldn't get away with it for very long.'

* * *

Soon after dawn the next morning Andrew Webb was eagerly approaching the site of his precious dig. There was a thin layer of frost on the fields, and it gave a satisfying crunch with each step of his heavy work boots. Such was his excitement that he hardly noticed the cold nipping at his cheeks and fingertips. When fired up, as he was now, Webb was extremely single-minded.

This was the find of his career. A Roman villa, with all early indications suggesting that it contained an underfloor heating process not dissimilar to our own modern-day central heating systems. He manhandled the tarpaulin protecting the area and cast it aside, then stood for a while inspecting his work. Just a few more feet and anything could be uncovered; a Roman bath, maybe. The possibilities were endless.

That mound in the next field caught his eye again. Tomorrow, perhaps? Yes, he would make that a priority for tomorrow.

* * *

Ashworth strode across reception and came to an abrupt halt at the desk.

'A word, Martin.'

'Is this a game, Jim, or what?' Dutton asked with his customary cheerfulness.

'Not quite,' Ashworth chuckled. 'I was at St Giles's Church last night giving some of the kids a lift home after the disco. The vicar's worried, and I share his concerns, so I was wondering whether we could get something organised. I don't know if any of your lads would be interested in a bit of unpaid overtime . . . ?'

'Running the kids home, you mean? I can't see why not, Jim. Most of the old lot like you and me, should volunteer, and the younger ones have got kids of their own, so they'll understand.'

'Good man,' Ashworth said, patting the sergeant's shoulder. 'If we could get say, two cars at every function to taxi the children home, it might also act as a deterrent.'

'No progress, then?'

Ashworth shook his head.

* * *

Jan Morrison's sleuthing instincts were fully aroused and as a result she was finding it impossible to stay away from Lime Street. With a shopping bag over her arm she acted out the part of a harassed housewife as she quickly paced the length of the street only to double back at the top. Number nine was drawing her like a magnet and, once there, she dropped the persona of innocent passer-by and stood, quite openly, viewing the house. It looked respectable enough. Its net curtains were crisp and white behind the double-glazed windows.

Double glazing, she thought with a gasp; if the house is double-glazed, then those screams from inside must have been awfully loud to be heard in the street. It was while she was reflecting on this that the front door opened and Gilbert Randall stepped into the front garden.

Had her imagination gone into overdrive, or was he really staring in her direction? Jan's face reddened and without further thought she turned and hurried away. She was certain that the man had something to hide, and after about forty yards she glanced back. Randall was still intent on watching her.

* * *

It was Saturday before Andrew Webb got around to what he now thought of as the burial ground in the adjoining field. The dig had indeed produced the remains of a Roman villa, and a large one at that; and Webb, with his considerable knowledge, suspected that it was one of the finest to be unearthed in recent years. Even the small floor tiles were still intact, and excitement gripped every one of the team when pots were found, complete and undamaged, along with leather sandals and a vast array of weapons.

But by mid-morning, unable to quell his curiosity any longer, he chose two of his team to go along with him and left the rest busily dusting and bagging the precious relics. Scott, Webb's young assistant, and an intense student named Val, hurried to keep abreast of their mentor as he literally ran to the new site.

They toiled earnestly, taking turns, the hole swiftly deepening. Far greater care was needed below the level of four feet and therefore their progress was slowed somewhat but their interest never flagged and it was not until the five-feet mark was reached that Webb began to suspect that his assumptions might have been wrong.

'Andrew,' a man called from the original site, 'we've found a helmet.'

'Carry on, guys,' Webb said. 'I need to take a look at that.'

He tore across the field and was examining the helmet when Scott let out a hideous cry. Webb glanced up to see his assistant motioning for him to get over there quickly, while Val was on her knees staring down into the hole.

Thinking that they had discovered something of huge interest he hastened towards the gate with a rising sense of expectancy. But as he drew closer Webb noticed that Scott's face was grey, and then Val vomited.

CHAPTER 10

Of all the places Ashworth might have chosen to spend a Saturday evening, the mortuary was not one of them. Yet there he now stood, with Holly at his side, staring down at a badly decomposed body on the slab while Alex Ferguson gave them the gruesome results of his examination.

'It's very interesting, actually,' he remarked, with a detachment only a pathologist could possess. 'I'd say the time of death was around eighteen months ago. The body is that of a female child, eight or nine years old. I can't give a cause of death, but the stomach and bowel are completely empty which can only point to starvation. She was a redhead and, even at her tender age, had two quite large fillings in the upper molars. They should make identification easier, shouldn't they, Jim? If she was reported missing, that is.'

Holly studied the pile of decay which was hardly recognisable as a child, and swallowed hard.

'How can you tell all that?' she asked.

Ferguson gave a dry laugh. 'Easy, we were lucky with this one. You see, the body was buried in very wet soil — if you study the lie of the land, all water from the surrounding area drains into that field and in a really wet season I'd imagine it's almost a lake. Now, what results in those conditions is a process called saponification whereby usually semi-liquid fats present in the body turn into a hard substance, almost like suet. This ensures the formation of adipocere—'

'Hold on, Alex, you're losing me here,' Ashworth said. 'How about using plain English?'

'Okay, well, the gist of it is, most of the body's internal organs were protected due to the wet conditions. Otherwise, I would've been able to tell you very little.'

He turned his attention back to the remains. 'Absolutely fascinating. I haven't seen anything like this for years. As I said, we've been very lucky.'

'Thank you, Alex,' Ashworth said, eager to leave. 'I look forward to receiving your report.'

'You'll have it by Monday morning, Jim.'

'Do you feel lucky, guv?' Holly whispered on their way to the door.

'No, just sick.'

They stood in the cold night air, breathing deeply and willing the sharp breeze to rid them of that unique mortuary smell.

'Right, then, we'd better get on to dental records,' Ashworth said.

'I'll get Josh to do it guv. He's already at the nick, going through the computer records on missing persons.'

'Good. You know what this means, Holly?'

'Yes, I've worked it out' she said, shuddering slightly. 'It means there could be any number of kids buried out there.'

'But we've only had two local children go missing, so where in God's name did that poor girl come from?'

Holly shrugged. 'Maybe they're getting more confident, guv. Maybe they picked her up miles away, and when she died they thought here would be a good place to dispose of the body. After all, they could cover the whole of the countryside with graves and in most cases we'd be none the wiser.'

Suddenly Ashworth clicked his fingers. 'Jan Morrison. She saw that man climbing over a gate at Anderson's Farm, remember? She said he was carrying a spade, and she thought there was another man behind him.'

'Do you think—'

'I know, Holly. Let's get back to the station. I'll get Newton on the phone. I want a police team on that field first thing in the morning.'

'Huh, you don't think he'll agree to that, do you, guv?'

'He'll have to,' Ashworth replied doggedly. 'If we could find a more recent body, the information that Alex and Forensic could supply us with would be invaluable.' He opened up the passenger door. 'Let's go, Holly, I feel in the mood to upset somebody, and the superintendent will do very nicely.'

* * *

It was almost 9 p.m. when Superintendent Newton burst into the CID office, looking rather incongruous in a splendid tuxedo.

'What's the meaning of this, Chief Inspector?' he spat. 'You've dragged me away from an extremely important dinner party.'

'Oh, really, sir? I am sorry,' Ashworth said, settling back in his chair to study the superintendent. 'It's just that DS Bedford and I have been attending a post-mortem on an unidentified young girl.'

'I'm well aware of that,' he said, his eyes skimming the full ashtray on Holly's desk. 'But surely this could have waited until Monday morning?'

'I disagree, sir,' the chief inspector said, with a definite edge to his voice. 'I need authorisation to dig up part of a field on Anderson's Farm first thing tomorrow morning.'

Some of the colour drained from the superintendent's face, much to Ashworth's delight and he growled, 'For God's sake, why, man? I'm trying to trim the budget. The last thing I need is a dozen police constables on double time, not to mention the whole of CID.'

Ashworth inhaled and paused for roughly ten seconds. 'Because, sir, as you well know we've had a report from a member of the public that a man was seen carrying a spade as he climbed over the gate to get out of that field. I did investigate, and although the field has been ploughed, it seems there were signs of the earth having been disturbed prior to that.'

'Refresh my memory, Chief Inspector, and tell me who reported it.'

'Mrs Janet Morrison, sir.'

'Exactly,' Newton said, glowering. 'Your supergrass, as she's known by the lower ranks. I believe she made a nuisance of herself in Leeds when she lived there, always calling the police—'

'Walking with a purpose,' Holly interjected, a sarcastic smile on her face.

'Thank you, DS Bedford, but I don't need to be reminded of what Home Secretaries, past or present have said on the subject of law and order.'

He shot another pointed look at her laden ashtray, and Holly responded by lighting a cigarette.

'Very well, Chief Inspector, I'll authorise the excavation of the field and leave you to make the arrangements.' He strode to the door and turned back, his grin mocking. 'But I'd be very careful of that supergrass of yours. We don't want the added expense of having to provide her with a new identity — passport, birth certificate, et cetera — now, do we? Oh, and DS Bedford, I would request that you refrain from smoking in the office. There's a part of the canteen allocated for those who indulge in the habit.'

'Enjoy your sweet and coffee, sir,' Ashworth said, his disdain barely hidden.

'Thank you.'

The door had hardly closed behind the man before Holly started waving two fingers at it and muttering, 'Prat,' rather loudly.

Josh came bustling into the office. 'I've just passed the super, and he didn't look too happy.'

'The superintendent and happiness are not comfortable bedfellows, I fear,' Ashworth remarked. 'Has anything turned up?'

'Yes, guv, but you're not going to like this,' he said, sinking into his seat. 'I managed to get an identification from her dental records. The body is Jade Vale, ten years old, and she vanished in Manchester twenty-one months ago.'

Ashworth let out a dismal sigh. 'So, what are we dealing with here?'

'A paedophile ring, by the looks of it,' Holly said. 'And a nationwide one, at that.'

'It certainly seems that way,' he murmured, wandering across to the glass wall. 'This thing isn't confined to Bridgetown — I realised that with the attempted abduction of Amy Byron. If the man had been local, there's a chance she would have recognised him.'

'Not necessarily, guv,' Josh said. 'The town's expanding. There're new people coming to live here all the time.'

Ashworth sighed. 'You're right, unfortunately, Josh. I still think of Bridgetown as the small tight-knit community it once was. Anyway, be at Anderson's Farm on the stroke of nine in the morning.'

* * *

Saturday night was known as pub night in the Leeds suburb where Jan Morrison had lived, with the streets often becoming rowdy and dangerous places after 9 p.m., and although she was now far away from that large city, the apprehension of venturing out still remained with her. However, the pull of Lime Street was proving too strong to be denied and if she should encounter a few drunks on the way there, then so be it. By this time Patch was familiar with the route and was pulling on his lead as they approached the expressway.

Jan had been christened Miss Marple by her old neighbours and she had to admit that the name pleased her. While she kept a vigil outside number nine, she wondered what the super sleuth would do if she were here now. Break in, maybe? Jan soon dismissed that idea; it was much too risky, even for her.

The house appeared to be in total darkness, with all curtains closed, although she did note that they were lined which meant that the lights could well be on but unable to penetrate the thick material. Concentrating hard, she listened for any sounds above the traffic roar of the expressway, but could detect nothing and was about to head for home when she spotted a man walking his Labrador on the far side of the bridge.

'Heel, Rocky, heel,' he grumbled, when the dog caught Patch's scent and pulled the man towards them.

'Evening,' he said to Jan. 'Bit chilly tonight.'

'I'll say.' Her heart was racing. Should she enlist this man's help? Should she pump him for information while their dogs sniffed noses?

'I, er, I was wondering . . .' she said. 'Do you happen to know who lives in number nine?'

'That I do — a right rum character called Randall,' the man said. 'Doesn't have much to do with anybody.'

'Oh, it's just that I was here the other night and I thought I heard screaming . . .'

'There's always something going on in there, missus — screaming, shouting, loud music. Should be reported. Anyway, I'd best be on my way.'

As she watched him walk off Jan was all the more determined to continue with her investigation. She would observe number nine Lime Street, and the next time she heard screaming she would telephone the police.

CHAPTER 11

A slight mist hung over Anderson's Farm the following morning as bleary-eyed police constables donned overalls and collected spades in a lane adjacent to the field. Ashworth had taken Holly to have a word with Sean, the attentive ploughman, whose curiosity in the investigation was instantly eclipsed by his interest in the shapely detective sergeant.

'Now be as exact as you can,' Ashworth said. 'Where was the grass that was taken from the side of the field?'

The ploughman, managing to drag his eyes away from Holly's figure, slowly pointed a finger. 'It was over there,' he said. 'Yes, I'm sure it was there.'

* * *

The officers split into three teams of four and worked in rotation, digging for hours. All were aware that the next shovelful of earth could reveal a foot, a hand, or part of a face, and each one hoped that his spade would not be the one to deliver. The work was hard and tedious and, after drawing a blank at the first site chosen by Sean, utterly frustrating. A second spot was targeted, mere feet away from the first, and that too proved fruitless. Holly stood at the gate and gazed around the vast area.

'This is a needle in a haystack job,' she remarked to Josh.

'That's if there's a needle out there, Hol.'

Ashworth was in earnest discussion with Sean at the centre of the field. The ploughman was becoming more agitated as the digging progressed, realising as he did that valuable police resources were being wasted.

'I'm sorry, Mr Ashworth,' he said, for the umpteenth time. 'I could have sworn it was there.'

Strain was showing on the chief inspector's face, but his tone remained kindly, as he said, 'It's all right son, just take your time. Have a good look round and see if you can line up with any landmarks.'

Sean scratched his head. 'I know it was in line with the gate, and I've been looking at where the grass was torn up from under the hedgerow . . . God, Mr Ashworth, I hope I'm right this time, but I reckon it's here.'

Ashworth glanced back to the second hole, a good nine or ten feet away. There was nothing else for it but to start again.

'All right,' he called to the officers. 'Let's try it here.'

The men moved straight away but there was a definite weariness in their steps, and fatigue showed clearly in the speed with which they struck the earth. By 4 p.m. Ashworth was thinking of calling a halt when a shout went up from the sergeant in charge.

'Over here, Jim, we've got a result.'

The CID team quickly made their way across the field, but Holly and Josh held back as they neared the hole and therefore Ashworth was the first to look into the unseeing eyes of Nicky Waldon. Her naked body was partially covered by the grey blanket, but her bruised and bloated abdomen was in full view.

Holly was already radioing for the police surgeon, the pathologist, and the Forensic department, while Josh set about organising the erection of a large tent over their grisly find.

* * *

Three hours later Alex Ferguson emerged from the well-lit tent, his face fixed with a grim expression.

'Walk with me, Jim,' he said, clearly shaken.

Ashworth frowned. 'Are you all right, Alex? You're not usually affected by your work.'

'It's far easier to work on a decomposed body, you know — far easier for me to cope with, I mean.' He let out a long breath. 'When I see a youngster like that, so recently dead, well, I can still imagine her laughing, playing . . .' He gave a tiny shake of the head and attempted to pull himself together. 'Anyway, Jim, she's been dead for about two weeks. Starved to death, I'd say. There's evidence of severe sexual assault over quite a long period of time — months, probably. I also found a high degree of physical abuse: cigarette burns all over her body, two broken ribs. I've an idea she was suspended by her arms at some time, and she was definitely gagged.' He cast a wretched glance at the chief inspector. 'What kind of bastard does that to a child, Jim?'

'I've no idea,' he replied slowly.

'I attended a lecture on paedophiles once,' Ferguson said, stopping by the hedge. 'They actually delude themselves into thinking that the children enjoy what's being done to them. They think the kids love them for it. Talk about sick people . . .'

'They're not sick, Alex, they're evil.'

'I'd have to agree with you there. Oh, by the way, Jim, I don't know what Forensic might tell you, but by the look of the blanket she was wrapped in, I'm almost certain that she was kept somewhere damp with a lot of loose debris about.'

Just then there was a commotion by the gate, a woman haranguing the police constable on guard whose patience was fast wearing thin. Their voices sounded clearly in the quiet evening air.

'I'm sorry, madam, this area is sealed off,' the constable repeated for the third time.

'But I have to see the chief inspector. It's very urgent.'

'I'll try and contact him on the radio, madam, but you can't go into that field.'

'Please hurry, this could be a matter of life and death.'

Ashworth was intrigued and, after excusing himself, he made for the gate.

'What's the problem, Gordon?' he asked PC Bennett.

'The lady here wants to see you, sir.'

Ashworth peered through the gloom. 'Mrs Morrison?'

'Have you found anything?' she asked, clearly emotional.

'Well, I'm not really allowed to say . . .' He hesitated. 'Yes, Mrs Morrison, I must confess that it hasn't been a waste of time.'

'When I heard the police were digging up this field,' Jan said, edging closer to the gate, 'it gave me the courage I needed to come and talk to you. You see, there's something else I want to report.'

* * *

Shannon was huddled beneath the blankets, the cold seeping into her very bones. She had been given nothing to eat all day, which was worrying for they had so far fed her well. She was, however, a child of the streets and her strong survival instincts were at last flooding to the surface.

If she stayed where she was then she would die, Shannon had already realised that much. She understood too that if she were to make an escape it would have to be now. Today. The repeated beatings were sapping her strength and hunger pains would only worsen her predicament, so she would take her chance while she still could.

Feeling better now that she had made a decision, Shannon pulled the blankets tighter around her chin and settled back to devise a plan.

* * *

Superintendent Newton slammed into the station, and every door between reception and his office was forcibly banged shut behind him.

'You're making a habit of this,' he ranted to the chief inspector standing in front of the desk.

'I need a search warrant, sir' Ashworth said, remaining quite calm.

Forty-five minutes later he was anything but calm, and he strode into CID looking far from pleased.

'Have we got the green light, guv?' Holly asked eagerly.

'No' Ashworth huffed. 'He's thinking about it.'

'But it's all bloody there,' she erupted. 'Jan Morrison heard screams outside number nine Lime Street, which is where Randall lives. He has a conviction for child pornography and two or three feet of false wall behind his lounge, which could fit in with what Alex Ferguson said about Nicky Waldon being kept somewhere damp with a lot of rubble on the floor. What more does he want?'

'I know,' Ashworth snapped, 'but he's weighing up the pros and cons.'

* * *

When that now familiar and dreaded shaft of light cut across her cell, Shannon lay perfectly still, her breath held fast. Then the light was shut out, all was black once more, and she listened hard for the click of the closing door. It came, but no sounds of sliding bolts followed. Good, the door wasn't locked. Now, all she had to do was remember where the light had been.

The rasp of fevered breath was heading towards her, a hand slapped the wall as it groped in the dark, and the sounds of concrete bits crunching beneath rubber soles were almost upon her. A hand touched her shoulder.

'Shannon,' the voice whispered, 'it's time for your treat.'

* * *

Ashworth was glaring at the telephone, willing it to ring. When it did, he jumped and hurriedly snatched up the receiver. 'Yes?'

'I've organised the search warrant,' Newton's frosty voice informed him. 'With considerable difficulty, as you can well imagine, at this time of night.'

Ashworth gave Holly a winning grin and motioned wildly for her to get moving. She grabbed her shoulder bag and ran from the office.

'Now, Chief Inspector, you'll want some uniformed officers with you . . .'

'Yes, sir, but we can arrange that.'

'Good. Well, I just hope this exercise proves to be worthwhile. If it's not, we're going to look pretty silly.'

'Thank you, sir,' Ashworth said, already on his feet.

He found Holly in reception, almost pleading with Sergeant Dutton.

'Honestly, Holly,' he was saying, 'I'm getting my lads there as quickly as I can. Sunday's a busy night.'

'They're on their way, are they, Martin?' Ashworth asked. 'Believe me, Jim, by the time you get there, half a dozen of my lads'll be waiting.'

'Good man. Let's go, Holly. Where's Josh?'

'Already in his car, guv.'

Dutton's expression was sceptical as he watched them disappear through the swing doors.

'You're taking a chance, Jim,' he muttered, glancing towards the ceiling. 'And I think there's someone not a million miles away from here who wouldn't mind seeing you fall flat on your face.'

CHAPTER 12

Shannon felt the cold prickles of fear inch along her spine as the man shook her shoulder and ordered her to stand, his large hands pulling at the blankets with a vicious force. Obeying meekly, she held her breath so she could hear his more clearly.

With infinite care she eased her foot along the floor, little by little until it touched his shoe. Then she moved it the other way until she again connected with the smooth feel of leather. Sure now that she was correctly positioned, Shannon brought up her knee with all the strength she could muster.

The man howled at the pain in his crotch and slackened his grip for just a second. But that was all the time she needed. She was running in the direction of the light but misjudged and collided heavily with the wall. Momentarily dazed, Shannon stumbled backwards, all too aware of the man feeling around for her in the dark, his angry curses bouncing off the high ceiling.

Managing to compose herself, she edged along the wall. The door must be somewhere . . . it must be. Yet all she touched was cold, damp, uneven brick. The man was crashing about behind, his breathing ragged and coming closer.

Shannon's spirits sank and hot tears were stinging her eyes when her hand finally rested on wood. Whimpering softly, she fumbled until her fingers found the handle. Hurriedly she pushed it down and pulled back. As the door swung open a bright harsh light hurt her eyes but she raced towards it heedlessly.

'I'll kill you for this, Shannon,' the man hissed.

She was running blind; having spent so long in darkness her eyes were unable to adjust. Everything was blurred, fuzzy, and his venomous voice was getting nearer.

* * *

Ashworth's adrenalin was racing when he turned left into Lime Street, and he shot Holly a triumphant smile when they caught sight of the patrol cars parked outside number nine. He brought the Scorpio to a halt and glanced back to see that Josh was pulling in behind. Police Constable Bobby Adams was there to greet them as they climbed out of the car.

'The back of the house is secure, sir,' he said. 'It's the embankment leading to the expressway. Gordon Bennett and John Dickens are already there.'

'Good,' Ashworth said, his gaze directed to the front door. 'No movement from inside?'

'None, sir.'

Holly started across the front garden. 'Let's do it, guv.'

* * *

Shannon was screaming as loud as she could, hopeful that someone might hear. She dared not stop to get her bearings but ventured on, crashing into walls and objects, unmindful of her painful shins and of the large bruises that were even now developing on her arms.

She could feel the man's breath on the naked skin of her back, and although her lungs hurt with each laboured cry she opened her mouth and let out a raw piercing shriek.

* * *

'What's that noise?' Ashworth muttered, stopping in his tracks.

'Somebody's screaming,' Holly said. She raced to the door and pounded on it with her fists. 'Open up. Police.'

The screams grew louder.

* * *

The man was almost upon her when Shannon made out the hazy outline of a door. Her mouth was dry, her heart beating frantically as she hastened towards it, still screeching, and turned the handle.

* * *

The door swung open to reveal Gilbert Randall standing on the threshold, seemingly unconcerned by the cacophony of screams filtering into the hall.

'What the hell's going on here?' he demanded to know.

Holly took an angry step forward. 'We're police officers, and we've got a warrant to search your premises.'

'I know who you are,' he sneered, 'but you've got no right—'

'Balls,' she said, pushing past and almost knocking him back against the wall.

Those distressing sounds were coming from the lounge and she raced towards them, kicking the door with some force. Gerald Clark was sprawled on the settee, his eyes on the blaring television. Holly watched the images. It was a horror film, the vampire obviously closing in on his victim whose mouth was open to emit one last blood-curdling cry before his fangs sank into her neck.

Clark straight away jumped to his feet. 'Hey, what are you doing here?'

'Shut it,' she spat, crossing to the television set and pressing the off switch.

Randall came hurrying into the room, closely followed by Ashworth and Josh.

'It was the TV, guv,' Holly said flatly.

'You'd better have an explanation for this,' the man ranted. 'You can't just come bursting into my house without so much as a by your leave.'

Ashworth swallowed nervously; he was feeling slightly sick now. 'We do have a warrant, sir,' he said. 'And, tell me, do you always have your television on so loud?'

'We were only watching a video, as we often do,' Clark said, glaring pointedly at Holly. 'But that moron turned it off.'

She glowered back at him, was about to offer a stiff retort, when Randall launched into a verbal attack directed at the chief inspector.

'I mean, what the hell are you doing here?' he yelled. 'I'll be complaining to the highest authority about this—'

'Like the chief inspector said, we've got a warrant,' Holly interjected. She swiftly produced it from her pocket and held it out, but Randall merely pushed it aside.

'I couldn't give a damn what you've got,' he said, still scowling at Ashworth.

'Calm down,' Gerald Clark advised. 'You're playing into their hands, Gilbert. This is exactly what they want. They'd just love you to over-react.'

Still seething, but visibly controlling his temper, Randall said to Ashworth, 'What are you actually looking for, then?'

'I don't know if you're aware of it,' he said, crossing to the fireplace and tapping the wall at various intervals, 'but behind here there's at least two feet of the house that was once joined to yours.'

The two men exchanged a look. 'So what?' Randall said, shrugging.

'This is a cock-up,' Josh whispered to Holly.

'Not necessarily,' she hissed back. 'They could've been using the loud videos to cover the sounds of a screaming child.'

Ashworth was instructing one of the uniformed officers to examine the wall, and while PC Dick Gibbins set about the task, he wandered over to watch with Holly and Josh. All was quiet as Gibbins systematically rapped the wall starting at floor level and finishing at ceiling height. By the time he had covered the complete wall his expression was one of dejection.

'Sorry, sir,' he said to Ashworth, 'but it's all solid brick.'

Randall threw back his head and let out a sarcastic laugh. 'Well, of course it is. You didn't think there was some sort of secret opening in it, did you?'

The answering grin froze on Clark's face when he saw Holly disappear into the hall. He followed quickly and found her staring up the stairs.

'What are you doing now?' he asked.

'Searching,' she replied. 'As in search warrant.'

He leant back against a door and fixed her with a derisory look. 'You didn't happen to have a grandfather called Adolf, did you?'

She laughed pleasantly. 'No, but I did have a famous ancestor, oh, way back. His name was Attila. Actually, they say I take after him.'

He took a threatening pace forward, and Holly deliberately stepped on his foot, her whole weight centred on the high stiletto heel that dug into his instep.

'Oh, sorry,' she said, her innocent look further fuelling the man's anger.

'You bitch . . .'

'Excuse me,' she said, pushing him to one side.

The door on which he had been leaning opened up to reveal a built-in cupboard of considerable size. And there was a puzzled frown on Holly's face when she saw a large bookcase positioned against its back wall.

'Guv,' she called. 'I think I've got something.' Ashworth came hurrying from the lounge with a highly flustered Gilbert Randall at his heel.

'There's a bookcase in this cupboard, covering the whole of one wall,' she said, stepping aside for the chief inspector. 'It's a funny place to put a bookcase, don't you think, guv?'

'Interesting,' Ashworth mused. 'Dick, come and check this out.'

'You can't do this,' Randall yelled, as PC Gibbins hurried into the cupboard. 'This is private property, for God's sake.'

When Randall tried to manhandle the constable back into the hall a scuffle ensued and Josh and Bobby Adams, alerted by the noise, came rushing from the lounge. By this time Ashworth and Holly had the man in a firm grip, but he continued to rant.

'Bobby, get him away from here,' Ashworth said.

He nodded and grabbed hold of Randall's arm. 'Come along with me, sir.'

'Get off,' he shouted. 'Just take your hands off me.'

'Control yourself, sir,' Bobby said, 'or I'll have to restrain you.'

The mêlée continued until Randall was herded into the lounge, with Josh following behind holding a far more subdued Gerald Clark. Then Holly helped PC Gibbins to empty the shelves. With most of the books stacked in haphazard piles, the constable began his test of the wall.

'Brick,' he muttered, moving speedily. 'Brick.'

When the majority of the wall had been covered he went down on his knees and lifted out the books from the bottom left-hand corner. The first tap hit a solid structure.

'Brick,' he murmured automatically, before tapping six inches to the right. 'Bri . . .' Gibbins spun around. 'This isn't brick, sir.' He hit the wall again and grinned at the hollow sound thrown back at him.

'Let's get it off the wall,' Ashworth urged.

'It's secured with a screw in each corner,' Gibbins said, producing a small screwdriver from his tunic pocket and setting to work. 'Sir, these screws are coming out easily. Could mean they've been in and out on a regular basis.'

The bottom two were out and Gibbins hastily got to his feet and started on the top. Ashworth watched the screws coming out, turn by turn, his hands bunched into impatient fists.

'Here we go,' Gibbins said as he slid the bookcase away, setting Holly's teeth on edge as it scraped across the concrete floor.

With the bookcase gone a piece of plasterboard was exposed, and behind that a hole about two feet in diameter where a number of bricks had been removed.

'Well, what do you know?' Holly said, with a victorious whoop.

'Give me your flashlight, Dick,' Ashworth said, as he knelt in front of the hole and peered through. He switched on the torch and manoeuvred his head and shoulder inside, his nostrils instantly flaring at the strong smell of damp.

'I can't really see anything,' he muttered glumly.

'Guv, give me the torch and I'll go in,' Holly said.

'No, I'll get one of the uniformed lads to do it.'

'There could be a child in there, guv. I'm best equipped to deal with this.'

'All right,' he said, still reluctant. 'But just be careful. We don't know what state the floor's in.'

'Yes, Dad,' she mumbled, taking the torch and preparing to wriggle through the hole.

She went in feet first, writhing and pushing her way forward like a limbo dancer, and was almost through when she stepped on a small chunk of concrete and badly ricked her ankle. Her muttered curse gave off a hollow echo in the chill confined space as she struggled to her feet.

The cavity was possibly wider than two feet and had a strange feel to it, for evidence of its former inhabitants was all around. In the dim glow of the flashlight Holly could make out an old iron fireplace attached to a chimney breast still covered with wallpaper, the large pink roses that made up its pattern now faded and forlorn. Indeed, the arc of the torch picked up nothing but reflections of the past: a discarded lampshade, also pink and edged with white fringe; a child's rag doll, its right arm missing.

Still whispering curses to herself Holly slowly picked a path to the left, careful to avoid the numerous jagged stones that were strewn about for their sharp edges would easily tear the thin soles of her shoes. There was an unnatural silence all around which caused her heart to thump and her skin to prickle. It was almost as if, by coming through the hole in the wall, she had entered into another world that had been deserted and forgotten for twenty years.

Shrugging off a distinct feeling of doom she edged along and came upon a door, its green paint bubbled and chipped. She gave a tentative push and started violently at the sound of its squealing hinges. But then her inquisitive nature took over, for beyond the door were a number of wooden steps that seemed to lead down to a small room.

Something caught her eye, something grey, and with rising anticipation she took a hesitant step on to the first stair to test its support. The wood creaked and groaned beneath her weight, and at each step threatened to collapse, but with a child's life uppermost in her mind Holly inched her way down.

On the middle step she could see that the object was a grey blanket thrown over . . . what? The moment her feet touched the stone floor, she hurried across to investigate.

* * *

It took the brawn of all attending officers to get Gilbert Randall and Gerald Clark to Bridgetown Police Station. The two men struggled all the way to the patrol cars and were still objecting as they were led into reception.

'Interview rooms one and two,' Ashworth ordered harshly.

'I won't say anything until I've spoken to my solicitor,' Randall warned at the top of his voice as he was dragged away.

Ashworth turned to Holly and Josh. 'Right, we'll take Clark first. For all his brag and bluster, it's not his property and he's going to want to get himself out of this. You come in with me, Holly.'

'Will do, guv.'

'Josh, you stay by the phone. I want to know the minute Forensic come up with anything from Randall's house.'

Holly followed him through to interview room number one. Clark was sitting at the table, idly toying with a packet of cigarettes, and she straight away moved to the tape recorder as Ashworth acknowledged the uniformed officer at the door and pulled up a chair.

'Mr Clark,' he began, his manner abrupt.

'I've got nothing to say.' Clark lit a cigarette and threw the lighter on to the table. 'You've got no right to hold me here.'

'I've every right,' Ashworth assured him. 'We found the bodies of two young girls this weekend.'

'That's got nothing to do with me. You can't prove I was anywhere near those kids.' His tone was strong and confident, but even as the words were uttered the colour drained from his cheeks.

'I could have a try,' Ashworth retorted. 'After all, you're very fond of videos that contain explicit sex with children, torture, and—'

'But they're not my tapes,' Clark insisted.

Ashworth watched him closely, noted the panic in his eyes, the almost imperceptible shake of his hand as the cigarette was brought to his lips.

'So, you didn't know those tapes were there?' he said eventually. 'You didn't know they were sitting in that hidden annexe to the house? The videos will be fingerprinted, you know.'

'All right, all right, I knew they were there,' Clark threw back, mercilessly grinding out the cigarette. 'In fact, I've watched them. Gilbert gets them from the Continent. So what? It's no big deal.'

Holly strode across to the table, a murderous light in her eyes. 'And have you and Mr Randall ever been tempted to turn fantasy into reality?' she spat. 'Have you ever been tempted to abduct a child?'

'Of course we haven't,' Clark blustered. 'People in this country are far too narrow-minded.'

'In as much as we put the protection of children before all else?' Ashworth said, glaring at the man. 'Well, I can tell you now, in that respect I'm positively old-fashioned.'

'Are you going to charge me with anything?' Clark asked, with a cool detachment.

Ashworth got to his feet. 'Our investigation is still ongoing. You'll be here until it's completed.'

Holly terminated the interview for the benefit of the recorder, and then stomped out to Ashworth in the corridor.

'Bloody tape recorders,' she fumed. 'If it wasn't for them we wouldn't have to be so polite to creeps like him.'

'I wonder if there's anything come in from Forensic.'

'Shouldn't think so, guv, it's too early. They won't have had time, yet.'

He exhaled sharply. 'No, I suppose not. Come on, Holly, let's see what Mr Randall has to say.'

CHAPTER 13

Shannon lay shivering on the cold floor, with huge tears of frustration tumbling down her cheeks. She had been so close to freedom. The door had opened up in front of her and she had thrust herself out into the night. Straight into the arms of a so-familiar figure.

She had smiled up into that welcome face and babbled on about the man chasing her, the man who had held her prisoner. But no response came from the woman in whose arms she felt safe and Shannon pulled back, horror widening her eyes.

'Oh, no,' she had whimpered. 'Not you as well?'

She tried to break free but it was hopeless, the man had caught up by then. And the woman smiled at him.

'Our little playmate almost escaped,' she said. 'But don't worry, it's only a cry to be punished. She does like that.'

* * *

Gilbert Randall stared straight ahead, refusing to meet Ashworth's gaze. He was concentrating on the whirl of the tape recorder in the background, and Ashworth's impatient sighs.

'I'm not saying anything until my solicitor gets here,' he said, banging his fist on the table. 'I've made a request for him to be present, and you're denying me my rights.'

'I'm denying you nothing,' Ashworth barked, his temper beginning to fray. 'Your request has been logged, so it's on record. But it's very difficult to get a solicitor at midnight on a Sunday night.'

'I'll be making a complaint about you,' Randall threatened. 'And that bitch over there.'

'For the benefit of the recording,' Ashworth said loudly, 'Mr Randall has just referred to DS Bedford as a bitch which, I'm sure, will be taken into account when a decision is reached on who was acting unreasonably.'

'I want my solicitor,' Randall repeated stubbornly.

'I'll chase him for you,' Ashworth said, getting to his feet. 'But it really is a waste of time. You see, Mr Clark has already told us what we want to know.'

Randall gave a tight smile. 'Gerald's done no such thing. I know him. All he's said is that the tapes belong to me, a fact that I'd have great difficulty in denying, in any case. But that's all he's told you.'

Ashworth leant across the desk and stared into Randall's eyes. 'So, you're admitting there's more — am I right? Is this nothing more than a damage limitation exercise? You'll get your brief, hold your hands up to the videos, then try and dodge any further questions? Is that it?'

'No, no,' Randall stammered, with a vigorous shake of the head. 'You're trying to trick me. That's not what I said.'

'I see, so you're willing to talk about the videos, but nothing else.'

'I've told you, I'm not willing to discuss anything until—'

'Until your solicitor is present — yes, I know. Well, I'll tell you the first thing I'm going to do — I'm going to bring in the girl who was nearly taken from outside the church school and see if she can identify you. That'll be in the morning. Until then, you and your friend can stay in our custody.'

Randall's mouth sagged open. 'You can't do that. You've got no right to do that.'

'Now, look here,' Ashworth said, his face pushed close to Randall's, 'I'm getting very tired of you telling me what I can and can't do.'

'You're wasting your time,' the man insisted. 'I wouldn't do anything like that. I mean, what sort of person do you think I am, Ashworth?'

The chief inspector was striding towards the door, intent on putting space between them; but when the tape recorder clicked off he seemed to pause for thought.

Turning slowly, with a contemptuous expression darkening his face, he said, 'Randall, I think you're the lowest form of life I've ever had to deal with.'

That said, he marched into the corridor and Holly hurried out to him.

'I'll second that, guv,' she said, her smile supportive.

He shot her a regretful look. 'I shouldn't have said it, Holly. I'm irritable, I suppose; it's long past the time for my whisky nightcap . . .'

'You don't have to make excuses for your feelings,' she said quietly. 'Caring deeply about something doesn't make you any less of a man, you know.'

'Maybe not,' he muttered, staring at the opposite wall. 'Holly, these people make me feel so angry . . .'

Just then Josh pushed through the swing doors at the end of the corridor and Ashworth hastened towards him.

'Any news from Forensic?'

'One big fat zero, guv. If a child's ever been held in that hidden recess, the signs have been well and truly covered up.'

'I suppose that's just about what I expected.' He let out a frustrated sigh. 'I've been doing some research on paedophiles, and it seems they often operate in teams or rings. One of the patterns to their behaviour is that those abducting the children are rarely the ones indulging in the sexual abuse or torture.'

'I don't follow,' Holly said.

'It's simple. If the abductors are identified and their premises searched, there's never any sign or trace of the missing child, and it can be very difficult to get a prosecution under those circumstances.'

'That figures,' Josh said.

'And they're very loyal to the ring,' Ashworth went on.

'So, we could have someone in custody,' Holly said, nodding towards the interview room, 'who's abducted a number of children, but he'd rather keep quiet and go inside than shop the other members of the ring?'

'That's about it,' Ashworth said. 'According to my research, they'll admit to the lesser charges if they have to, but that's as far as they'll go. Another thing I've learnt is that they often use a woman to help with an abduction. A child will trust a woman far more than a man. All in all, that's why so few of the rings are ever broken.'

'We're really up against it, then,' Josh ventured.

'Yes, but I'll promise you something, here and now — this is one ring that's going to be prosecuted, believe me.' Without another word, he strode off and disappeared through the swing doors.

'What about Randall and Clark?' Josh asked Holly.

'We're holding them overnight. The guv'nor wants to see if Amy Byron can identify Randall. Come on, let's go home,' she said, linking her arm through his.

Holly's mood was pensive as they shouldered their way through the doors, and she was still silent when they trudged wearily down the stairs. Josh cast her a surreptitious glance.

'What's the matter, Hol? You're too quiet.'

'I'm worried about the guv'nor, Josh. You know how he usually rants and raves . . . Don't you think he's being too controlled on this one, as if he's bottling it all up? I just sense he's like a time-bomb ticking away. You know as well as I do that he's a pussycat where kids are concerned.'

'This case is affecting all of us.'

'Huh, tell me about it.'

'Listen, I'm sure that whatever happens, at the end of the day he'll behave like a true professional. He's a good copper . . .'

'Maybe, Josh.'

Reception was empty as they made for the car park, and once outside Holly stopped to light a cigarette. Beyond the gates a group of drunken teenagers passed by, chanting, 'Pigs, pigs.'

'Up yours,' Holly muttered. She leant back against the wall and inhaled deeply. 'Just look at them, Josh. They work all week to get their money, then spend the weekend pissing it up the wall. They're on their way to the chippy now, I'll bet, and in half an hour they'll be throwing up all over the place.'

'Oh dear, we are depressed.'

She drew on the cigarette and smiled. 'I suppose I am, just a bit. And it's too late for us to go for a drink.'

'Have you got anybody at the moment?' he asked, after a long pause.

She shook her head. 'This case has even turned me off that. Look, Josh, shall we go to my place and have a few drinks there? You can crash out on the settee.'

'Okay, but only if you promise not to try and convert me,' he said, hoping to lighten her mood.

She grinned. 'Shit, I was going to get you drunk and grope you.

'Come on, Bedford, take me home,' he said, pulling her towards their cars.

CHAPTER 14

Amy Byron gave a positive identification of Gilbert Randall at the police station next morning. She was certain he was the man who had tried to tempt her into his car outside the school gates. Her reasoning was clear and precise: it was his eyes she remembered, she said, and his ginger hair sticking out from under his cap.

Even as she was talking, Ashworth could see the complications. The girl would have to attend court and give evidence. It would be difficult, however grown up she thought she might be. As soon as Randall was taken away, he broached the subject to her parents.

'Do I have to go to court now?' Amy asked excitedly, jumping from her chair.

'Not at this precise moment,' Ashworth said, his smile warm. 'But at some time in the future, if the case goes to court—'

'I'll have to go then.' She straight away shot an apologetic glance towards her father. 'Sorry, I know it's rude to interrupt, but sometimes when I know what's coming I can't help it.'

'Well, I think on this occasion we can overlook it.' Ashworth chuckled.

He wanted to speak to her parents alone. They at least needed to be told of the difficulties attached to a court case, and therefore he asked Sergeant Dutton to take Amy to the canteen in search of orange squash.

'Now, I want you both to think this through carefully,' he counselled, the moment their daughter had gone. 'A court case is an extremely traumatic experience, especially for a child.'

The Byrons exchanged a glance and linked hands. 'What are the chances of a conviction, Chief Inspector?' Larry Byron asked.

'Only fifty-fifty,' he was loath to admit. 'It would go to a jury and would depend on them linking the possession of child pornography with the attempted abduction. If they went the other way, then they could quite easily find that talking to a child was not an offence in itself.'

'Have you found the little girl who went missing recently?' Mrs Byron asked.

Ashworth shook his head.

'The thing is,' she said, 'we've talked this over at length. It could so easily have been Amy that went missing . . . Anyway, we feel we have to go ahead with it, if only to deter others from doing the same thing.'

* * *

Gilbert Randall glanced up when Ashworth ushered Holly into the interview room. Beside him at the table was his solicitor, Benjamin Fox, a man in his forties who possessed the worst toupee that Ashworth had ever seen. It resembled the fur on a child's teddy bear, and its auburn colour in no way matched Fox's own deep brown.

'Ah, Chief Inspector, at last,' the solicitor said. 'Now I must insist that you make it clear if you intend to bring any charges against my client.'

'Mr Fox, isn't it?' Ashworth said, easing his bulk into a chair facing the two men. 'Well, Mr Fox, I intend to charge Mr Randall with the possession of pornographic video tapes, and also with the attempted abduction of a minor.'

Fox gave a tight smile. 'My client intends to plead guilty to the pornographic tapes charge, but vigorously denies having anything to do with the attempted abduction.'

'He's still going to be charged with it,' Ashworth replied, in a flat hard tone.

'Come, come, Chief Inspector,' Fox cajoled. 'You haven't got a hope in hell of making that stick.'

'We've got a positive identification, and Mr Randall drives a grey car which happens to be the colour we're looking for.'

'You're looking for a *small* grey car, if the newspapers are to be believed. My client drives a Ford Granada which, as you know, is quite large.'

'A child can make a mistake about the size of a car.'

'And also about who was sitting in the driver's seat,' the solicitor countered cleverly.

Ashworth took in a deep breath. 'We'll wait and see, shall we?' He fixed Randall with a hostile stare. 'Now, I'd like to ask your client about the disappearance of other children in the area.'

'Mr Randall doesn't want to discuss any such thing. His only comment with regard to this matter is that he knows nothing about any of the children who have disappeared.'

'So he's refusing to answer questions?'

Fox cast an uneasy glance at his client and noisily cleared his throat. 'That's not what I said, Chief Inspector. Mr Randall will answer any questions you put to him.'

'Fine.' He rested his gaze on Randall's face. 'Where were you on the night Shannon Dixon disappeared?'

'When was that?' Fox interjected.

'It's okay,' Randall said softly. 'I read the papers, I watch TV, I know when it was. And as it happens I know exactly where I was that night. I went to the Apollo Club. After my work-out I went to the bar for a meal and a few drinks.'

'You were there all evening?'

'All evening,' Randall said firmly. 'From seven to around eleven.'

'How convenient that you remember so clearly,' Ashworth said, with heavy sarcasm.

Fox leant forward. 'With respect, Chief Inspector, I would suggest that you're behaving in a very vindictive manner. If Mr Randall could not remember where he was that night, you'd accuse him of being evasive.'

'You were nowhere near the recreation ground on the council estate that evening?'

The solicitor inhaled sharply. 'My client has already told you where he was.'

Ashworth rose abruptly to his feet. 'Right, Mr Randall, you'll be charged in due course and appear in court later today.'

'Will you be opposing bail?' Fox asked.

'I most certainly will,' Ashworth told him.

* * *

Holly left the interview room to find him pacing the corridor.

'What do you think, guv?'

He scowled. 'Randall's tied up in all this somehow, but everything we've got on him is paper thin.'

'Will the abduction charge stick?'

'I can't see why not. It'll go through the magistrates court, and I'm sure the CPS will endorse it. But Randall will get bail, that's what's getting to me.'

'At least he'll know we're watching him, guv. That should stop him doing anything else.'

'Holly, could you and Josh check out the Apollo Club tonight? I've no doubt that Randall was there the night Shannon Dixon disappeared, but check out who he mixes with. I've a strong feeling that man's the key to this whole thing.'

'Will do, guv. What about Gerald Clark?'

'Thank Mr Clark for his help and then let him go.'

* * *

Every inch of Shannon's body ached. The night before, she had been kicked and punched around the tiny cell until she passed out. The same had happened many times, but last night was worse for there were more than two people kicking out at her. She could almost feel their rage poisoning the air. They seemed to be blaming her for something that had happened to a man called Randall.

All sense of time had long since departed but her tormentors, during their embittered talk, had revealed that it was night, therefore she assumed it was now daytime and that she had been unconscious for just a few hours. She was able to reach such an accurate presumption because of the relatively small amount of stiffness in her joints on waking. They had bound her hands and feet during her black-out, as they always did; and sometimes, after lying prone for a long time, her numb limbs needed much coaxing before she was able to shift her position.

Shannon tested the rope that held her hands securely behind her back. It was tight around her wrists, digging into her skin, and would not loosen no matter how hard she tried. Quite breathless, with arms aching, she rested. And it was while her thoughts were wandering that she remembered something she had touched yesterday on her way to the door. If only she could find it again. If only she could reach it . . .

* * *

When Gilbert Randall was brought before the magistrates that afternoon it was swiftly decided that there were indeed cases to answer on both charges. The man exuded an air of innocence throughout the proceedings and when the chairman of the bench bailed him to appear before them in one month's time he nodded his gratitude.

Ashworth was seething. He had strongly opposed bail and had hoped that the magistrates would uphold his application in view of the seriousness of the charges. One month was necessary because the Crown Prosecution Service would need that time to decide whether or not to go ahead with the attempted abduction charge. Nevertheless, Ashworth was none too pleased with the prospect of having to keep tabs on the man for four weeks.

As Randall was led from the court he cast an amused glance at the chief inspector, whose impassive expression betrayed none of the bubbling anger that was eating away at his insides. Ashworth had begun to take things personally.

CHAPTER 15

Vic Meadows signalled to overtake the Cortina and pulled out into the middle lane of the motorway. His huge lorry took time to pick up speed and the car was dwarfed in its shadow for the few minutes that Vic dawdled alongside. Then, grinning widely, he inched in front and roared past, throwing up sheets of spray from the wet road as he swung in front of the car.

His grin became a belly laugh as Vic imagined the driver cursing and swearing at the spray on his windscreen obscuring his view. This was a game he often played on long distance runs; it helped to ease the monotony. Today's haul was from Manchester to London and was one he had done so many times he could negotiate it with his eyes shut.

Vic was sixty years old and had been driving heavy goods vehicles for the past forty. Forty years in which he had married, fathered four kids, paid off the mortgage, and for what? So he could enjoy the retirement that now loomed on his horizon? No way; he dreaded it. His wife was all right in small doses, but the thought of seeing her day in and day out filled him with loathing. The truth was, Vic loved young shapely prostitutes and his job gave him ample opportunity to indulge his passions with no one, his wife especially, being any the wiser.

Junction six one mile ahead, the signs told him. Great, he could get off at six and pass through Bridgetown. It was about time he caught up on the action there.

* * *

Holly took hold of Josh's arm as they strolled towards the Apollo Club. It was a new establishment of the kind that had become the vogue in recent years for those upwardly mobile types who, after working hard, liked to play hard, too. It offered its members a large well-equipped gymnasium, saunas and massage parlours, plus a sumptuous restaurant and numerous bars in which to relax afterwards.

Holly was in a buoyant mood and was looking her best in a black trouser suit worn over a white roll-neck sweater. As the automatic doors opened up and welcomed them into the impressive foyer they were approached by the steward, a huge man in evening dress.

'Good evening,' he said, smiling. 'Are you members?'

Holly tore her gaze away from the pink scalp shining through his severe crewcut and said, 'Yes . . . members of Bridgetown CID.' She produced her warrant card which the man scrutinised closely.

'Okay, so what can I do for you?'

Josh jumped in quickly. 'Actually, we'd like to see the manager.'

'Sure,' he said. 'Just wait here.'

Moments later the manager, a slight well-groomed man in his thirties, came hurrying into the foyer, his eager smile at odds with the concern showing in his eyes.

'Hello, there,' he said, holding out a hand. 'How can I help you?'

Holly put on a serious expression. 'DS Bedford, sir, and this is DC Abraham. And you are . . . ?'

'John Headson. Look, there's nothing wrong, is there?'

'This is a very delicate matter,' she said, leading him to one side. 'We've been getting reports about girls on the game using your bars and massage rooms.'

'What?' he said, his jaw sagging. 'I've seen no signs of that sort of thing and I can tell you now, I keep a very careful watch for it.'

'Don't take any notice of her, Mr Headson,' Josh said. 'She's mental, that's all.'

The manager looked from one to the other, his expression alternating between alarm and relief.

'We're making inquiries about one of your members,' Josh told him. 'A Mr Gilbert Randall.'

Headson relaxed. 'Ah, Mr Randall. I heard he'd been arrested. It was such a shock.'

'Were you surprised?' Holly asked. 'Discovering he was into child pornography, I mean?'

'I was astounded, actually.' His voice dropped to a whisper. 'To be honest, I always think of Mr Randall as the odd man out. All his friends are keen members of the church, and yet he shows no leaning in that direction at all, not that it's a crime. But buying those tapes, and then trying to take a young child off the streets . . .'

Their ears pricked at mention of the church, and Holly said, 'Does the youth leader employed by St Giles's use the club?'

'No, not him — he always claims he's too busy — but the vicar does.'

'The vicar works out here?' she asked casually, her sudden interest concealed.

'Well, he doesn't work out as such, he just uses the sauna. He brings some of the choir boys from time to time. I mean, if parents can't trust a vicar with their kids, who can they trust?'

'Who, indeed,' Holly muttered. 'Mr Headson, are you willing to tell us who Randall's friends are, here at the club, and perhaps mention their addresses?'

'Names and addresses?' He hesitated, fidgeting on the spot. 'I shouldn't really pass out that sort of information.'

Holly smiled sweetly. 'But you will, won't you? Just for me? Because you like me so much?'

Headson laughed loudly, despite his misgivings. 'All right, he's rather friendly with two couples. Robin and Marcia Scott — they run an insurance brokers and live in Sundial Lane.'

Holly found her notepad and scribbled the information in hurried shorthand.

'And Arthur and Jean Perry,' the manager continued. 'They live in one of the big houses in Lilac Avenue. I think they're in property. Both couples are impeccably respectable. All of this is going to come as quite a shock to them.'

'I'll bet,' Josh said. 'There's nobody else?'

'No, not really. Mr Randall is very popular here, but he doesn't . . .' Headson suddenly paused. 'Hold on, I don't know if this'll be of any use to you but old Tom Gardiner was in here last week. Have you heard of him? Awful character. Never washes. He just walked straight in and started talking to Mr Randall. I felt like asking him to leave.'

'Any idea what they were talking about?' Holly quizzed.

'None, but Mr Randall was quite amicable towards him. That's why I hesitated about throwing him out.'

'Thanks a lot, Mr Headson,' Josh said, shaking the man's hand. 'You've been very helpful.'

On the walk back to the car, Holly said, 'Funny how the church keeps coming into this. Have you noticed, Josh?'

'Yes, and what better cover for a paedophile ring than a place of worship?'

'And old Tom Gardiner's popped up again. I think we should have another look at him in the morning.'

'Holly, you can't really believe—'

'Listen, Josh, if you can believe a vicar could be taking these kids, you shouldn't have any difficulties in accepting an old pervert like Gardiner might be tied up in this somewhere. Like I said, we'll have another look at him tomorrow.'

* * *

Shannon crossed the cold rubbish-strewn floor, inch by painful inch, until she rolled into the wall. There, she began the arduous process of getting to her feet. Somehow she struggled upright and stood a while, gasping for breath. How much time had she got? Enough, she hoped, to find what she was looking for.

As soon as she felt able, Shannon worked her way along the wall, the rough bricks chafing the skin on her back. And then she found it. Controlling the joyous shout that threatened to erupt from her throat, she ran the fingers of her trussed hands over the sharp edges of the protruding brick.

Praying as hard as she could, she eased herself into position and started to rub the restraining rope against it. Would it work, or would she tire too soon? Even as those worries flitted across her mind, strands of the rope began to part. Encouraged, she rubbed harder and could soon smell burning, could feel heat caused by the constant friction scorching her wrists.

More strands separated, and then more. Shannon struggled to pull her arms apart and the rope gave way. She hurled the tangled mess across the cell, hardly able to believe she was free of it, then lost no time in crouching down to untie the rope around her ankles. Her thumbnail broke, the sharp pain bringing tears to her eyes, but she carried on. Finally the knot began to give, and then it came apart. Shannon pulled off the coarse rope and straight away felt her blood starting to flow again.

Almost whimpering with relief, she stayed on her haunches and made her way across the floor, her hands sweeping its surface in wide circles until they touched the filthy blankets. She quickly bundled them up and worked back in the direction of the stairs, finding them after three attempts.

Caution was not part of her plan now, so she scrambled up the steps and made a grab for the door. Beyond it the house was in darkness, but Shannon's night vision enabled her to see well enough. She stepped into the corridor and trod purposefully in the direction of the front door.

An object on the hall table caught her attention, made her stop dead. She stood for many moments, staring at it, unable to believe her eyes. Its very presence revealed the identities of her captors and utter disbelief tussled with revulsion in her young heart.

At that moment a kaleidoscope of light illuminated the hall as a car swung around a comer and stopped outside the house. Sounds of its engine dying and doors slamming shut rang out loudly as Shannon ran back through the rooms, her bare feet thudding on soft carpet. She opened a door and barged through to find linoleum beneath her feet, its touch cold and uninviting as she raced across the kitchen.

They were coming into the house. She could hear their key in the lock and its sound tore at her ears. Beyond a half-glazed door she could make out the garden. It was her only chance. Please, God, let the door be unlocked.

A blast of cold night air took away her breath as she wrenched it open and, swiftly wrapping the blankets around herself, she hurried towards a low fence and scrambled over it into the field beyond.

* * *

Not far away, Vic Meadows was steering his lorry back on to the trunk road, its massive wheels bumping precariously over the uneven surface in the transport café's car park.

He had managed to find a young girl with the unlikely name of Jezebel who had proved to be especially gifted in the finer arts of her chosen profession. Her fee was twenty-five pounds, and Vic felt he had enjoyed really good value for money.

Afterwards he treated himself to a jumbo-sized mixed grill and three mugs of tea. Now he needed to find a quiet lay-by, somewhere he could sleep in the cab after a pint or six in the nearest pub. Vic enjoyed his work.

CHAPTER 16

Those thin blankets gave little protection against the cruel frosty night but the bitter temperatures didn't worry Shannon, any more than the sharp stones that tore at her feet. She had outwitted her captors. She was free.

There was a road not far off. When she got there she would wave down the first passing car and ask to be taken to Bridgetown. She glanced nervously over her shoulder. Had they missed her yet? If so, what would they do, chase across the field after her? It was hardly likely; they wouldn't know how long she'd been gone. Okay, then, would they race to their car and scour the lanes and roads? That seemed the most probable scenario and was one that sounded a note of caution inside her brain.

She crouched by the fence, shivering violently. Two cars went by in close succession but Shannon was frightened to show herself in case it was them. Soon, though, her heart gave a leap for a vehicle far larger than a car came hurtling along the road. It was a lorry. Straight away Shannon ran out from her hiding place.

* * *

Vic Meadows let out a greasy belch and momentarily interrupted his whistled rendition of the 1960s Dion song, 'The Wanderer', and he was about to start again when he noticed something in his path. He leant towards the windscreen and peered harder. It was small and white.

'Jesus Christ,' he exclaimed.

It was a face, a young girl's face. He could clearly see her mouth opening and closing as she shouted to him.

'Jesus Christ,' he repeated, smashing his foot down hard on the brake pedal.

The giant wheels locked, their tyres screaming and burning into the tarmac, but it was too late. There was a thud and Vic could only watch in horror as the child's naked body was tossed into the air, grey blankets flying from it and billowing down on to the ground.

* * *

'Telephone, Jim,' Sarah called from the kitchen, her own path blocked by Peanuts who raced and barked around her feet in protest at the shrill ring.

'Yes, I think I can hear it Sarah,' Ashworth muttered good-naturedly. 'I tell you what, I'll get it.'

The dog was now yapping at his heels as he fought his way into the hall and snatched up the receiver.

'Jim Ashworth,' he said.

'Hello, Jim.' It was the warm Scottish lilt of Alex Ferguson. 'Apologies for disturbing you, but I've got something here that you'll want to know about.'

'Okay, Alex, what is it?'

'There's been a road accident a fatality.' Ferguson paused. 'I'm afraid it's young Shannon Dixon. She was knocked down by a lorry in Littlemarsh Lane. I was called in because of the suspicious circumstances. You see, she was naked and she apparently stepped out into the path of the lorry.'

Ashworth let out a dismal sigh. 'What did you find?'

'Plenty of signs of sexual abuse. There was physical abuse too, as far as I can tell. I can only suppose that she escaped from wherever she was being held and was trying to flag down the passing lorry.'

'Did she die on impact?'

'No, on the way to hospital. There's nothing you can do until morning, Jim, the lorry driver's in serious shock, but I just thought I'd let you know.'

'Thanks, Alex, I'm glad you did.' He dropped the receiver and stood for a while, his thoughts tumbling over themselves.

Sarah appeared at the kitchen door. 'Everything all right, Jim?'

'I'm afraid not. Shannon Dixon's dead. Run over by a lorry as she tried to get away from her kidnappers, apparently.'

Sarah gasped. 'Oh, no, this is getting worse.'

'I know, and what really worries me is the fact that every time one of these youngsters turns up dead, another one gets abducted.'

* * *

There was a purposeful stride to Ashworth's walk when he entered the CID office next morning.

'Alex Ferguson and Forensic have been on the phone, guv, Holly said.

'And?' he said, hanging up his waxed cotton jacket.

'Alex just wanted to confirm what he told you last night, and Forensic phoned to say that it looks as though Shannon had been kept in the same place as the other two girls.'

'I see,' Ashworth mused as he settled into his seat. 'And have they come up with anything from the scene of the accident?'

'Nothing. They were out there at first light trying to establish where she came from, but there're no traces of anything. She could have cut across the fields on either side of the road, or travelled any distance to arrive at the spot where she was run over.'

'What about the lorry?'

'Forensic did a thorough check. It's clean, and so is the driver, Victor Meadows. We phoned his employer. Meadows is from Manchester, on his way to London.'

'That's not much help.' Ashworth swivelled around and studied his map on the wall. 'Littlemarsh Lane,' he murmured. 'Now, across the field on one side we have the vicarage . . .'

'And on the other side, Tom Gardiner's place,' Holly remarked pointedly.

Josh dragged his attention away from the computer and said, 'But it's not as clear-cut as that guv, Holly's got a down on old Tom. If you look at the map, Lilac Avenue and Sundial Lane are very close to those fields. They're right on the edge of town.'

'What've Lilac Avenue and Sundial Lane got to do with this?'

Josh recounted the details given by Mr Headson at the Apollo Club and as he listened Ashworth sank back into his chair and thoughtfully drummed his fingers on the desk.

'I see,' he said, at last. 'I must confess that old Tom's not at the top of my list of suspects, but this church connection is starting to worry me. Now, we can't just go barging into either of those addresses, nevertheless I think discreet inquiries are in order and we should go there saying we're checking on Randall.'

'I still want to look into Gardiner,' Holly insisted.

'Don't worry, we shall. And I'll try and see the lorry driver at the hospital.'

* * *

Jan Morrison had really got the bit between her teeth now. On the day of Gilbert Randall's first appearance before the magistrates she had been sitting at the back of the court, and when he was brought in she thought how evil the man looked, and how guilty, too. By the time bail was granted a plan was already forming in her mind.

She was aware, from newspaper reports, that the police were seeking the driver of a small grey car in connection with the attempted abduction of Amy Byron, and yet Randall drove a large Ford Granada; she had seen it often enough, parked outside his house. Now, it didn't take a brain to rival Sherlock Holmes's to realise that unless the car turned up, the case against Randall could well fall apart. Jan had no intentions of letting such a thing happen, which was why she was yet again keeping an inconspicuous watch on number nine Lime Street.

She parked a little way along the road, as did all the best television detectives, and used her rear-view mirror for observation. After three-quarters of an hour her feet were like blocks of ice and she made a mental note that extra-thick socks would be needed for future surveillance.

She was trying to massage some warmth into her toes when Randall's Granada backed out of the drive, thick smoke escaping from its exhaust. Jan watched as he left his car to close the gates, and then ducked down in her seat as the vehicle moved slowly along the road. Starting the engine with an almost overwhelming excitement, she fell in behind it.

* * *

The doctors said he was suffering from shock, but he knew they were wrong. What Vic Meadows was experiencing as he lay in his hospital bed was deep dread of a police visit. There had been no witnesses to the accident so they could easily blame him. Thank Christ it happened on the way to the pub and not afterwards, when he would've reeked of beer. It was a selfish thought but one that continually went around his mind.

To his credit he was also nursing an intense feeling of guilt for he had hardly thought twice about the girl he had killed. He had tried, but every time his mind turned to that incident it just seemed to close down. All he could think about was losing his job, going to court — all the things that were likely to happen to him. More selfish thoughts. Perhaps he *was* in shock, and this self-interest was purely a symptom of it.

Voices in the corridor roused him from those depressing reflections, and he turned to see a huge man almost filling the doorway to his side room.

'Good morning, Mr Meadows,' he said. 'I'm Chief Inspector Ashworth, Bridgetown CID.'

CHAPTER 17

'How the other half lives,' Holly remarked, as she brought the Micra to a halt outside number twelve Sundial Lane.

'Yes, but think of the insurance premiums,' Josh replied.

They sat for a while and studied the house. It was a huge, detached dwelling, sitting prettily at the centre of its extensive grounds, its walls bedecked with the rust red leaves of a magnificent Virginia creeper. Leaving the car on the road they started the trek along its lengthy drive, immaculate but for the odd fallen leaf and bounded on both sides by neat well-maintained gardens.

As they approached the house, Holly spotted a young and extremely well-dressed woman intent on watching them at the leaded bay window of the lounge. When their eyes met the woman darted from sight. Josh pressed the bell and they stood outside the entrance porch to wait. Presently, the door was opened by a po-faced man, his glare as sharp as the perfect creases in his pin-striped business suit.

'Mr Scott?' Josh asked.

'Sorry,' the man said, pointing to a notice beside the door, 'but as you can see, we don't want to be bothered by salesmen or canvassers or any other such types.'

'Lucky for us we're police officers, then, isn't it sir?' Holly said, holding out her warrant card. 'We're from Bridgetown CID. I'm DS Bedford, this is DC Abraham, and you're Mr Robin Scott. Am I right?'

'Well . . . yes,' he said, his dour expression giving way to a flustered redness. 'What do you want with me?'

'We're making inquiries about Mr Gilbert Randall,' she said. 'May we come in for a moment?'

He stood aside immediately, and said, 'Yes, yes, of course.'

'Who is it, Robin?' The voice was young, female, and was coming from a room on the left of the hall.

'It's the police, dear.'

Holly was staring at the hall table on which a Bible took centre place when the woman came hurrying towards them.

'Whatever do the police want with us, darling?'

'They're making inquiries about Gilbert Randall,' he said, turning to the detectives. 'This is my wife, Marcia.'

Holly gave her a pleasant smile. 'We understand that you and your husband are friendly with Mr Randall . . .'

'Not friendly as such, no, I wouldn't say that,' she replied, her hands clutching nervously at her gold and pearl necklace. 'We've met him at the health club, had a meal and some drinks with him on a few occasions, but that's all.'

'So you don't know anything about his private life?' Josh asked.

'Only what we've been reading in the papers,' her husband said. 'I mean, we had no idea he was involved in anything like that.'

'And we'd rather it wasn't put about that we're friends of Mr Randall,' Marcia quickly said. 'We were merely acquaintances. Robin and I are heavily involved in the church, and if rumours start spreading, well . . .'

'Nothing to worry about, Mrs Scott,' Holly said. 'We're just talking to people who know Randall. We're not implying that you or your husband had any knowledge of his activities.'

'Well, thank God for that,' she said, a relieved smile dimpling her cheeks. 'And I can promise you one thing, we won't be having anything more to do with him.'

'Sorry to have taken up your time,' Josh said. 'But we do have to check up on these things. Anyway, thanks for your help.'

Robin Scott rushed forward to open the door. 'Not at all,' he said. 'Thank you for calling. Sorry we couldn't be of more help.'

As they trudged back to the car, Josh said, 'They seem respectable enough.'

Holly gave him a doubtful look, and then glanced back towards the house. 'Mrs Scott said thank God the way we'd say it, not like a deeply religious person would.'

'Are you kidding, Bedford?' Josh said, grinning.

'Noticing things like that is the mark of a good detective.'

'Oh, I see,' he said in a teasing tone. 'So if we go back and get one of them to say bugger, the case is solved. Brilliant.'

* * *

'Well, Mr Meadows, how are you feeling?' Ashworth asked as he pulled up a chair.

'Pretty rough,' he said, his eyes fixed on the ceiling. 'Am I in any trouble? I know that's a pretty selfish thing to ask, but . . .'

'No, it's not, it's quite natural, and I'm almost certain the answer is no. The girl you knocked down had been abducted some time ago. We think she was attempting to escape, which is why she was naked except for those two blankets.' He leant towards the bed. 'Do you feel up to telling me what happened?'

Vic was fiddling with the sheet screwing up its edges with huge anxious fingers. He swallowed noisily, then turned his gaze on the chief inspector.

'I've been trying to think it through . . . you know . . . but my mind just won't have it.'

'Try,' Ashworth gently urged.

Vic took in a deep breath. 'I . . . I was driving along the lane and all of a sudden there she was, just in front of the truck. I threw the anchor out the minute I saw her, but there wasn't time . . .'

'Was she waving her arms? Try to think because it's important.'

'No, no, she wasn't. All I could see was her white face, and she was shouting something. The blankets must have been wrapped round her. If it hadn't been for them I might have seen her.'

'That's the way we've put it together,' Ashworth said. He paused for a moment. 'After you hit the girl, what happened then?'

'Oh, God, I'm so ashamed of myself,' he muttered, his eyes tightly shut. 'It must have been a couple of minutes before I got out of the cab. I . . . I just sat there; I couldn't believe what had happened.' He turned towards Ashworth with a pleading look. 'Those couple of minutes didn't make any difference, did they? If I'd got the ambulance a bit quicker . . . ?'

Ashworth shook his head. 'No, Mr Meadows, it wouldn't have made the slightest bit of difference.'

'I didn't think so, but I can't help tormenting myself.' He fell back against the pillows. 'I reckon the kid knew she was dying, she asked me for a Bible.'

'A Bible?'

'Yes, when I got to her, she was saying, a Bible, a Bible . . .'

'I see.' Ashworth stood up and returned the chair to where he'd found it. 'That'll be all for the moment Mr Meadows, someone will be in later to take a formal statement. Try to rest now.'

* * *

It proved to be a particularly frustrating morning for Jan Morrison. Gilbert Randall visited the Save U supermarket, the bank where he worked, and then went on to several shops before returning home.

Jan doggedly sat in her car, a short distance along the road, and prepared to wait. Her mission was, after all, of vital importance and since she had recently acquired a microwave oven, meals were no longer a problem. When her understanding husband returned home from work he simply needed to pop a prepared dish into the oven and, hey presto, in a matter of minutes he had a meal fit for a king.

'So, Mr Randall,' she thought aloud, 'I'm completely at your disposal.'

* * *

Although Holly virtually ached for the Scotts' house in Sundial Lane, the one in Lilac Avenue had her positively drooling. The drive was far longer, the furnishings more expensive — those she could see, anyway — and the welcome equally frosty. Again they got no further than the hallway, and again their interviewees — this time, Arthur and Jean Perry — denied having any intimate knowledge of Gilbert Randall.

Yes, they knew him on a superficial basis, had shared meals and drinks with him at the health club where he proved to be the most agreeable company. Both were deeply shocked to read about his arrest and subsequent court appearance, and more than a little worried that their association with him, slight as it was, might damage their reputation at St Giles's Church.

Holly kept glancing back as they hurried along the drive. She could see the couple through the large dining room window, apparently locked in urgent discussion. Arthur Perry, tall, well-dressed, his brown hair thinning at the temples and greying at the sides, was doing most of the listening, while Jean, young and elegant in designer slacks and sweater — with a hairstyle that to Holly's mind must have knocked her back a couple of hundred pounds — was talking rapidly.

'She's a lot younger than he is,' she remarked.

Josh nodded. 'By a good ten years, I'd say. You know, I could see her as chairperson of the snotty tennis club.'

'I know what you mean, the pair of them ooze respectability, just like the Scotts did. But something I did notice, Josh—'

'I know what you're going to say. Their answers were identical to the Scotts', word for word. It's almost as if they'd rehearsed them together.'

'You've got it, lover.'

* * *

'Oh, Christ it's the bloody law again,' Tom Gardiner groaned, when Holly's Micra turned into his lane. Straight away he herded the dogs into the house. 'Get them in the other room, Rose, that Bedford girl doesn't like them.'

'I told you they'd come for you, Tom, I told you.'

'Shut up,' he yelled, pacing the kitchen. 'It's something and nothing, I know it is.'

'That Randall's grassed on you. He's trying to wriggle out of it by dropping you in it.'

Gardiner was about to bellow another rebuke when he saw the detectives picking a path through the wrecked cars littering his garden. Fixing a smile of welcome on to his face, he scrambled towards the kitchen door.

'Hello, Mr Abraham, it's nice to see you again. I put the dogs away, Miss Bedford, I know you don't like them.'

'Tom, do you mind if we take another look around?' Josh asked.

Suddenly, Gardiner's features matched the grey stubble on his chin. 'I'd rather you didn't,' he spluttered. 'I've got some stuff I'm trying to keep under wraps.'

'We'll just take a look in the barn,' Holly said, setting off across the yard.

Gardiner hobbled after her. 'Don't let her go in there, Mr Abraham. It's my competitors, you see. If they find out what cars I'm breaking, they'll flood the market with parts to drive the price down. That's all it is, honest.'

'Stop waffling,' Holly snapped.

She was about to enter the dilapidated building when Gardiner stepped in front to bar the way.'

'You've got no right to go in there without my permission.'

'Look, stop giving me verbal,' she said, a warning finger pointed at his chest. 'Now, just get out of the way.'

He studied the finger and Holly's resolute expression for a few seconds, and then his shoulders hunched resignedly but he continued to stand his ground.

'Rose is right, you've got it in for me,' he grumbled. 'I bet that Randall's dropped me in it.'

'Okay, Tom, let her through,' Josh said, taking the man's arm.

'You need a search warrant, Mr Abraham. If it was anybody else, you'd have to get one.'

'Do you want us to, Tom? We could radio in and wait here till the warrant arrived.'

Gardiner saw his last hope vanish. If he could just get rid of them for a couple of hours, he would have time to clear the barn.

'Oh, go on,' he scowled, shuffling away. 'Doesn't make any difference to me.'

'Keep your eye on him, Josh,' Holly said as she disappeared inside.

'Huh, I'm hardly likely to fly off to Brazil, now, am I, Miss Bedford?'

'We'll go in as well, shall we, Tom? Let's see what you're hiding in there.'

Holly was already negotiating a path around the clutter en route to the room at the back. She swung open the door and started down the small flight of stairs.

Mere seconds ticked by before she shouted, 'Nick him, Josh.'

CHAPTER 18

It was 8 p.m. before Jan Morrison returned home. Her long-suffering husband, Paul, was watching television.

'Any luck?' he asked, over the fading theme of *East-Enders*.

'No, I'm afraid not.' She sank into the armchair beside his and told him about Randall's movements earlier in the day. 'But after that, he didn't leave the house again,' she concluded wearily.

'And you were sitting there all that time? Jan, it's freezing out there . . .'

She pouted. 'You're going to tell me I'm a silly old woman, aren't you?'

'Now, come on, when have I ever said you're old?'

She laughed at the familiar joke, but sobered quickly.

'I know that man's evil, Paul, I *know* he is.'

'I'll make you a cup of tea,' he said, getting to his feet. 'And I'll put a drop of whisky in it. That should warm you up.'

She followed him to the kitchen and stood in the doorway while he filled the kettle.

'Paul, I keep thinking about those two men I saw in the lane . . .' She shuddered violently. 'They'd just buried that little girl's body, hadn't they?'

He plugged in the kettle and moved to give her a comforting hug. 'I was thinking about that while you were out. Are you sure Randall wasn't one of those men?'

'He definitely wasn't the one I saw climbing the gate.'

Paul Morrison stared down into his wife's face and smiled warmly. 'I realise this is something you need to do, Jan, but I want you to promise you'll be careful. That man could be dangerous.'

* * *

'No joy with the Perrys or the Scotts, guv,' Holly said, as she sauntered into the office. 'They've all enjoyed Randall's company over meals and drinks, apparently, but none of them want to be seen dead with him, now.'

Ashworth sat back in his chair and gave a loud sigh. 'And they looked all right, did they? Nothing to raise your suspicions?'

'Nothing,' Josh said.

'Both couples were whiter than the driven snow,' Holly added. 'In fact, the latest washing powder with secret ingredient QTS couldn't get my knickers any whiter.'

A smile hovered around Ashworth's lips while he fixed her with a reproachful stare. He picked up a folder from his desk.

'The report's come in from Shannon Dixon's post-mortem,' he said. 'She died from massive internal injuries received during collision with the lorry — but that's obvious, isn't it? There were signs of sexual and physical abuse, although her extensive injuries hindered Alex's search for the latter. He could say, however, that given her body weight and absence of stomach contents, she had been deprived of food for some time.'

'Sounds like she suffered the same treatment as Nicky Waldon,' Holly remarked.

Ashworth nodded. 'It does, indeed. Therefore, I think we can safely assume that the same people were involved in both cases.'

'It doesn't get us very far, though, does it guv?' Josh said.

'Anyway, what next?' Holly asked.

'I suppose we'd better interview old Tom,' Ashworth said. 'He's had plenty of time to stew.'

* * *

So, it was 9 p.m. and the end of a hectic day when Tom Gardiner was brought up from the cells and shown into the interview room where Ashworth was waiting with Holly. The man seemed to have developed a nervous tic, and his right eye blinked rapidly as his gaze fluttered over the two officers.

'Mr Ashworth, this is all a mistake,' he said, in a pitiful whine.

'Sit,' the chief inspector said, pointing to the chair opposite.

'This is one of those miscarriages of justice, you see if it isn't.'

Ashworth selected one of five video cases lying on the table and held it in front of Gardiner's brooding face.

'Tom, are you denying these are your property?'

'Mr Ashworth, I've never seen them before in my life,' he said, his twitch worsening with each word that was uttered.

'For the benefit of the tape recorder, Mr Gardiner has just been shown a selection of video cases with titles such as *Lust in the Afternoon* and *Erotic Housewives* . . .' Ashworth leant towards the man, a forbidding light in his eyes. 'Now, stop messing me about Tom. Forty of these videos were found in the cellar of your old barn.'

Gardiner's furtive gaze swept over the damning evidence on the table and then returned to the chief inspector's face. He said nothing.

'Where did they come from?' Ashworth persisted.

Finally, he let out a long breath, and said, 'From a couple of blokes at Bridgenorton market. They let me have them for four hundred quid, see, and I could have sold them on for eight hundred or even a thousand because they're made in Sweden. I mean, all the politicians keep telling us to get into the heart of Europe, don't they?'

Ashworth shot an exasperated glance towards the ceiling and heaved an impatient sigh.

'Tom, you said to DS Bedford that Gilbert Randall must have dropped you in it. Does he have anything to do with these tapes?'

Gardiner stared at the tabletop, his eye twitching. 'I've got nothing to say.'

Ashworth was about to launch into another attack when a knock came on the door and Martin Dutton popped his head around it.

'A word, Jim, if I may.'

'You would have to tell him about that,' Gardiner hissed to Holly when Ashworth had left the room. 'You've got it in for me, you have.'

Holly said nothing, simply lifted a knowing eyebrow, and all was silent until Ashworth re-entered the room, the beginnings of a smile on his lips. He leant back against the door and focused his full attention on Gardiner.

'Have you ever played any of those tapes, Tom?'

'No, I haven't got a video recorder.'

'Okay, then, I'll ask you one more time — does Gilbert Randall have anything to do with these tapes?'

'I've got nothing to say.'

'Tell me, Tom,' Ashworth said, resting his palms on the table.

Gardiner looked decidedly shifty, but seemed to be weakening under the chief inspector's formidable stare.

'I tell you what Tom, if you tell me about Randall, I'll let you off with a caution for the video tapes.'

'What, you mean do a deal with the police, like they do on the telly?' He turned to beam triumphantly at Holly. 'If I drop somebody else in it you'll let me off?'

'That's about it.'

'Well, that's fine by me, Mr Ashworth.' He pointed to the video cassettes. 'I'd got the stuff, you see, and I'd heard it put about that Randall and his fancy friends were into mucky films, so I went to the Apollo Club to see him. Well, the blokes who sold me the tapes wrote the titles out for me and when I showed a few to Randall he said they weren't the sort he was interested in. So, being a bit of a salesman, like you have to be in the scrap metal game, I said if you tell me what you want, I'll get it for you. Anyway, he hummed and hawed a bit and then said he was into child porn. Well, I wouldn't want to get involved in that, Mr Ashworth, even if I knew where to get it, so I said I'd see what I could do, and we left it at that.'

'I see,' Ashworth said, returning to his seat. 'When you said his fancy friends, who did you mean exactly?'

'His church friends,' Gardiner said with a derisive snort. 'They look down their noses at me when I go round their way with my rag and bone cart.'

'Right Tom, I think you've told us all we need to know. Sergeant Dutton's waiting outside, he'll take care of you.'

'Thank you, Mr Ashworth, sir,' he said, almost touching his forelock as he hobbled towards the door. 'If you ever need a spare part for your car, you just come and see me.'

'Guv, what are you doing?' Holly said, before the door was even closed. 'That's all recorded. You can't just let him walk, Newton will have a fit. That stuff's hard porn.'

Ashworth closed his eyes and chuckled. 'Even in the darkest hour, Holly, even in the darkest hour.'

'You all right, guv?'

'Perfectly,' he said, his shoulders heaving with laughter.

'Are you going to let me in on the joke?'

'Sorry, Holly, it's just that I keep thinking about poor old Tom paying four hundred pounds for those tapes.'

'And?'

'They were actually old cassettes sold off by the video hire shops for a pound apiece because they were almost worn out. Whoever sold them to Tom must have known he couldn't read, and also that he hadn't got a machine to play them on.' His laughter erupted again. 'Some of Martin's lads were assigned to watch the tapes to see what they contained, and that's how the scam came to light. Most of them were kiddies' cartoons, and not one of them contained any type of pornography.'

'Hah, I bet they were chuffed,' she said drily.

'God help Europe, that's all I can say,' Ashworth chortled. 'Anyway, at least what we already know has been confirmed. Randall and his friends are in the business of buying child pornography.'

'I wouldn't trust Gardiner on that one, guv. We've no proof that the Scotts or the Perrys go in for child porn.'

'No, we haven't,' he said, sobering somewhat. 'And to be honest I can't see how we're going to get any. Tell me, Holly, that grey Vauxhall Nova that was at Tom's place — is it still there?'

'It is, but not all in one piece. The wheels have gone, and the exhaust.'

'We could really do with the car Randall used when he tried to abduct Amy Byron,' Ashworth mused. 'That would really seal his fate.'

Josh appeared in the doorway, a wide grin on his face. 'I hear you two have been dealing with a very serious villain.'

Holly laughed. 'You bet, lover.'

'The superintendent left a message on your desk, guv,' he said. 'It seems tomorrow we're going to be assessed by a Dr Williams.'

'Assessed for what?'

'Our reaction to paedophiles, guv.'

'Our what? Without consulting me first?' Ashworth scowled. 'Just you wait, Newton.'

* * *

There was a heavy frost overnight and Jan's fingers tingled with the cold as she scraped her car windows at 8 a.m. the next morning. Pulling her scarf tighter and turning the heater on to high, she set off for Lime Street.

She got there to find the area almost devoid of parked cars which meant little cover for her surreptitious surveillance. But refusing to be discouraged, she pulled in a fair distance away from the house and settled back to watch.

By ten-thirty Randall had still not made an appearance and Jan was forced to start the engine in an attempt to keep warm.

At eleven-thirty she was so cold that her vigil was temporarily abandoned while she nipped into the café at the corner of Lime Street.

She felt a tiny pang of guilt for leaving her post. Miss Marple would surely have stayed put, cold or not. Still, it was while she was paying for her mug of tea and two cheese rolls that Jan realised there was a good chance the man would have to drive past the café on his way into town. So, with her conscience nicely assuaged, she chose a seat by the window, loosened her coat and with one eye on the road, began her attack on the rolls.

CHAPTER 19

Alice Williams caused quite a stir at Bridgetown Police Station. The psychologist was a good-looking woman with a vivacious personality and a body to match; indeed, even her plain navy suit could not hide her comely curves.

She was in Newton's office, sipping a cup of tea.

'I've finished my assessments, Superintendent, and for the sake of convenience I'll start with the one who should give you least trouble and work down. All right?'

Newton nodded. 'Yes, that seems like a good idea.'

The doctor replaced her cup on the desk and shuffled her papers.

'DC Abraham,' she began. 'Now, he's most definitely the easiest of the team to evaluate. He's a little highly strung, perhaps, but solid, very dependable. I think you can rely on him to abide by the regulations, whatever happened.'

'Good,' Newton intoned.

'Now we come to DS Bedford.' The doctor gave a smile. 'Here we have a very attractive woman who resents me because I've temporarily deprived her of male attention. I've studied her record and it seems she has a very tragic past. Her husband died of leukaemia several years ago, when she was only twenty-three.

'Basically she's quite an emotional woman, sensitive, but life has necessitated that she should become hard as nails. Also she's a career woman, no man to support her and no wish to be supported. So, in any situation she'd have many considerations to balance. Not least, that the police force is her chosen career with a good pension at the end of it. I believe that however much loathing she felt for those she was pursuing she would simply knuckle down and get on with the job, because that's what she's had to do in life.'

'I see.' Newton briefly studied his fingernails. 'And the chief inspector?'

'Ah, James Ashworth . . .' the doctor said, her blue eyes sparkling.

* * *

The café was warm and comforting, the tea more than palatable, but two facts weighed heavily on Jan's peace of mind. Firstly, she knew she mustn't drink too much, for there was no lavatory nearby. How would Miss Marple cope with that one? she briefly pondered. Secondly, and much more important, she would lose Randall if he set off in the opposite direction.

Her gaze fell on the wall clock behind the counter, and she was astonished to find that thirty-five minutes had passed — enough time for Randall to have slipped through her net. With her determination to hook him rapidly resurfacing in the warmth of the café, she gulped down the remains of her tea and prepared for another long cold wait.

* * *

'. . . the charming chief inspector.' Dr Williams paused, noting as she did the adverse change in Newton's expression. 'I've been studying his record, Superintendent, he's a fascinating man. A maverick, with a very strong will. I see he's had a number of disputes with authority over the years.'

Newton gave a grunt. 'Very true, and he's always got away with them.'

'You don't like him, do you?' she was quick to ask.

'Surely that's irrelevant,' he calmly replied. 'Please continue with your evaluation, doctor.'

'Very well,' she said, hiding a smile. 'Chief Inspector Ashworth is a man who sees things very much as black or white, right or wrong, and as far as he's concerned there's precious little between the two extremes. Let me illustrate. I often ask police officers if they believe in the death penalty. Most say yes, to which I always state that there is no evidence to support the claim that capital punishment acts as a deterrent. Now, the reaction to that always falls into two distinct categories. Some officers accept the fact while others, a minority, will question this lack of evidence . . .'

'And what answer did Ashworth give?' Newton asked, clearly not relishing the reply.

'The chief inspector quite simply said, if you hang a murderer he's not going to kill again, and he asked if I could present any evidence to the contrary. There you have a clue to the man's character. He thinks things through.'

'And he can't be wrong?'

'I think you're being unfair to him,' the doctor said quietly. 'He thinks things through, arrives at a conclusion based on his feelings, and that makes it right for him. He's obsessive, stubborn and, I'd imagine, very well liked.'

'Yes, the lower ranks,' Newton said, with a slight sneer, 'refer to him as a bloody good bloke.'

'That figures. I couldn't imagine him ever pulling rank, it's not in his character. Basically he doesn't give a damn what people think of him; it's what he thinks about himself that matters. If he doesn't agree with something he'll fight tooth and nail, and he'll go to extreme lengths to keep on fighting. On the other hand he's fair, honest, straightforward and, in most cases, understanding, and that tends to make him popular.'

'It sounds as if you've joined his fan club,' Newton huffed.

'The constraints of marriage and family,' the doctor went on, pointedly ignoring his remark, 'have probably helped him. Without them I'd say he would have been too headstrong to stay in the police force. As for the paedophile case, I'd say he's the wrong man to be working on it.'

'He could over-react, you mean?'

The doctor gave a nod. 'He has no understanding of the people he's dealing with. He sees them as totally evil, whereas most in my profession see them as deeply disturbed. If you could replace Ashworth on this case, Superintendent, then do it.'

'That's impossible,' he said, with a vigorous shake of the head. 'He's my most experienced officer and, I have to admit, the best I've got.'

'Well,' the doctor said, getting to her feet, 'at least you've been forewarned. I'd advise that you keep a tight rein on the chief inspector while he's dealing with this case.'

'You can be sure I'll do that,' Newton replied, as he ushered her towards the door. 'Thank you for all that you've done.'

'My pleasure. Goodbye.'

He closed the door and leant against it, a sardonic smile on his lips. 'Yes, Ashworth,' he murmured. 'You could well slip up on this one.'

* * *

It was mid-afternoon and Jan worried that if she stayed there much longer her legs would fall off, they were so very cold. Not that she could spend much more time there, anyway. Paul was one hundred per cent behind her on this, but even his patience had its limit.

As that thought flitted across her mind the first rain-drops hit the windscreen and trees on the pavement were buffeted by a sudden wind. Jan opened the car door and almost whooped with joy when warm air met her skin. This change in the weather had been promised for days, and it had finally arrived. Now she could wait a little longer without freezing to death.

And wait she did. The minutes ticked away into slow-moving hours; her husband temporarily forgotten. Darkness fell, and here and there the orange glow of street lamps illuminated wet pavements and windswept trees. Jan glanced at her watch; it was 8 p.m. She would *have* to go home now. With a sigh she turned the ignition key, pushed into first gear and gazed into the rear-view mirror. And what she saw made her heart thump.

Gilbert Randall was coming out of his front door and there was something about his body language that alerted Jan. He seemed cautious, hurrying to the gate then casting sly glances along the road as if making sure no one was watching. Obviously satisfied that all was clear, he opened the gates and steered the Granada out on to the road. Jan was quick to duck down in her seat until he had travelled past and then she set off in pursuit.

As she watched the spray being thrown up by the wheels of Randall's car, she prayed that other vehicles would appear so that her own presence would go unnoticed. Her prayers were finally answered when Randall turned onto the main road. There, Jan managed to tuck herself two cars behind his in the light evening traffic.

He went along the high street, over the bridge spanning the River Thane, and it was at this point that the traffic began to thin again. The car in front of Jan turned left, leaving just one vehicle between them. At the next junction that car signalled right and she was forced to wait while he watched for a gap in the traffic. All she could do was vent her frustrations on the steering wheel and stare at the Granada's tail lights as they disappeared into the distance.

The car in front finally turned right and Jan quickly went through the gears. The Granada, only just in view, signalled left and Jan tried desperately to pinpoint the spot as she raced towards it. Her side of the road was clear now so she slowed at the first left turn which led to a long straight lane with not a car in sight. The second was a cul-de-sac and she scrutinised the parked cars, but Randall's wasn't there. She had lost him.

With a bitter sigh of disappointment she crawled forward to the next turn. It was another long road with cars parked on either side. Jan was about to drive on when she noticed, about a hundred yards along, a vehicle with its hazard lights flashing. That might be Randall, she thought as she cruised towards it.

Her stomach gave a lurch when she drew level. It was indeed his car, but it was empty. She looked around; he could be in any of the houses or he could have abandoned the Granada and continued on foot. Maybe he knew she was following and that's why he had dumped the car.

A familiar noise caught her attention — metal grating on metal — but she couldn't quite place it. Then there was a rattling sound, and it came to her in a flash. Metal up-and-over garage doors were being opened. She eased the car a little further and stopped suddenly, for to her right was a row of lock-up garages and the fourth door along was open.

Just then Randall's head spun round, and alarm flitted across his face when he caught her watching. Jan was oblivious to the look, however; her attention was fully taken up with what the man was doing.

* * *

Police Constable John Dickens stopped his patrol car on the deserted country lane and turned to Police Constable Gordon Bennett.

'Well, that's it, Gord,' he said, studying his watch. 'We've patrolled the town for hours now, so it should be quiet till the pubs turn out. How about a smoke, eh?'

Bennett was peering through the windscreen. 'We've got more than smoke, John,' he said, with urgency in his voice. 'We've got a bloody great fire over there.'

Dickens viewed the red ball in the distance. 'Oh, shit, the little darlings have done a car again.'

'It's going like the bollocks,' Bennett observed.

'We'd better get there. Come on.'

They cut through two short lanes and then Dickens brought the panda car onto a bridle path. The vehicle bumped and shook on the rutted surface and came to a halt in front of the raging fire. The stench of burning rubber was thick in their nostrils as they scrambled from the car.

'The front end's alight,' Bennett shouted. 'I might be able to get the reg number before the tank blows.' He set off towards the blaze.

'Be careful,' Dickens called, as he radioed central control. 'Hello, Sarge, it's Dickens. We're in the lane behind the gravel pit. There's a car well alight. Gord's done a Tom Cruise and gone to get the number.'

Bennett's frantic coughing could be heard minutes before he emerged from the dense grey smoke. He shouted the registration number for Dickens to pass on to the station.

'I'd say we've got plenty of time for a ciggie now, Gord, while we're waiting for the fire brigade.' He took out a packet of Benson and Hedges as they watched the columns of orange flame leap towards the sky. 'Did you ever torch cars when you were a kid?'

'No, but if I had my time over again I would, and I'd give the birds a miss.' The words were said with a rueful snort; Bennett's marital problems were legendary.

'Yeh, I know what you mean.' Dickens passed across a lighted cigarette. 'Here you go.'

And then the petrol tank exploded.

CHAPTER 20

'Ah, good, you're still here, Jim,' Sergeant Dutton said from the doorway of CID.

Ashworth glanced at the clock. 'Can you pretend I'm not Martin,' he asked wearily. 'I was hoping to get home for half nine.'

'You've got a visitor,' Dutton said, grinning. 'Jan Morrison.'

Holly giggled.

'And you can shut up,' Ashworth warned her with a smile. 'What does she want, Martin?'

'I don't know. She just said it's important, and she'll only speak to you.'

'She's at a funny age, Martin,' Holly cut in.

Ashworth exhaled sharply. 'All right, young lady, maybe you'd like to sit in on this.'

'Don't worry, guv, I'll make sure she behaves herself.' She turned to Dutton and grinned. 'It's really hard working for a sex symbol, you know.'

The sergeant laughed. 'I've put her in number one interview room, Jim, with a cup of tea.'

* * *

Jan looked up when they entered the room and, as always, was hit by a terrible shyness when faced with the chief inspector. She often likened the feeling to that she'd had for her English teacher at grammar school; she'd nurtured a huge crush on him for all of three terms. Straight away, her gaze dropped to her teacup.

'Mrs Morrison, this is DS Bedford,' Ashworth announced.

Jan gave a shy smile. 'Hello.'

'It's Holly, actually,' she said, smiling back. 'Do you mind if we call you Janet?'

'I prefer Jan, if you don't mind. It's less formal, isn't it?'

'All right, Jan,' Ashworth said, drawing up a chair. 'What have you got for us?'

'Well, Chief Inspector—'

'He prefers Jim, actually,' Holly interjected. 'It's less formal.'

She ignored Ashworth's pointed glare and gave the woman an encouraging smile.

'All right . . . Jim. I've been keeping my eye on Gilbert Randall, following him about watching what he gets up to, that sort of thing.'

'You shouldn't really be doing that,' Ashworth said, concern heavy in his tone. 'This man could be dangerous, and we think he's part of a large organisation, so you must be careful.'

'Well, I *have* been doing it,' she replied stoutly. 'And tonight I think it's paid off. You see, I followed him to a row of lock-up garages in Broadmead Avenue, and when I drew level he closed the garage door and got into a grey Vauxhall Viva.' Jan gave Ashworth the registration number.

Suddenly Ashworth was interested. 'You're sure about this, Jan? It could be of vital importance to our investigation.'

'Absolutely certain, yes. I took down the number and then drove straight here.'

'That's great work,' Holly said, quickly taking notes. 'Now, you said there was a row of garages — which one was Randall using?'

'It was the fourth from the left, as you're facing it from the road.'

Ashworth cleared his throat; his mind already racing ahead.

'Jan,' he said, 'you realise, don't you, that if this gets to court you may have to give evidence?'

'Of course,' she said, beaming. 'And I don't mind one little bit.'

* * *

'What now, guv?' Holly asked, as they made their way back to the office.

'Where's Josh?'

'He's got a date tonight.'

'Oh . . . pity. Anyway, what can we do? We haven't got enough to pull Randall in again. What we need is a good look at the inside of that garage.'

'Already under way, guv. While you were walking Jan to the car park I checked with uniformed. The garages are owned by one Dev Patel. He owns takeaways, flats and garages. He's a little bit iffy, and every time our lot confront him he pretends he doesn't know any English.'

'Do we know where he is at the moment?'

'Yes, guv, at the Star of Bombay. It's one of his takeaways, and it's quite close to the lock-up garages.'

'Right, let's go and pay him a visit. I'm sure he'll want to communicate with me.'

* * *

The delicate scents of spices and oils in the Star of Bombay set their mouths watering the moment they pushed through the door. Indian music was playing softly in the background, and behind a high counter at the rear of the room could be seen the heads and shoulders of Mr Patel and a spotty English youth.

'Evening, folks, and what can I do you for?' the young man asked.

Ashworth disregarded the question and turned instead to the proprietor.

'Are you Mr Patel?' he asked.

The man, quick to spot the law, shrugged his thin shoulders and held up his hands.

'Bridgetown CID,' Ashworth said, sticking his warrant card under the man's nose.

Patel ran a hand over his well-oiled hair and pointed towards the youth.

'He's telling you to give your order to me,' he said.

'Tell him I don't want to order anything,' Ashworth snapped.

'Can't, I don't speak his lingo.'

Impatience showed clearly on Ashworth's face, as he said, 'Mr Patel, we're police officers and we want all available keys for garage number four in Broadmead Avenue, and also the name of the person who rents it from you.'

Patel spread his hands, his mouth firmly closed, and pointed again to the youth.

'Right,' Ashworth said, banging a palm on the counter. 'Your radio, DS Bedford, please.'

She passed it across and Ashworth pretended to press the button. 'Chief Inspector Ashworth here. I want the environmental health inspectors at the Star of Bombay, right now, to close it down. After that, I want them to visit every takeaway owned by a Mr Dev Patel and the same course of action followed.'

Patel gulped and immediately placed a ring containing two keys on to the counter.

'Thank you, sir,' Ashworth said, handing back the radio. 'Now I want the name of whoever rents it from you.'

'Mr Smith,' the man said grudgingly. 'He pays by post, every month in cash.'

'And would you recognise Mr Smith if you saw him?'

'No, you all look the same to me,' he muttered, making no attempt to disguise the insult.

'Thank you for your help,' Ashworth said, 'and rest assured that I shall remember you very clearly.'

Outside, he turned to Holly. 'All we need now is a patrol car outside that garage.'

'Bobby Adams is already there, guv.'

'Good, let's join him, then.'

* * *

Bobby had parked his panda car across the entrance to the garages and was standing nearby, enjoying a cigarette. Police officers were not allowed to smoke on duty in public areas and when Ashworth's Scorpio pulled up unexpectedly he swiftly dropped the offending exhibit behind his back and trod on it, thankful that he had not been caught. However, there was little he could do about the smoke trailing from his mouth, as he said, 'Good evening, sir.'

'Nobody's been near the garage, I take it?'

'No, sir.'

'Good,' Ashworth said, throwing the keys into the air. 'Let's take a look inside, then.'

With the padlock undone he retrieved a handkerchief from his pocket and wrapped it around the handle before opening the door. It swung upwards, its metal screeching, and an empty garage yawned back at them.

'Damn,' Holly muttered. 'Whatever Randall did with the car, he didn't put it back in here.'

'And we could really do with that car,' Ashworth said, as he closed and locked the door. 'Never mind, though, Forensic might well come up with something from the interior.' He turned to the young constable standing so upright, so eager to please. 'Bobby, I'm sorry about this, son, but—'

'You want me to stand guard on it all night, sir?'

'That's about it. I'll get the lab boys here first thing in the morning.'

'No problem, sir,' Bobby said, his cheerful tone not quite coming off.

'We'll leave you to it, then.' He motioned for Holly to follow.

'Hol,' Bobby hissed, 'I haven't got enough ciggies to last till morning.'

She delved into her shoulder bag and handed over a packet. 'There's about twelve in there,' she whispered.

'Thanks.'

Her radio started bleeping on the walk back to the car. 'Bedford.'

'Ah, my little ray of sunshine,' PC Doug Saunders cooed.

'Hi, Doug, what have you got for me?'

He gave a lewd laugh. 'You shouldn't ask me that, Holly, I might tell you one of these days.'

'Get on with it, Dougie.'

'Sorry, my little love, to be serious for a minute, I've run a trace on that registration number you gave me and believe it or not it's turned up on fire by the gravel pit. And I'm afraid the number plates were false.'

'Really? Go on, Doug, you're starting to excite me.'

'We got the chassis number and checked that. It was a Vauxhall Viva, stolen three months ago in Birmingham.'

'And it's completely burnt out?'

'As in cinders.' He paused and gave a chuckle. 'Now, as for your question about what I've got for you . . .'

'Keep taking the tonic, Doug, and in a couple of months you might be up to it.'

Ashworth was waiting with impatience by the car, and he listened intently while Holly told him what had been discovered.

'So, Randall was getting rid of the evidence,' he mused.

'Do we pull him in in the morning, guv?'

'Yes, I think so. I don't think Jan Morrison's testimony will be enough on its own, but if Forensic can come up with something in that garage . . . Yes, it's looking good. Right, Holly, do you want me to take you back to the station for your car, or shall I give you a lift home?'

'The lift sounds good, guv, it's not far from here.'

Ten minutes later he was pulling up outside her modest two-bedroom semi. She hesitated before opening the door.

'I suppose it's too late to invite you in for a drink?'

'It is, really. Sarah will be wondering where I am.' He glanced at her. 'You look a bit down.'

'Oh, I don't know, guv, I suppose I'm just jealous,' she said with a shrug. 'I mean, Josh could be starting a big love affair, and we used to spend such a lot of time together. I'm lost without him.'

Ashworth gave her a sympathetic look and said hesitantly, 'I wish you'd meet someone and settle down, Holly.'

'Oh, no, guv, I've been there once. Anyway, thanks for the lift.'

'You were out of line, telling Jan Morrison to call me Jim,' he said, as she climbed out of the car, 'but I've decided to let you off without a smacked bottom.'

'Sod your luck, Bedford,' she muttered, as she watched him drive away.

CHAPTER 21

A lot of Randall's bluster evaporated when Ashworth revealed next morning that they now had a witness who could put him at the lock-up garage in possession of a grey Vauxhall Viva. And the chief inspector took great pleasure in watching the man struggle to regain his composure.

'I wasn't there,' he eventually said. 'And I want my solicitor.'

'Your solicitor can't help you now,' Holly said. 'We've got you.'

Randall was thinking on his feet. He shot her a scathing glance, and said, 'What have you got? One witness, that's all. It'll be my word against theirs.'

'We've also got forensic evidence,' Ashworth cut in.

'Okay, tell me what exactly.'

The man leant back, a smug look on his face, and Ashworth's body tensed. Before him sat an intelligent and articulate man, seemingly well liked by highly respected members of the community. And yet what sort of practices did he indulge in? How much misery had he already inflicted upon God knows how many children?

'You all right, guv?' Holly asked.

Ashworth swallowed. 'Yes, fine.'

'What's this evidence that you've got?' Randall persisted.

'We're waiting for the forensic results.'

Ashworth had instructed Josh to report their findings as and when they came in, and now he was beginning to regret his decision to bring Randall in before the results were available.

'You've got absolutely nothing,' the man mocked. 'That's what you've got and you know it.'

They were interrupted by a knock on the door, and Ashworth breathed a sigh of relief when Josh entered the room. He stood up, his huge hands bunched into fists as he looked down at Randall, and then he joined Josh in the corridor.

'I hope you've got something for me.'

'Sorry, guv, there were no fingerprints at all. Whoever's been using that lock-up was wearing gloves the whole time.'

'So we've come up with nothing,' Ashworth growled accusingly.

'Not necessarily. There're no fingerprints, guv, but they're still running other tests. You did ask me to keep you informed as and when information came in.'

The red mist of anger before Ashworth's eyes slowly dispersed to reveal an offended frown on Josh's face.

'I'm sorry, son, Randall's getting to me, that's all, but I shouldn't take it out on you.' He looked towards the interview room. 'I just wish you'd given me something I could use to nail that . . .' He sighed deeply. 'Oh, well, I'd better get back in.'

Holly tried to read his expression as he returned to the table, but his eyes divulged nothing.

'Now, Mr Randall, shall we talk about your friends . . . the other members of your ring?'

'No comment,' he said, turning his slippery gaze to the ceiling. 'Now, will you either get my solicitor here and charge me, or let me go?'

'Randall,' Ashworth bawled, suddenly leaping towards the man.

'Guv,' Holly said, heading for the door, 'could I have a word, please?' He remained with his eyes fixed firmly on Randall's face. 'Please, guv?'

In the corridor she rounded on him. 'What's the matter with you?'

'I'm all right,' he insisted harshly.

'No, you're not. For a start your face is as white as a sheet, and you keep giving that bastard looks that could kill.'

He let out an exasperated sigh and focused on the opposite wall, unwilling to meet her gaze.

'That man's getting to me, Holly. If Forensic don't come up with something, he's just going to walk out of here.'

'But we've been here with other cases, guv. Just calm down.'

He made no response.

'Look, when we go back in there, can I take over the questioning?'

'All right.'

Randall watched with amusement as they filed back into the room.

'Okay, Mr Randall,' Holly began. 'Either you or one of your friends stole that car in Birmingham and changed the number plates, then you used it to abduct children.'

'Is that a fact?' he said, looking with interest at his fingernails.

'Oh yes, that's a fact.' She leant forward. 'Don't forget, we've got a child who's identified you, and now we have a witness who links you to the car.'

Randall made a great show of stifling a yawn, and said, 'Prove it in court.'

'Tell us who your friends are,' she said.

There was another knock, and Josh was again motioning for Ashworth to join him. After several minutes of earnest whispering, Ashworth turned to Randall.

'Right' he rasped. 'I'm now in a position to tell you what we've got with regard to forensic evidence, Mr Randall. Inside the garage were hairs which match those of all three dead girls: Jade Vale from Manchester; and Nicky Waldon and Shannon Dixon, both from Bridgetown, which means that at one time or another they all passed through that garage. And the only other person we can be certain passed through it, too, is you.'

'So wouldn't you like to tell us who your friends are?' Holly urged.

Randall shook his head.

'All right, you'll be charged with the murder of all three girls,' Ashworth said.

Holly terminated the interview and was turning off the tape recorder when Randall whispered to her, 'You'll never make it stick, you know, we've been here before. You won't get your witnesses to court.'

She spun round, a look of utter disbelief on her face. 'What did you say?'

He gave her a mocking smile. 'Nothing.'

Ashworth witnessed their aggressive interplay and returned to the table, his eyebrows arched quizzically.

'A word, guv,' she said, heading for the door.

In the corridor she told him what Randall had said.

'Bravado?' he suggested.

'I don't think so. I was watching him carefully. After the initial shock of realising he was in all sorts of trouble he became a little too sure of himself — didn't you notice? as if he'd thought it through and knew the rest of the ring wouldn't let him go down for this.'

'If you're right Holly, then Amy Byron and Jan Morrison could be threatened in some way.'

'That's how I read it, guv.'

Ashworth paced the corridor, a thoughtful expression on his face. 'I've decided to go through the Nicky Waldon file again. I remember her parents' statements; they said their daughter didn't know Randall. But in light of what's come up, I'm just wondering if she knew the Scotts or the Perrys.'

'The girl was a member of the church, guv. She used to attend a lot of the functions, if I remember rightly.'

He suddenly brightened. 'I think our days of stumbling about in the dark might soon be over, Holly. Right, I'm off to get that file. You charge Randall with murder and the abduction and torture of Shannon Dixon, and then get ready for the flak.'

* * *

Josh went over it again and again but the computer could not link Gilbert Randall to any other paedophiles anywhere in the country.

He let out an impatient sigh. 'It's no good, guv, I just can't tie Randall in with any of the known rings. I suppose he could be with one that we don't know about.'

'And nothing's come up about his friend, Gerald Clark?' Holly asked.

'Only what we already know. He's gone back to Manchester where the local police are keeping an eye on him, but there's nothing to link him with a paedophile ring outside his association with Randall.'

'Did you find anybody else local?' Ashworth asked.

'No. Anyway, if there was anybody local, we would've pulled them in by now, wouldn't we?'

'I know, I'm just hoping for anything at the moment.'

'Randall could have been bluffing in there,' Josh reasoned.

'Something tells me he wasn't,' Ashworth said, as he stalked from the office.

'Daly works at the same bank as Randall,' Josh said to Holly.

'And Daly is your new boyfriend, I presume?' she said in a sour tone.

He nodded. 'I met him when we were making inquiries there, and he's confirmed what the others told us. Randall was very popular but didn't have any really close friends at the bank, and everybody's totally surprised that he'd have anything to do with the disappearance of those kids.'

'One thing really bothers me, Josh. With Randall's arrest, it looks as though this case is over on paper, at least — but—'

'Yes, on paper, but it's not over, Hol, because these scum can't keep their hands off kids.'

CHAPTER 22

Larry Byron tucked his daughter into her bed and paused at the door to look back. Amy was lying snug between a huge teddy bear and her favourite rag doll in Victorian dress. She was almost asleep and looked so young and vulnerable without that adult expression she worked so hard to cultivate. He smiled fondly and was overwhelmed by a strong surge of parental love which was still with him when he joined his wife in the lounge.

'Has she gone down?' Jilly asked, on her way to the drinks table.

He laughed. 'Yes, but only after she'd finally stopped going on about the new computer she's expecting for Christmas.'

'I'm just pleased she's set her heart on something that'll help with her studies. We will be able to afford it, won't we?'

'We'll afford it love, even if we have to go into debt.'

She passed him a scotch and ginger and he was about to take a sip when the telephone rang out in the hall. Pulling a face, he put his drink on the carpet and went to answer it.

'Hello, Bridgetown 7294.'

The line crackled, and then a muffled voice was in his ear.

'Hello, Mr Byron, I'm a little worried about Amy.'

'What do you mean? Who is this?'

'Let's just say I'm someone who has your daughter's interests at heart.' There was an ominous pause and humour sounded in his voice when he went on, 'Now, I'm against the course of action my friends have decided to take, so I thought it best to warn you.'

'Who is this?' Byron whispered harshly. 'What are you talking about?'

'I'm talking about the trial, Mr Byron. If Amy goes ahead and gives evidence against Gilbert Randall, she's as good as dead.'

The man rang off and he was staring dully at the receiver when Jilly came hurrying from the lounge.

'What's the matter, Larry?' she said. 'You look awful.'

* * *

Ashworth and Holly were looking forward to an early night, and the chief inspector was switching off the office lights when the telephone rang. Holly swore under her breath as she watched him stride across the darkened room and snatch up the receiver.

'Ashworth,' he barked.

But then he listened. Casting a worried glance towards Holly he snatched up a notepad and scribbled furiously for several minutes. Finally he dropped the receiver back into its cradle and rubbed a hand across his tired eyes.

'You haven't got anything planned for this evening, have you, Holly?'

'Only a couple of things I don't usually get time for nowadays, like taking a bath and getting some sleep.'

'Cancel them,' he said. 'Amy Byron's parents have had a phone call. The girl's life is at risk if she gives evidence against Randall.'

She flicked on the light switch and hurried back into the office. 'Have central control asked for a trace on the call?'

He nodded. 'It came from a payphone on the council estate. They also ran a check on Clark, via the Manchester police, and they say he's at home.'

'I suppose we'll have to go and see the Byrons and take a statement,' she said, perching on the edge of his desk.

'For what it's worth, yes.' He wandered across to the glass wall and stared out over the illuminated town. 'I'm taking this threat seriously, Holly. These people are not only willing to kill, they enjoy it. If Amy and Jan Morrison back out now — and I wouldn't blame them if they did — we wouldn't have a case against Randall.'

'But if they really meant to go through with it guv, why would they tell us in advance?'

'Because they like to play games, Holly.'

* * *

'We've agreed not to tell Amy about the call,' Larry Byron told Ashworth. 'And as far as possible we want her to carry on living a normal life.'

'And we shall be taking all possible precautions, Mr Byron, you can be assured of that,' said Ashworth, his feelings of impotence growing before their frightened eyes. 'If it makes you feel any better I can tell you that this type of threat, although often made, is very rarely carried out.'

'But you won't just ignore it, will you?' Jilly Byron asked.

'Oh no, of course not,' Ashworth quickly replied. 'First thing tomorrow morning we'll be making visits to Amy's school and to the vicar and his youth leader, to ask that everyone concerned with school and after-hours activities be extra vigilant where Amy is concerned, without unduly alarming the child.'

They talked for some time, the Byrons seemingly reluctant for them to leave. Nevertheless at 9.10 p.m., after further reassurances, the detectives left the house and headed for home.

* * *

Jan Morrison could sense fame hurtling towards her. Surely after the trial, at which she would be the key witness, the newspapers would want her story and TV chat show hosts would be queuing to have her as their guest. In her mind's eye she could see herself sitting with Clive Anderson.

You've been likened to Miss Marple, he would say, smiling; is that how you see yourself?

Jan gave her most charming laugh and scrubbed even harder at the brown stains on the dinner plate.

'Oh no, Clive,' she said aloud. 'I'm afraid real life is nowhere near as glamorous as fiction.'

She would touch his knee and, with perfect timing, add: In any case, I'm much too young for the part. And then she would settle back in her chair while the studio audience erupted into laughter. Just then the shrill ring of the telephone brought her back to the real world.

'Jan,' her husband called, 'it's for you.'

Drying her hands quickly she went through into the hall where the receiver was lying on the table. From the lounge came the chanting of a football crowd on the television.

She picked up the receiver. 'Yes?'

'Jan, it's Holly Bedford. Sorry to disturb you at this time of night, but Amy Byron's parents have had a threatening phone call. They've been warned against letting her give evidence at Randall's trial. I just thought I'd warn you, in case you received anything similar.'

Jan smiled broadly. She felt very much a part of the team now. 'Thank you, Holly,' she gushed. 'But I wouldn't let anything like that frighten me.'

'I didn't think so, but I thought I'd let you know anyway. Have to dash, I've got the bath water running. Bye.'

'Bye.'

She replaced the receiver and was shocked to see that her hand was trembling slightly.

'Kick it man,' Paul shouted from the lounge.

'I won't tell him, he'll only worry,' she murmured, returning to the washing up.

CHAPTER 23

Reverend Thorne was waiting on the steps of the vicarage when Ashworth's Scorpio turned into the drive. He looked every inch the small-town vicar as he hastened towards the car, his hands clasped in front of him, an anguished look fixed firmly on his face.

'Good morning, Chief Inspector, how nice to see you again. When you said you wanted to speak to Noel and myself, I took the liberty of inviting him here.'

'Good, that should save time,' Ashworth said shortly, his shoes crunching on the frosty gravel.

Thorne led him into the drawing room where Harper was at the window, staring out across the large garden.

'Noel, you know Chief Inspector Ashworth, I believe,' Thorne said.

Harper smiled warmly. 'Of course.'

'Oh, if only I could dress like that,' the vicar said, indicating Harper's fashionable blue jeans, white sweater and high-necked black leather waistcoat. 'I would be as popular with the youngsters as he is, then. But alas, for me it's a dog collar, which always seems to suggest gloom and boredom to the younger generation.'

'It's my electrifying personality that makes me popular.' Harper grinned.

'Are you suggesting it's my lack of it that makes me unpopular?'

Although the exchange was quite jovial, Ashworth momentarily wondered whether the two men were affected by professional rivalry.

'May I have your attention, please?' he said, feeling rather like a schoolmaster in front of a class of boisterous boys.

They straight away fell silent and turned their intense gazes on the chief inspector.

'I'm afraid that last night Mr Byron received a threatening call to do with Amy giving evidence at the trial of Gilbert Randall.'

'You mean Amy was threatened?' the vicar asked, his mouth gaping open.

'That's right, yes. So, I'd like you to keep a very close eye on the girl while she's attending any church functions. She doesn't know about the threat, so I want you to be very surreptitious. I don't want her alarmed.'

'That's terrible,' Reverend Thorne said, shaking his head. 'And do you think it's likely that these people will carry out their threats?'

'We've no reason to believe they won't,' he said grimly.

'There's a junior disco tonight. I'll personally see that Amy gets home afterwards.'

'No need, I'll be with her,' Harper quickly said. 'After all, David, if you start keeping a watch, she may sense there's something wrong.'

'Quite so,' Thorne conceded.

'Now, gentlemen,' Ashworth said, 'it appears that two couples deeply involved in the church are also good friends of Mr Randall. I refer to Mr and Mrs Scott and Mr and Mrs Perry. Can you shed any light on that?'

'What? Robin and Marcia? Arthur and Jean?' The vicar looked astounded. 'You must be mistaken, Chief Inspector, those kind people are so respectable. Why, Robin and Arthur take the plates round at church services.'

'Did you know they were friends of Randall?' Ashworth persisted.

'I had no idea,' Thorne said.

Harper gave a discreet cough and fixed the vicar with a challenging stare. 'You did mention to me that you'd seen them with Randall at the Apollo Club. Don't you remember, David?'

'Well . . . yes,' he said, highly flustered. 'I mean, of course I remember. But they were only having a drink, and I only mentioned it after that chap Randall had been arrested. I believe I said, it just goes to show you never know who you're mixing with at that sort of place. I never actually implied they were friends.'

'I just thought it might help the chief inspector, David, that's all.'

Ashworth got to his feet. 'Well, thank you, I won't take up any more of your time,' he said, heading for the door.

As he eased the Scorpio along the drive his thoughts centred on the obvious fact that Thorne and Harper had little liking for each other. That fact went against any idea of the two men colluding within a paedophile ring. But then again Ashworth had little knowledge of the type of person inclined to such things and as he steered the car towards the police station he decided to keep an open mind.

* * *

Noel and Beth Harper were listening to the closing bars of a Take That number and watching the children dancing beneath the strobe lighting. As usual, loud groans went up when the record finished and the main hall lights came on.

'Okay, gang,' Harper said. 'That's it for tonight.'

The youngsters booed.

'And don't forget the Bible class on Sunday,' he said, grinning.

That was followed by even louder jeers but even so, the children were obediently filing towards the cloakroom when Reverend Thorne pushed his way towards the stage.

'Noel,' he said. 'A word, if I may.'

'Yes, David, what is it?'

'I hope you haven't forgotten about taking Amy home.'

'I'm hardly likely to, am I?' Harper retorted. 'I arranged it with her earlier.'

'I know I'm fussing, but I'm so very concerned about this whole business,' he said, with a quarrelsome light in his eyes. 'What with you throwing doubt on the integrity of four members of our congregation earlier today . . .'

'Look, David, I only told the chief inspector what you told me. And in any case, no one's whiter than white just because they go to church . . . not even the vicar.'

Thorne's mouth hung open, but he let the insult pass. 'I just thought as both couples help you with your youth work—'

'Oh, look, here comes Amy,' Harper said, putting on a pleasant face. 'She's waiting for her lift, no doubt.'

'Noel,' she said, 'I'd like to get off now, please. My mum and dad seem really worried about something, and I want to make sure they're all right.'

'Okay.'

Harper took her hand and steered her towards the doors. Outside the night was cold and he hurried her towards the car and swiftly opened up the passenger side.

'Right, let's go,' he said cheerfully, starting the engine.

They had just reached the exit gates when he glanced into the rear-view mirror and saw the vicar emerging from the hall and waving for him to stop. Harper sighed and pulled on the handbrake.

'I won't be a minute, Amy. Lock your door.'

He ran back to meet Thorne, his impatience growing with each step.

'What is it now?' he demanded.

'You're going off with the money for the disc jockey.'

'No, I'm not, I left it with Beth.'

'But I can't find her.'

'She's ferrying the kids out to their parents' cars,' he said, pointing to his wife who was leading three children across the car park.

Harper was about to mutter an exasperated remark, but the words never left his mouth for Amy had started to scream.

CHAPTER 24

Salty tears were streaming down Amy's face and stinging her eyes. She was sitting on her father's lap in their cheerful lounge, sheer terror making her cling to his chest. Her fearful mother was crouched by the side of the chair, every so often wiping the tears from her daughter's face.

'Tell us in your own words,' Ashworth said, his voice soft and gentle. 'Just take your time.'

She looked up at him but said nothing.

'If you're not up to it, we could come back tomorrow,' Holly suggested.

Amy swallowed hard. 'No, it's all right I'm acting like a child, I know I am.'

'But you are a child, Amy,' Ashworth said, stooping down in front of her. 'And there's nothing wrong with being frightened.'

Her eyes were huge in her pale face, and the pain showing in them went deep into Ashworth's heart when she said, 'Next to my mum and dad, I like you the best in the whole world.'

He turned away for a moment, his eyes smarting. Presently, he said, 'Do you want to tell us now?'

'It was all so sudden,' she began. 'Noel had gone back to talk to Reverend Thorne and a man came running up to the car. He tried to open the passenger door, but I'd locked it like Noel told me to. Then he went round to the other side and opened that one . . .' She suddenly heaved a huge sigh and clung to her father, her arms entwined around his neck.

'I was frightened,' she said, her voice pitifully small. 'He had a mask on, and it covered all of his face. I could only see his eyes and mouth. He said, just tell your mum and dad I could be driving you away now. Tell them to think about it, he said. I started screaming, I couldn't help it . . .'

Ashworth glanced at Holly, and then said to the girl's parents, 'Look, as a police officer I shouldn't be telling you this, but if Amy decided she didn't want to give evidence at Randall's trial I for one wouldn't blame you for pulling her out.'

'What would happen if she didn't give evidence?' Byron asked.

Ashworth gave a resigned shrug. 'The abduction charge would collapse. In fact, if Amy withdrew her evidence now, the Crown Prosecution Service wouldn't let the trial go ahead.'

Byron looked from Ashworth to Holly and back again. 'I can't put her through this,' he blurted. 'I just can't take the chance.'

'I'd have to back my husband on this,' Jilly said. 'What happened tonight has badly shaken us and in any case Randall's still on a murder charge, it isn't as if he's going to get off scot-free.'

'No,' Ashworth said, his tone doubtful. 'As I said, this is your decision, and if that's how you feel . . .'

'It is,' Byron said firmly. 'I'm sorry, but well . . .'

'We do understand,' Ashworth said. He stood up and pointed a finger at the little girl. 'Now, you take care of yourself, young lady.'

She managed a weak smile. 'I will.'

Jilly Byron seemed embarrassed as she showed them out. 'I really am sorry,' she said lamely.

'Don't be, Mrs Byron. We can see that nothing is more important to you than Amy's safety. Good-night.'

When they were in the car, he sat staring at the dashboard. 'No one's approached Jan Morrison yet?'

'No, guv, I would've mentioned it if they had. I've rung her three times today.'

'It's collapsing, isn't it? The whole case against Randall is falling apart.'

'It would be if Jan decided not to give evidence, but that's not happened yet.'

'Even though it's been through the magistrates court, the CPS will throw it out without her evidence.'

'But no one's approached her yet, guv, so you're a bit premature to start worrying about it now.'

'Oh, face it Holly, they've already scared Amy and her parents witless to get Randall off the attempted abduction charge. They'll approach Jan, just you see if they don't.'

* * *

Fireworks were going off in the distance and every so often the night sky was lit up by a profusion of colours, closely followed by riotous explosions that sent the radiant sparks cascading in all directions. Jan tut-tutted and closed the bedroom curtains as Patch began to bark in the kitchen.

'I don't know,' she said to Paul, already in bed. 'In our day fireworks were let off on November the fifth, but now it goes on for weeks. Where do they get the money from? That's what I want to know.'

Her husband yawned. 'Yes, dear,' he mumbled. 'Or no, dear, as the case may be.'

Jan went out onto the landing, all the time making soothing noises to the dog who was now barking hysterically. There was another loud explosion.

'Oh, for God's sake give it a rest,' she muttered. 'It's no good, Paul, I'll have to go down and try to get him settled.'

Still cursing, she padded down the stairs and into the kitchen. At the sound of her voice Patch immediately calmed and sloped off to his bed, scratching at the blankets for a few moments and then curling up in a ball. He watched her with big doleful eyes.

'Good boy,' she cooed. 'Now, you just go to sleep.' She glanced at the kitchen clock 'Holly said she'd call tonight. She must have forgotten.'

As if on cue the telephone rang. Fearing that it would start the dog off again she hurried into the darkened hall and snatched up the receiver.

'Hello?'

'Hi, Jan, it's Holly. Sorry to call so late, but things have been a bit hectic again tonight No one's contacted you, have they?'

'No.'

'Well, my guv'nor's really worried about this—'

'Oh, poor Jim,' she interjected.

'Yes.' Holly paused. 'The thing is, Jan, he wants to put monitoring equipment into your house so that if they do make contact we'll at least know what the voice sounds like.'

Jan grinned inwardly, her chest puffing up with self-importance. 'Fine, if you think it's necessary,' she said.

She was thinking how caring the chief inspector was when a bang on the front door made her start.

'Open up . . . police,' a male voice called.

'Hold on, Holly, it's your colleagues knocking on the front door. I'll just see what they want.'

'Jan, don't open it. Jan . . .'

But the receiver was already on the table, and Holly's voice was drowned by another explosion of fireworks and Patch's bewildered barking.

Jan drew back the bolt and pulled open the door. It took a few seconds for her to register that the two men standing in her porch were not police officers. And then one of them punched her in the face.

* * *

Ashworth was not well pleased as he pulled up outside the Morrisons' house at 11.15 p.m. A glass of malt whisky had been poised at his lips when central control rang to tell him of Jan's attack. The uniformed division had offered to handle it but Ashworth, out of concern for the woman, declined the offer and promptly called Holly. She was now climbing out of her Micra, her freshly scrubbed face like thunder.

'Hello,' he said tersely, as he locked his car. 'These people are beginning to get on my nerves.'

'The bastards are pissing me off,' she mumbled, following at a distance as he stomped up the garden path.

In answer to his loud knock, Paul Morrison pulled back the lounge curtain and peered out into the darkness. Ashworth strode to the window and pushed his warrant card close to the glass. The man nodded, and they waited on the step while he opened the door.

'You'd better come in,' he said. 'Jan's in the kitchen. Follow me.'

She was sitting at the table with a glass of brandy in her hand, the bruise on her cheek already beginning to show.

'Are you all right?' Holly asked, with real concern.

'Of course I am,' she replied, with a cavalier wave of her hand. 'It was just a shock, that's all. Please sit down.'

They settled into chairs around the table while her husband stayed by the door.

'You should go to hospital and have that looked at,' Ashworth advised.

'It's nothing, Jim,' she said, placing her glass on the table.

Holly felt naked without her make-up and somehow less able to undertake her duties as detective sergeant. However, unwilling to show such feminine cracks in her tough exterior, she strove to put the feelings behind her.

'Did the men say anything to you?' she asked.

'Not a word, no. One of them punched me and then they ran off, so I came back on the phone to you.' She lowered her gaze, her self-assurance momentarily crumbling. 'Was it an attempt to frighten me, do you think?'

'We'll have to treat it as such,' Ashworth said.

'Well, it's not going to work. I'm not going to let those people terrorise me, Jim. I saw what I saw, and I'm going to stand up in court and say so.'

'That's all well and good,' her husband said from the doorway. 'But they're getting violent, and—'

'I don't care, Paul, I'm going to see this through.'

'We'll do all we can,' Ashworth assured the man. 'We'll have a patrol car keep an eye on the house every time it's in the vicinity. And it might be as well to check the identity of any callers before you open the door.'

'We shall, Chief Inspector, don't worry about that.'

'He prefers to be called Jim,' Jan said, with a vague look in her eyes. 'I suppose I should start carrying a personal alarm.'

'It might help,' Ashworth said. 'And you really should have that bruise looked at.'

'Nonsense,' she replied, with much bravado. 'It's nothing that a little make-up won't cover.'

'Oh well,' he said, leaving his chair, 'there's nothing more we can do tonight.'

Jan favoured him with a warm smile. 'Thank you for coming, Jim.'

He inclined his head. 'Our pleasure.'

Paul Morrison at last moved from the doorway and stood before Ashworth, his frame pulled erect.

'I must tell you, Chief Inspector, that if anything like this ever happens again, I'll do my level best to persuade Jan not to give evidence.'

'We'll do all we—' Ashworth broke off in midsentence. The man looked grey with concern, and there was precious little the police could do, so what good were empty pledges?

Morrison showed them to the door, and when it was closed behind them they stood for a few moments in the damp cold air that reeked of gunpowder.

Holly said, 'I think her husband will have a job on his hands getting her to back off, guv. After that bloke punched her, she came back to the phone and couldn't apologise enough for not having a description of him because it had all happened so quickly.'

'She's a very brave woman.' He paused to watch a rocket explode in the sky. 'It's a pity so many at the station see her as a joke.'

'I'm sorry I had to bother you with this, guv. I passed it on to central control like I had to, but I thought uniformed would deal with it.'

'They were going to, but I thought it better that we should.' They reached the end of the garden path, and Ashworth stopped and managed a smile. 'You know, Holly, this is getting to be a habit, the two of us standing on street corners at midnight.'

'Huh, it's a habit I wouldn't mind giving up, guv.'

'Me too, Holly, me too.'

CHAPTER 25

Fast-falling temperatures heralded another severe frost, and Reverend Thorne shuddered with cold as he opened up the church doors next morning. Inside, he worked his way along the pews, placing prayer books for a funeral service due to take place at 11 a.m. But his mind was far removed from that sad event; indeed his thoughts were edged with selfish gloom. If the rumours started to spread again, then this time he would be in real trouble. Oh, why was he always placing himself in such inextricable situations?

He had explained to Mrs Drive that after the other children had left the prayer meeting last Sunday, her daughter, Emily, had stayed behind and asked him to tie up her shoelace. As he did so, he noticed that the five-year-old girl had a bad bruise on her left leg, just below the knee. Of course, he was concerned and had asked her about it. That was all. But then he had glanced up to see the utter shock on her mother's face when she entered the hall to find him touching the girl's leg.

He put down the last of the prayer books and sighed deeply. His explanation had pacified the woman, he was certain of that — or was he? How could he be certain of anything with that infernal Chief Inspector Ashworth always asking questions, and everyone being so suspicious of motives just lately?

* * *

Although she would never admit such a thing to a living soul, Jan's attack had seriously unnerved her. Yet she was determined to overcome her fears. She would out-bottle her attackers — that was how she saw her mission now. Indeed, she was already thinking ahead and restructuring her strategy. As events had now turned physical, she momentarily wondered whether she should leave behind Miss Marple's woolly-cardigan-and-cocoa type of sleuthing and change instead to more of a *Prime Suspect* technique.

Jan smiled to herself as she sorted through the freezer compartment at her local supermarket, unable to decide between Birds Eye fish fingers or the supermarket's own brand. Somehow she couldn't quite see herself as Jane Tennison, jumping into bed with big butch policemen — even if the officer in question was Jim Ashworth. Mind you, he did make her legs go just a tiny bit weak.

She laughed aloud at the notion, unmindful of the other shoppers staring at her as she placed the Birds Eye fish fingers into her trolley. On second thoughts, perhaps she should stick with the sedate, non-sexual Miss Marple; it would be easier all round.

At the checkout, Jan packed her groceries into two shopping bags and headed for the door.

'Hey,' a male voice called from behind.

She swivelled round, her heart beating frantically against her ribcage. The man was huge and made to look even bulkier in an ill-fitting blue anorak, his face partly covered by a large crash helmet.

'What do you want?' she demanded, gripping the handles of her bags tightly and preparing to swing out with them if necessary.

‘Sorry, love,’ he said, taken aback, ‘but you left your fish fingers in the trolley.’

‘Oh . . . oh,’ she said, sighing with relief. ‘Oh, thank you.’

* * *

Jan’s daughter, Diana, visited in the afternoon, and baby Harry dutifully slept in his carrycot throughout his grandmother’s detailed account of her exploits. With such a fertile imagination Jan could not help but colour reality a little, and by the time the words left her mouth Ashworth’s promise of occasional police surveillance had become round-the-clock protection, with the chief inspector in constant contact via the telephone.

Jan rarely allowed the truth to spoil a good story, but that was not her only reason for the exaggeration — she didn’t want Diana worrying about her safety; the girl had enough on her plate coping with Harry.

‘My goodness, is that the time?’ she exclaimed, when her daughter pointed out it was 4 p.m. ‘It doesn’t seem as if you’ve been here for five minutes, and you’ve hardly said a word.’

‘I couldn’t get one in edgeways,’ Diana muttered, as she headed for the front door.

‘Now, you mustn’t worry about me,’ Jan said, helping the baby into the car seat. ‘I shall be all right.’

‘Yes, Mum. Bye, Mum,’ Diana said, waving a hand as she pulled out into the road.

The trouble was, she did worry. Having a mother like Jan was a constant worry. She reached the junction at the end of the road, and it was while she was signalling left that Diana noticed two men walking purposefully towards her mother’s house. She pulled onto the main road, her mind dwelling on them. Say they were going to her mum’s, and this time she’d get more than a punch in the face? The baby woke up then and started crying hungrily.

'Oh, be quiet,' she murmured.

Her nerves were already stretched to breaking point by the sleepless nights she had suffered, listening to that very sound. And now there was the added worry of her mother.

With the traffic lights on red, Diana brought the car to a halt, grabbed her mobile telephone and punched out Jan's number.

'Hello . . . Mum?'

'Diana, what's the matter, dear?'

'Oh, nothing, I, er, I just thought I'd left Harry's bottle, but I've found it now. Are you okay?'

'Fine, dear—'

'Sorry, Mum, the lights are on green, I've got to go. Bye.'

Thank God for that. The two men hadn't called at the house and murdered her in cold blood on the doorstep. And as an added bonus, Harry had stopped crying and was gurgling quite cheerfully on the back seat.

As the bricks and mortar of the town gave way to vast green fields Diana started to relax. She even turned on the car radio and allowed the soothing sounds of classical music to wash over her. Always mindful of the baby she drove slowly and carefully, never allowing the needle to pass the thirty mark on the narrow snaking roads.

After a few miles she became aware of a Mini behind her. It pulled up close to her back bumper and made her feel extremely nervous. When she came to a straight stretch of road the driver of the Mini fell back and sounded his horn. Diana straight away touched the brake pedal and signalled for him to pass, but he continued to lean on the horn. All too soon the harsh noise had the baby crying again.

'Oh, come on,' Diana snapped. 'Just get past.'

The driver dropped back and then increased his speed.

'About time,' she said aloud, waiting for him to overtake.

But he didn't pull out; he was hurtling forward, in direct line with her car.

'Christ, no,' she shouted, as the Mini loomed large in her rear-view mirror.

At the very last second there was an horrendous squeal of brakes and the vehicle clipped her back bumper. That sudden impact shunted her forward, the seat belt digging into her breasts, and before she had time to recover he hit her again, harder this time, and she could hear sounds of metal bending and twisting above Harry's lusty sobs.

'Please, don't,' she whimpered, as the Mini pursued her for a third time and smashed into the back of her car with a dull thump.

Diana could no longer keep hold of the steering wheel and it spun from left to right, reeling around while she let out a frightened yell. And then the car mounted the grass verge, ploughed into a ditch, and all was silent.

CHAPTER 26

A dogged scowl was taking permanent root on Ashworth's face as he strode across reception to where Sergeant Dutton was busy at the front desk.

'What's happening with Jan Morrison's daughter, Martin?'

'She's all right, Jim, so's the baby. They're just badly shaken.'

'Well, that's something,' he said, leaning on the desk. 'Have your lads interviewed her yet?'

'Yes, very briefly. She can't give a description of the driver, outside the fact that it was a man, and she didn't get the registration number, but the Mini was green. After she went into the ditch, he just drove off. There's no doubt that he deliberately intended to run her off the road.'

'And there's no doubt why it was done,' Ashworth added, his scowl deepening.

'To put the frighteners on her mother,' Dutton said.

'That's about it and it'll work, too. If it was just her own safety at stake Jan would hold out, but if members of her family become involved . . .' He shook his head.

'No new leads in the Nicky Waldon case, then?'

'Not as such, Martin, no, but I've been going through the file. As far as her parents are aware Nicky didn't know

Gilbert Randall. And it seems she couldn't stand Reverend Thorne — used to call him a creep, apparently — but she had a big crush on Noel Harper.'

Dutton's eyebrows rose. 'But Nicky was only eight. A bit young for crushes, wasn't she?'

'Puberty can start as early as nine nowadays, Martin. Old-timers like us tend to forget that.'

'Hmm, suppose so.'

'Of course we spoke to Thorne and Harper at the time, but not as suspects. We needed to establish if they had any ideas of where Nicky could have gone.'

Dutton frowned. 'But now you think they might have had something to do with her murder?'

'I'm ruling nothing in and nothing out, as they say, Martin. I am thinking of having another word with Harper, though. Why did Nicky think of Reverend Thorne as a creep? Was it something she sensed, or had he tried to touch her?'

Dutton shook his head. 'I'd tread very carefully, Jim, if I were you. My lads on the beat are reporting a large section of the public up in arms about this church connection. If you start interviewing Harper or Thorne again those people might well jump to conclusions.'

Ashworth fixed him with a determined stare. 'Nevertheless, I've got to dig, Martin, and I'll keep on digging until I unearth something.'

* * *

Noel Harper was pulling on his polo-necked sweater when he opened the door.

'Chief Inspector,' he said, surprised. 'What brings you here?'

'Hello, sir, I don't think you've met DS Bedford. I wonder if we might have a word?'

'Yes, come in.' He stood back, still tucking the sweater into the waistband of his jeans. 'This way.'

They were led into the lounge where Beth Harper was sitting on the settee, watching the television. A friendly smile was on her face when they filed in.

'Hello,' she said. 'Chief Inspector Ashworth, isn't it?'

He nodded. 'And this is DS Bedford.'

Her open smile was transferred to Holly as she stood up. 'Let me get you a cup of tea.'

Ashworth straight away held up a hand. 'No, it's all right thank you. We just want to ask your husband some questions. They won't take long.'

'What sort of questions?' Harper asked, settling on the arm of the settee.

'We believe that Nicky Waldon had some sort of crush on you, sir,' Holly said.

He looked surprised. 'Well, yes, along with most of the other girls in the youth club. I try to discourage it of course, but in my work it helps to get close to the kids and in doing so crushes sometimes happen.'

'Mr Harper, I know this is ground we've already covered,' Ashworth said, 'but any new information you could give would be of great assistance. Now, you say you need to get close to the children — does that mean they might sometimes confide in you? Did Nicky ever confide in you, sir?'

'Often,' Harper readily replied. 'About boys she liked, problems with her parents . . . These were only slight I must add — getting told off for playing pop music too loud, things like that.'

'Did Nicky get on well with Reverend Thorne?'

'Yes . . . yes, I think so.'

'But it's been brought to our notice that she often referred to him as a creep. That would suggest to me that she had little liking for the man.'

Harper laughed. 'That's just the way kids talk, Chief Inspector. I must admit though, David doesn't relate too well with youngsters. He's far too serious, too stuffy. I'd expect most of them call him a creep, or even worse.'

Ashworth considered this. 'It's long been my contention, Mr Harper, that Nicky Waldon went off with someone she knew. After all, it happened on a summer's evening — it was still daylight — and no one ever came forward to claim they saw her being accosted. I'm certain she would have struggled if a stranger or someone she disliked had tried to abduct her.'

'Hold on, now just hold on,' Beth said shrilly. 'What are you actually implying here? Are you saying you think Noel had something to do with her disappearance, because—'

'Beth, calm down,' Harper interjected. 'They're only asking questions.'

'But they're not — can't you see? They're saying she wouldn't have gone off with David because she couldn't stand him, but you . . .' She left the sentence unfinished.

'That was not my intention, Mrs Harper, believe me.'

'Well, that's how it sounded.' She pointed an accusing finger. 'You keep on trying to link church members with those deaths, and you've no idea of the damage that's caused. People are staying away from church functions in droves—'

'Mrs Harper,' Ashworth said, his temper wearing dangerously thin. 'We are not trying to link the murders to the church, we're simply making inquiries. Now, we always hope that members of the public will help us in every way possible, which is all I'm asking from you and your husband.'

Beth bristled under his stare and turned away. 'Just consider this, Chief Inspector — when looking at those working in the church, who comes under most suspicion? Noel does, because he works with the kids.'

'Thank you for your help,' Ashworth said shortly. 'I think we'd better leave.'

Harper ushered them into the hall. 'Don't take any notice of her,' he said, his tone subdued. 'It's true, though, that the kids have stopped coming to the discos and the Sunday classes.'

'I'm sure that's no reflection on you, sir,' Ashworth said. 'It's just a case of parents keeping their children at home until this matter can be cleared up.'

Harper sighed. 'That's not what the gossip-mongers are saying. In any case, Beth and I feel so deeply for those kids. They're either at or approaching a time when it'll seem like almost every adult in the world is out to harm them. We try desperately to make them see that's not the case, otherwise they'll end up thinking everybody over the age of twenty-five is a pervert.'

'I take your point, sir,' Ashworth said, anxious to be away. 'Once again, thanks for your help.'

They were driving back to the station, when Holly said, 'What do you think of him, guv?'

'I don't like him. He spreads the sincerity on like butter. But we've got nothing on him, so we'll have to leave it there.' He huffed. 'That wife of his only makes matters worse — the more indignant she gets, the more tongues will wag. You see if I'm right, Holly.'

* * *

Superintendent Newton was a staunch believer in the five-day week, so he was far from pleased when events necessitated his attendance at Bridgetown Police Station on Saturday morning. A glower darkened his features as he sat at his desk, his gaze resting accusingly on Ashworth.

'Chief Inspector, I've been approached by the *Bridgetown Post*. They want to know if there's any truth behind the rumour that Mr and Mrs Harper have been interviewed in connection with the abduction and murder of Nicky Waldon.'

Ashworth shifted his huge bulk in the inadequate chair and matched his superior's formidable glare.

'We've had a word with them, yes, sir, but I don't see why the press should have picked up on it. We've spoken to a number of people. This is, after all, a murder inquiry.'

'Yes, yes, I realise that,' Newton muttered. 'And did your inquiries lead you anywhere?'

'No, sir. It seems Nicky had a crush on Harper, but we haven't been able to connect him with her murder.'

Newton rose from his seat and stomped across to the window. 'This is most inconvenient you know. I'd better tell them that a number of people have helped us with our inquiries, which are ongoing, and I don't wish to comment beyond that.' He sighed deeply. 'That will, of course, be taken as an admission that we have talked to the Harpers.'

Ashworth frowned. 'I can't understand how the press got hold of this.'

Newton turned, a bitter smile on his lips. 'They're grubbing around for a story, and they'll keep on poking their noses in where they don't belong.'

'We do have to speak to people, sir, if we feel they may be of help,' Ashworth ventured.

'Yes, yes, yes, of course you do.' He gave a dismissive wave of his hand. 'But these reporters are going to keep on asking their damned questions, hoping to rake up some dirt on Harper. So, although there'll be nothing in print, rumours and distortions of the facts will spread like wildfire. It'll be trial by newspaper, Ashworth — and the chief constable won't like that one little bit.'

* * *

At the Sunday morning service Reverend Thorne stood in the pulpit to address an almost empty church. While he preached a sermon involving the evils of malicious gossip, he gazed upon the few stalwarts that were there. The Scotts and the Perrys stared back at him, their expressions impassive. There were one or two unfamiliar faces at the back — parishioners with morbid curiosity come to gloat? — and as always in her usual place sat Sarah Ashworth.

Afterwards he stood in the porch, shaking the hands of his dwindling congregation, while he waited for Sarah to reach him.

'Ah, Mrs Ashworth,' he said, 'I'm so glad you're the last to leave. Could I possibly have a word with you?'

'Of course, vicar,' she said, smiling warmly.

'Please walk with me, Mrs Ashworth,' he said, pausing for her to fall in beside him. 'No doubt you've noticed my diminishing flock?'

'I'm afraid so,' she said, picking a path through a churchyard filled with headstones from another era.

'And no doubt you're aware of the reason for it?'

'That young man, Noel Harper,' she said bluntly.

'Among other things.' He gave a dejected sigh. 'It seems that because of your good husband's investigation, people such as the Scotts and the Perrys have come under scrutiny. Your husband hasn't any evidence against them, has he? Or perhaps I shouldn't be asking you such questions.'

'You shouldn't,' she said with a slightly scolding look. 'But if he did have evidence, I'm sure they would have heard by now.' She stopped and stood in front of him. 'Look, vicar, people are frightened, that's all. There are so many rumours flying about but it will blow over, you'll see.'

'I'm not so sure,' he said, his hands clasped to his chest. 'I've received a petition, you know, from the parents of all children connected with the church. They're demanding that Noel Harper be sacked. They're over-reacting—'

'They're very frightened,' she said again. 'And who can blame them? Two local girls have gone missing, and both of them found dead. It's no wonder they're all looking over their shoulders and pointing fingers.'

'Those poor children,' he said, wringing his hands. 'May God rest their souls.'

'Vicar, do you think Noel Harper had anything to do with this?'

'No, of course I don't, any more than I believe the Scotts and the Perrys are involved. But can you see my dilemma? All I have to do is get rid of Noel, ask four of the longest-serving church members to stay away, and the flock will return. Simple. But if I do that it will be seen as an admission that I think they are involved.'

'Let's just hope the police soon catch whoever is responsible and clear the whole matter up.'

'Amen to that.'

CHAPTER 27

Monday morning brought the news that all in CID had dreaded.

'Randall will be out on bail by Wednesday,' Ashworth announced as he sat behind his desk.

'Does that mean Jan Morrison's withdrawing her evidence?' Holly asked, lighting a cigarette.

'Yes. I spent the best part of yesterday afternoon with Jan and her husband, and she's decided she can't go through with it. So, the CPS won't proceed with the case, which means we've got him for the pornographic video cassettes and nothing else.'

Josh shook his head. 'It doesn't make any sense, guv. We only questioned the Scotts, the Perrys and Harper — we were looking for information, not accusing them of anything. But now the whole town's ready to lynch them, while Randall will just go back to his normal life.'

'They've simply homed in on the church connection, Josh. Most of them want to believe it, so they do.' He huffed. 'This is fast becoming a case of, you lose some and then you lose some more.'

* * *

'Noel, I must ask you for your resignation,' Reverend Thorne said, trying hard to sound firm. 'It's been three weeks since the congregation started staying away from the church, and all its functions. You must see the predicament I'm in.'

Harper rounded on him. 'No, I don't,' he retorted. 'It's you who must see mine.'

They were in the drawing room at the vicarage and this was the fourth such meeting they'd had over the past few weeks. Nothing had been resolved, however. Each talk had ended in stalemate, and the vicar saw no alternative now but to offer his ultimatum.

'Noel,' he implored, his face reddening. 'I've said I'll do my level best to secure a post for you in another area, well away from here. There's no reason why your leaving should be linked to local events. In fact it could even look like promotion.'

'I like it here, David. Beth and I enjoy the work.'

Thorne took in a long breath and exhaled slowly. 'But, Noel, there isn't any work. And there isn't likely to be any while you're here.'

'And there you have the problem,' Harper spat. 'My move would make it look as if I had something to hide, and I'm not going to have that on my record.'

'Oh, Lord, what can I do to persuade you? Noel, I would hate to have to go over your head with this. I did so hope that we could somehow sort it out between ourselves.'

'That's a threat Thorne,' Harper said, pointing an accusing finger. 'And that's something I'm not willing to tolerate. Don't forget, the public could well be suspecting you if the facts were known.'

Thorne's eyes narrowed. 'And what do you mean by that?'

'You know well enough.'

'So, that's it. So many times you've hinted at it, and now it's out in the open. But I have to remind you that no one ever proved anything.'

'They haven't proved anything against me, either, and I'm not moving until my name is completely cleared.'

Something seemed to go out of the vicar then and his shoulders slumped, making his stoop even more pronounced.

'Very well, Noel, you win, but I really can't see any way out of this predicament.'

* * *

Amy Byron sauntered across the school playing fields, her hockey stick swinging at her side. Her team had just thrashed that of the lower third and she was in good spirits. Suddenly she spotted Noel and Beth Harper waiting at the touchline and a wide smile lit up her features as she hastened towards them.

'Well done, Amy,' Harper said, while he and his wife clapped heartily. 'You played a terrific game.'

'Thank you,' she said, grinning. 'It was easy, really.'

'When are we going to see you at the church disco again?' Beth ventured. 'It's been three weeks now.'

The girl pulled a disgruntled face. 'Mum and Dad said I'm to stay away from the church until they're sure it's safe.'

'But it is safe.' Beth laughed. 'Surely you know you can trust us?'

Their conversation was cut short by Miss Rolands, the sports mistress. The moment she spotted them talking to the girl she rushed over.

'Amy, go and get changed.'

'Yes, miss,' she said, skipping off and waving to them.

'What are you doing here?' the teacher demanded to know.

Harper looked severely taken aback by the hostility in her voice. 'We're just trying to drum up support for the church,' he said. 'We're regular visitors to the school, so why—'

'Are you trying to tell us we're not welcome here?' Beth asked tersely.

Miss Rolands turned away. 'I think in the circumstances it would be better if you didn't come to the school for the time being.'

'Oh, come on, Noel,' Beth flared. 'We're wasting our time with these people.'

'I'm sorry,' the teacher said, a hot flush burning her cheeks.

'You're sorry,' Beth threw back scornfully. 'My husband hasn't done anything. The police haven't even formally interviewed him. You're ruining our lives for no reason — can't you see?'

She strutted off before the teacher could reply. Highly embarrassed now, Miss Rolands turned to Harper.

'I am sorry,' she repeated, her eyes cast down.

'Beth's right, you know. You're all treating us like lepers, and we haven't done anything — or even been accused of doing anything by the police.'

'I'm . . . I'm sorry.'

Harper shrugged and set off in pursuit of his wife.

* * *

Jilly Byron went to collect her daughter from school as usual, and while she sat in the car waiting for Amy to come out she noticed Noel Harper standing on the opposite side of the road to the school gates. Quite curious, she watched and waited. After a few minutes Amy came running along the pavement and Harper waved to her, signalling for her to cross the road and join him.

Straight away Jilly was gripped by panic and was struggling out of her seat belt when she saw Amy shake her head and start towards the car. She breathed a sigh of relief and went to greet her daughter, all the while glaring at the man.

'What did Mr Harper want, Amy?' she asked, taking the girl's hand.

'He wanted me to go across the road, but I said I couldn't because you were waiting for me.'

'Good girl.'

'He was at the hockey match this afternoon, Mum. I think Miss Rolands told him off for talking to me.'

Jilly's heart skipped a beat 'You're to stay away from him. Do you understand, Amy? Stay away from him, and his wife.'

CHAPTER 28

'Amy's gone,' Jilly Byron sobbed into the telephone.

'Sorry, madam, could you repeat that?' the police constable asked.

'Our daughter's gone,' she cried. 'Just get somebody here.'

'Calm down, madam, and give me the details.'

'Oh, please get somebody here—'

Her husband snatched the receiver. 'For God's sake, man, just tell Chief Inspector Ashworth that Amy Byron's vanished.'

* * *

Holly had a job to keep up as Ashworth hurried to the house, and they had hardly reached the front step when Larry Byron snatched open the door.

'Thank God you're here,' he said. 'I can't do anything with Jilly.'

'Right,' Ashworth said, shouldering his way into the lounge, 'tell us what happened.'

'Amy's gone,' Jilly shrieked from the settee. 'She's gone. What more do you need to know?'

Holly made straight for the woman and whispered calming noises while Jilly collapsed on to her shoulder, her body racked with sobs.

'Mr Byron?' Ashworth said.

'She only went into the garden,' he began, perilously close to tears. 'She'd been helping Jilly with the washing up. She was just taking the scraps out to the rubbish sack.'

'If only I'd taken them out,' his wife wailed. 'Amy would still be here now if I had.'

Ashworth frowned. 'She vanished from the garden?'

'Yes, our fences are very low,' Byron told him. 'And there's access out the back for the garages.'

'What time was this?'

'About seven p.m.'

'Would you show me the garden?' Ashworth asked.

Byron ushered him into the kitchen and opened the back door. Ashworth went out onto the patio and strained his eyes in the darkness. All of the perimeter fencing was made of wire and was no more than three feet high. At the far end of the garden he could make out the dark outline of a garage and beside it a low gate leading into the vehicular access beyond.

'Someone must have been standing at the gate and called out to her,' Byron said, his voice breaking. 'She must have gone down to him.'

Ashworth turned to the man. 'She wouldn't do that surely?'

'I think you'd better listen to what my wife has to say.' He caught Ashworth's arm, his fingers digging into the flesh. 'If you find out who's taken Amy, you'll be able to get her back, won't you?'

'If we find out for certain who's abducted her then, yes, there's every chance we can get her back,' he said, wishing he felt the confidence that his words implied.

'Good,' the man said, seemingly pacified. 'Now come and talk to my wife.'

In the lounge Holly was still attempting to comfort the distraught woman, and when she caught sight of Ashworth, she said, 'It's going to be all right, Jilly, just tell the chief inspector about Noel Harper.'

Jilly looked at their faces in turn and made a concerted effort to calm down.

'It was two days ago,' she said haltingly. 'Harper was waiting outside the school. He was on the opposite side of the road, as though he didn't want to make himself conspicuous. Anyway, when Amy came out he tried to get her to cross the road, but she wouldn't . . .'

She stopped to fight back fresh tears, screwing a handkerchief between her fingers.

'Amy said he'd been at the hockey match that afternoon and only went when her teacher, Miss Rolands, told him off for bothering her.'

Ashworth thought for a while, and then said, 'If Harper was waiting at the gate, do you think Amy would have gone to him? After all, she didn't go to him outside the school.'

'Only because I was waiting for her,' Jilly said. 'Otherwise she would have gone. She felt safe with him, you see, she never believed the things everybody was saying about him.'

'We'll have the man in for questioning right away,' Ashworth said, already moving towards the door. 'If his answers don't add up, we'll apply for a warrant to search his house. And I'll get one of my officers to take a statement from the teacher — Miss Rolands, is it?'

Jilly nodded. 'Kathy Rolands, yes.'

On the drive back Holly radioed in with a request that Noel Harper be brought in for questioning, and an order that Josh be dispatched to the house of Miss Rolands for a statement. Fifteen minutes after their arrival at the police station, Harper was led into the interview room by PC John Dickens.

'Mr Harper,' Ashworth said, 'would you like to take a seat?' He indicated the chair.

Harper sat down and folded his arms, his brows raised expectantly. 'What's all this about?'

'I believe you were at St Giles's school two days ago, talking to Amy Byron.'

'So?' he said, his eyes taking in the whirring tape recorder on an adjacent desk.

'And outside, after school, you tried to entice her across the road,' Ashworth went on, his unflinching gaze resting on the man's face.

'I didn't try to *entice* her anywhere, I merely waved to her. Look, Amy's a very special child, you know that, Chief Inspector. It just breaks my heart to think I got so close to so many wonderful children and now it's all been taken away from me.' He leant forward, his expression earnest. 'I'm just trying to build bridges with the kids, show them they've got nothing to be frightened of.'

'Amy's gone missing,' Holly said, as she wandered across to the table. 'She was snatched from the back garden of her home earlier this evening.'

'I don't believe this,' Harper said, rushing to his feet. 'And you think . . . ?'

'Sit down,' Ashworth ordered.

* * *

Kathy Rolands was in her forties and had never married. Indeed, there were many who believed that her preferences lay with her own sex. But this was a charge often made against unattached women of a certain age, especially those like Miss Rolands who were rather masculine in appearance and manner.

She shyly welcomed Josh into her tiny flat which was situated above the offices of a travel agent in Bridgetown's high street. He accepted her invitation for him to sit and proceeded to take out his notepad and pen while she settled herself opposite.

'Did you know that Amy Byron had been abducted?' he asked.

'No, I didn't,' she said, her eyes wide with shock. 'Oh dear, when was this?'

'Earlier tonight. Now, we've been told that you were forced to speak to Mr Noel Harper two days ago, concerning his behaviour towards Amy. Is that right?'

'Yes, yes, it is,' she said, nodding furiously. 'Mrs Harper, as well, as it happens. They were watching the hockey match on the school playing fields, and when it was over they waylaid Amy.'

Josh frowned. 'When you say waylaid, what do you mean, exactly?'

'Precisely that. The pair of them made a beeline for her. It looked to me as if they'd singled her out. They totally ignored the other children.'

'And what did you do?' Josh asked.

'Well, I was a bit suspicious, what with everything that's going on at the moment. So I confronted them in the most diplomatic way I could and more or less told them to stay away from the school. The headmistress has instructed us to use our own judgement in such matters,' she added quickly, 'because of what's been happening.'

'I see. And in your opinion Mr and Mrs Harper seemed to be accosting Amy, is that what you're saying?'

'Most certainly. I found it very alarming.'

'Good . . . thank you.' He glanced up. 'Did you know any of the other girls who vanished?'

'I knew them all. Of course, none of them attended St Giles's . . . apart from Amy, that is. Do you know, I really can't believe this. I used to coach her in the evenings, after hours. She has the makings of a fantastic hockey player.'

'And you knew the other girls . . .'

'Oh, yes, so many schools are selling off their playing fields nowadays. I think about six others pay to use ours, at the moment.'

'Miss Rolands, do you think Amy would have gone off with someone she knew?'

'She wouldn't have gone off with someone, exactly,' the teacher said, after a thoughtful pause, 'but I reckon she would have gone to someone she trusted, just like she did at the playing fields.'

'But not the other girls?'

'I don't quite see what you're getting at.'

'Well, we've reason to believe that the other girls were taken forcibly, but that doesn't seem to be the case with Amy.'

'The others were more streetwise — I believe that's the expression, isn't it? Amy is far too trusting.'

Josh snapped shut his notepad and stood up. 'Thank you, Miss Rolands, you've been a great help.'

'I do hope so,' she said, leaving her seat. 'Let me show you out. These old buildings are littered with steps where you don't expect to find them.' She led the way to the outside door, switching on lights as she went along.

'I don't mind telling you, constable, I'll be glad when you've found the murderers. All those in charge of children will tell you the same thing. Parents are so frightened just lately, they're suspicious of everybody.' She opened the front door and stepped aside. 'Do mind the stairs, they are very steep.'

'Thanks again.'

The door closed and Josh negotiated the steps with care.

'Definite lesbian,' he muttered. 'But kids? Maybe not.'

CHAPTER 29

'Have you got any more questions to ask me, Chief Inspector?' Harper asked hotly.

'Plenty,' Ashworth assured him.

He was about to elaborate when they were disturbed by a knock at the door. Josh hurried in, a number of papers in his hand.

'Miss Rolands' statement,' he whispered in Ashworth's ear.

While Josh made a discreet exit, Ashworth picked up the pages and studied them for many moments, occasionally glancing up at Harper.

'Well,' he said, 'it seems your behaviour and that of your wife raised the suspicions of the games mistress at St Giles's School.'

'We were talking to Amy. What's wrong with that?'

'That's not what the teacher says in her statement. She says that your behaviour caused her some concern.'

'This is ridiculous,' Harper said with a scornful laugh.

Ashworth leant across the table. 'You were at the playing fields, acting suspiciously,' he said, placing heavy emphasis on each word. 'Then, outside the school, you tried to entice Amy across the road.'

Harper shook his head.

'Then tonight you went to her house,' Holly said. 'You went along the service road at the back and you waited for her to come into the garden. You knew she'd come to you — she trusted you — and then you snatched her. You fancy her, Noel, don't you? Come on, tell us, you'll feel better.'

'No, no, no,' he yelled, his fist repeatedly hitting the tabletop. 'I couldn't fancy a child, I couldn't—'

'Where were you tonight at seven p.m.?' Ashworth asked. 'Were you at Amy's house?'

'I was at home,' the man shouted.

'Was anyone with you?'

'My wife. We were eating dinner.'

'Your wife,' Holly said with a vicious sneer. 'The same person who was with you when your behaviour was giving rise for concern at the school. That doesn't look too good, Noel, does it?'

'I'm going to apply for a warrant to search your house,' Ashworth said abruptly.

'You don't need a warrant,' Harper said, his voice now weary. 'I'll give you my permission.'

The chief inspector stood up and motioned for Holly to join him in the corridor.

'Would you like a cup of tea, Mr Harper?' he asked.

'No,' he said, slowly shaking his head. 'I just want this over with.'

The uniformed division was changing shifts so the corridor was busy with groups of boisterous officers. However, one caustic glance from Ashworth brought about an almost reverential silence.

As soon as they were alone, Holly said, 'We're not going to break him, guv. And if the search at his house doesn't reveal anything, we'll have to let him go.'

'His behaviour at the school . . .' he thought aloud. 'It's almost as if he wanted to put himself in the frame.'

'Of course, the other alternative is he's telling the truth.'

'Possible. All right, get Josh and we'll go and have a look at his house.'

'Are we taking Harper, guv?'

'Yes. I think so.'

* * *

Holly sat with Harper in the back of Josh's car, and the tail lights of Ashworth's Scorpio were ahead of them as they negotiated the long winding lanes.

'We'll find her,' she said, continuing with her gentle persuasive approach.

'I just hope you do. And I hope you find her in time.'

'I think you've got her.'

'Oh, do you?' he scoffed. 'So I let you search my house, knowing you'll find her there.'

'That only means she's not there,' Holly countered. 'How about if you left her with the Perrys or the Scotts?'

Harper let out a derisive laugh.

'You see, we've already worked out who the other members of your ring are. It's just a matter of time before we get all of you.'

'If this wasn't so tragic, it could almost be funny,' he said. 'You're wasting your time harassing me, when you should be out there looking for Amy.'

'It must play on your mind,' Holly said. 'I mean, we've already found three bodies. We're going to get all of you, so wouldn't it be better for you to make a statement now? Somebody's bound to crack sooner or later, and when they do they'll want to put themselves in the best possible light.' She paused, gave time for her words to sink in. 'Perhaps Gilbert Randall will be the one to crack. Is that why you all intimidated the witnesses? Are you frightened he'll crack, Noel?'

He made no response, simply continued to stare out into the dark. Presently the Scorpio's brake lights glowed red as Ashworth pulled up outside the house. Josh parked behind and Harper was manhandled onto the grass verge. Beth was soon running towards them.

'Noel,' she cried, 'what's happening?'

'They're going to search the house,' he told her. 'They think we've got Amy Byron in there.'

'What? Noel, I don't want them in the house. This is our home,' she screamed at Ashworth, 'and you're violating it.'

'Your husband has given his permission,' he calmly said. 'But if he wants to withdraw that permission, we can apply for a search warrant.'

'Let them look, Beth,' Harper chided. 'They won't find anything, so let them look and let's just get it over with.'

Still protesting, she led the way into the house and her angry words turned to screams and shouts as the three detectives crossed the threshold. So intent were they on proving Harper to be a liar that they failed to notice a solitary figure standing across the lane, partly concealed by the darkness and a low hedgerow.

'Where do you want to look first?' Beth shrieked.

'Would you please calm down, Mrs Harper?' Ashworth asked. 'I must remind you that your husband invited us in.'

She seemed on the point of another screamed attack, but subsided and flounced into the lounge to sit rigid in an armchair.

'Have you got a cellar, Mr Harper?' Ashworth asked.

'Yes, I'll show you where it is.'

At the far end of the kitchen Harper opened a door and flicked on the light. Josh went with the chief inspector down a number of stone steps. There was a strong musty smell and the rough brick walls were cold and mildewed.

'You've got damp, Mr Harper,' Ashworth remarked.

'Most cellars have,' he replied dully.

The space was lit by a single naked bulb and was completely empty. At one time the walls had been emulsioned white but were now a dull grey, the paint flaking. Ashworth paced about, staring up at the exposed joists.

'Empty . . . as you can well see,' Harper said, folding his arms. 'Are you satisfied?'

'Not completely,' he said, almost to himself as he moved to the wall on his left. 'Above here must have been the chimney breast in the kitchen.'

Harper shrugged. 'I suppose so. What about it?'

Ashworth felt around the bricks. 'Now, the support for that chimney breast comes right down into the cellar. Most of them are just two vertical pillars of brick, open at the front. But this one's different . . .'

'It's the priest hole, Chief Inspector, it's been boarded up. Look, you can still see the bricks across the top.'

Ashworth felt a growing sense of excitement as he viewed the six lines of bricks that formed an arch between the two uprights. He could almost believe he was on to something but for the laid-back attitude of Harper who was clearly enjoying the history lesson.

'It was bricked lower down originally,' he went on. 'Close to the floor some of the bricks were loose and they could be removed for the priest to crawl through and then be replaced. At some time part of it must have collapsed, leading to it being boarded up. Shame, isn't it?'

'Maybe we should take the board down and have a look behind,' Ashworth said.

Harper smirked. 'Easily done, Chief Inspector, one corner's loose. See? It comes away from the wall.' He reached up and pulled the plasterboard aside. 'There, now you can see behind it.'

Ashworth peered into the dark empty space which was barely large enough to accommodate a standing adult.

'Bad luck.' Harper chuckled. 'You really thought you'd found something then, didn't you?'

'We'll take a look upstairs, if we may,' he said, crossing to the stairs.

'With pleasure.'

Harper's eyes held a mocking light and Ashworth had to take a long breath to calm himself as they hurried back up the steps. Holly had stayed in the lounge with Beth, and their raised voices could be heard all the while Josh followed the chief inspector from room to room, with Harper close behind. The first floor produced nothing, but Ashworth had expected as much.

The old stairs creaked beneath their weight as they returned to the ground floor where Harper darted in front, eager to show them the dining room. Ashworth surveyed the long table and dark oak chairs with a gloomy expression. Already seeds of doubt were in his mind, and they blossomed instantly when his gaze took in the well-thumbed Bible on the hall table. Maybe Harper and his wife were victims of malicious gossip, after all.

'I do hope your report will state that we cooperated with you fully,' Harper said.

'You can be sure of it, sir. All our reports are completely factual.'

They entered the lounge to find Beth rising from her chair and glaring accusingly at Holly.

'You should wash your mouth out with soapy water,' she spat.

'We're very sorry to have disturbed you, madam,' Ashworth said quickly, before Holly could make matters worse. 'Thank you for your help.'

'We didn't have much choice in the matter, did we?' she said, the anger in her words following them to the front door.

Ashworth let out a long-suffering sigh.

'And I don't want that person in my home ever again,' she yelled, her finger pointing aggressively towards Holly.

Cold air rushed in as Harper let them out, and he could be heard trying to pacify his wife as they hastened down the path.

'What's her problem?' Ashworth asked Holly.

She shrugged. 'I think the woman's got silly cow disease, guv.'

'Chief Inspector, could you hold on a minute?' Harper called, as he ran to catch them up.

'Yes, sir?'

'Sorry about that,' he said, keeping his voice low. 'Beth's had it up to here. Now she's worrying about what people are going to say when they find out you've searched our home.'

It was then that Ashworth's attention was caught by a shadowy figure crossing the road. He strained his eyes and tried to identify the man. Something in his walk warned Ashworth that this was no ordinary citizen out for an evening stroll. Presently, Larry Byron emerged from the gloom.

'Have you found her?' he demanded. 'Have you found Amy?'

Straight away Ashworth moved to intercept him. 'No, we haven't, Mr Byron. Now, I want you to go home.'

'Home,' he echoed flatly.

'I'm so sorry,' Harper said. 'Amy's a very special little girl. I'll of course do anything I can to help.'

'You've got her,' he whimpered, his eyes clouding over. 'I know you have.' Then he lunged towards Harper, and Ashworth had to put out a hand to restrain him.

'Sir,' he said, 'will you please go home?'

'You've got her, you bastard. Tell me where she is.'

With lightning speed he dodged around the chief inspector and started raining blows on Harper's head and chest. Ashworth dashed forward to grab the man's flailing arms. Byron resisted but then, with Holly's help, he was dragged away. Harper stood shocked, his nose bleeding badly.

'You'd better calm down,' Holly cautioned.

'But he's got Amy. Oh, Christ, just let me get at him.'

'Mr Byron, stop it,' Ashworth yelled.

The man was still wrestling, but Holly finally managed to twist his arms behind his back. He stood there, sobbing and trembling, his struggles now ineffectual.

'We've searched the house,' Ashworth told him, 'and we haven't found anything. Do you understand me, son? Now I want you to go home, your wife needs you there.'

'I know he's got her,' Byron wept. 'I just know he has.'

'Mr Byron, listen to me,' Ashworth said, speaking slowly. 'Amy is nowhere in that house. How did you get here?'

'I walked,' he mumbled. 'I'm going out of my mind.'

'Let him go, Holly.'

She released her grip and he stood with head bowed, shoulders slumped.

'Now, sir, I'm going to get one of my officers to drive you home, and I want you to stay there. Do you understand me?'

He nodded.

'Good. Josh, take Mr Byron home.'

Byron allowed Josh to take his arm and lead him away, all the fight knocked out of him.

'Poor devil,' Ashworth murmured, as he watched Josh settle him into the passenger seat.

Blood was pouring from Harper's nose, and he was having to use a handkerchief to stop the flow. Ashworth noted the lack of animosity on his face; in fact all that showed there was sadness for the Byrons' plight. Once again, doubts about the man's guilt bubbled to the surface of his mind.

'Are you all right, Mr Harper?' he asked gently.

'Oh, yes,' he said, as blood seeped through his fingers and dripped on to the ground. 'I think this proves what Beth was saying, though, and I must ask you to stay away from us unless you have something you can prove.'

CHAPTER 30

Larry Byron couldn't sleep that night. Even a full bottle of scotch failed to bring any respite from the terrible gnawing anger that consumed him. All night he sat in the darkened lounge with the curtains tightly shut.

He could hear his wife crying upstairs, deep racking sobs that brought on fits of coughing now and then. He knew he should go to her, offer comfort, support; but the thought of what Amy might be going through at that very moment made any such move impossible. He was tied to the chair by invisible bonds of hopelessness. What comfort and support could he offer his wife when he was in need of help himself?

By the time chinks of daylight showed through the curtains his head was thumping badly from the scotch, and he looked up with shame-filled eyes when Jilly finally joined him. She seemed to be in a daze and her own eyes were red and puffy, the dark shadows beneath them angry and exaggerated. Trance-like, she pulled back the curtains and greeted the new day with a sob.

Without a word she went into the kitchen and he listened while she filled the kettle. Minutes later she reappeared clutching two mugs of steaming tea. Placing one beside his chair, she sat down to face him. Still neither spoke, simply stared straight ahead while the tea grew cold.

At 9 a.m. PC Gordon Bennett and PC Bobby Adams called at the house. Jilly became very animated, certain that they were bringing good news, but her husband remained seated, staring ahead, his eyes unseeing. Bobby's gaze took in the empty whisky bottle, the overturned glass.

He cleared his throat. 'We've nothing to report,' he said sadly. 'But we're working flat out to find Amy. We just wanted to make sure you were all right.'

Jilly sank back on the settee, her hopeful expression chased away by despair. She said nothing.

'Is there someone you could get to come and stay with you?' Bennett asked. 'A relative? Friends?'

'No,' she muttered. 'We don't need anybody.'

'I think the chief inspector is planning to call by later today,' Bobby said. 'And if any information comes in, we'll let you know straight away. We're doing all we can.'

'I know,' Jilly said. She tried to smile as she got to her feet. 'Thanks for coming. I'll show you out.'

At the garden gate, Bobby glanced back. 'They need some help, Gordon.'

'We can't force it on them,' he said, shrugging. 'I suppose we could ask for a WPC to stay at the house, but our bastard of a superintendent isn't known for an abundance of the milk of human kindness, is he?'

'He's a prick,' Bobby said with feeling. 'I think I'll have a word with Jim Ashworth. Byron looks like he could do something stupid.'

Bennett's radio bleeped. 'Control to all mobiles . . .'

'Gordon here, Sarge. We're in Ladbrook Close.'

* * *

'What are we going to do?' Jilly asked.

'I can't just sit here, love,' her husband replied, his voice firm and controlled. 'I've been thinking it through. We know

Harper took Amy, and we know the police are never going to be able to do anything. So, we've . . . I mean, I've got to do it.'

'Please don't do anything silly, Larry. Leave it to the police.'

He left his chair and crouched by her side. 'They can't do anything, love. It's our daughter we're talking about. God knows what they're doing to her.'

'Don't, Larry, I . . .' She started to cry.

'Jilly, I can't just sit here and wait for her to turn up dead.'

'I said, don't,' she wailed, her hands clamped over her ears. 'I don't want to hear.'

'But that's what's going to happen unless I do something now. All I'm asking for is your support. I want you to help me save Amy's life.'

She threw her arms around his neck. 'Oh, Larry, I'll do anything . . . anything to get her back.'

* * *

Ashworth's frustration was growing. With a scowl on his face, he systematically went through the file, examining and re-examining everything, only to find himself back where he had started.

'Nowhere,' he intoned. 'No forensic evidence. Nothing concrete against any of the main suspects. No garage has reported carrying out crash repairs on a green Mini . . .'

He had pinned a lot of faith on someone coming forward with information about the car used to frighten Jan Morrison's daughter. But no one did. He had investigated everything and everybody to the limits of his powers, and he had come up with nothing.

And to make matters worse, Beth Harper had heatedly reported that Larry Byron was following her husband. Everywhere they went nowadays, Byron would turn up. No words were exchanged; the man would simply stare from a distance. As Byron had already attacked Harper once it was quite possible that he could do so again. Therefore Ashworth had no choice but to send Holly and Josh to warn the man off.

Silently cursing all of the rules and regulations that so successfully hemmed him in, Ashworth turned his thoughts to the publicity, both local and national, attached to this emotive case. His only hope now was that someone, somewhere, would hand him the information he needed to break this awful deadlock.

* * *

Larry Byron had no stomach for work on Monday morning. All he could think about was Amy. Where was she? How could he get her back? Try as he might, he could not clear from his mind images of her predicament. Dreadful thoughts crowded into his consciousness until he was certain he would go mad. A hatred of Noel Harper was flourishing rapidly inside him like an ungodly foetus, feeding off his gruesome notions and growing fat.

Jilly was worried for both of them. She knew that his plans would bring him into conflict with the police and the courts. What if he was taken from her? What would she do then? She had already lost her daughter.

Oh, yes, even though her brain was cocooned by shock, she had accepted that Amy was gone. Grief would surely follow in the weeks and months to come, when no news was forthcoming . . . or when Amy was found dead. That thought always caused her stomach to turn and bile to rise in her throat.

She must support her husband, she *must*, in every conceivable way. The police were impotent; there was not a thing they could do. At least Larry's idea gave them a glimmer of hope to cling to.

* * *

Noel Harper called in at the church hall to check if anyone had turned up for the junior disco. Deep down he knew he was wasting his time, and one look inside confirmed that assumption. The hall was empty.

Harper dug his hands into the pockets of his jeans and reflected that soon, very soon, things would have to come to a head. If David Thorne wanted him gone, then he would have to go to the bishop and formally request that he be removed from his job. Harper smiled. He knew full well why the vicar hadn't already done so, and almost gloated over the fact that, even now, he would find that course of action so difficult. Should he talk to the police and get this whole thing sorted, once and for all?

His gaze strayed across the car park. Heavy snow was falling, and already the scene before him was picturesque. The driving storm was blowing full into his face so he turned up the collar of his coat, glad of his warm sweater, as he reached to lock the doors to the hall.

Suddenly the quiet of the night was pierced by urgent sounds from behind. Footsteps? Harper was turning to look when a hefty shove sent him crashing into the unlatched doors. They sprang open and he went sprawling across the floor, his body jarring badly as it met the hardness.

He rolled over quickly, ready to defend himself, and saw Larry Byron lurking on the threshold, his outline dark against the snowy background. In his hand was a thick iron bar, about two feet long, and on his face was the look of a madman. Echoes of his footfalls bounced off the high walls as he moved into the room and stopped just short of Harper's prone figure.

'Where's Amy?' he snarled.

'Larry, listen to me,' Harper said, inching away. 'You've got it all wrong . . .'

Byron let out a horrifying cry, then raised the iron bar and brought it down with a mighty crash on to a chair to the left of the door. Sounds of the splintering wood were exaggerated tenfold by the perfect acoustics in the hall as the chair collapsed in a heap. And then the bar was raised again.

'Tell me where she is, or I'll kill you. I mean it.'

Harper cringed.

CHAPTER 31

It was 10.30 p.m. when Beth Harper reported her husband missing. The officer on the line, although sympathetic, was forced to point out that there was little they could do. A person was not technically considered missing until after twenty-four hours had passed. Her husband was merely late coming home. He could well have been delayed, or decided to call on some friends; indeed, there could be a hundred and one reasons why he had still not returned.

It was while the constable was patiently relaying these facts — at the same time imagining the workload should they be required to pursue every wayward husband — that his fellow officers were checking all local hospitals in case there had been an accident admission bearing the name of Noel Harper. Having received negative replies from them all, the constable had no option but to advise Beth to ring back in the morning.

He was replacing the receiver when his brain promptly connected the name, Noel Harper, with the hunt for the missing child. Should he tell the chief inspector about the call? Maybe not. He'd telephoned Ashworth at home on a previous case and had got an earful of mild abuse for his trouble. No, he'd phone Holly instead.

The ringing tone sounded for many seconds, and he was about to drop the receiver when the connection was made and Holly's intimidating voice could be heard on the other end.

'Hello, Holly, it's Derek Saunderson.'

'Hi, Del, what do you want? I'm in the middle of washing my hair.'

'Oh, sorry, it's just that I've had a call from Beth Harper — she's reported her husband missing — and I thought I'd let you know before I passed it on to central control. I've already checked the hospitals—'

'How long's he been missing?'

He hesitated. 'About two hours.'

'Two hours? Del, are you pulling my plonker?'

'Look, Holly, I know he's probably with a bit of skirt, but I thought what with everything that's happened I'd better let you know, just in case Larry Byron's tied up in it somehow.'

She sighed. 'Yes, okay, Del, put it through to control and tell them I'm on it.'

He rang off and stared at the telephone. 'I didn't know she'd got a plonker.'

* * *

Josh was in the middle of dinner with his new boyfriend when her call came through, and he was still grumbling when he met Holly outside the Harpers' cottage.

'Thanks for phoning,' was his opening remark.

'Oh, stop moaning, for God's sake.' She reached for the doorbell.

Beth looked frantic with worry. She was convinced that something terrible had happened to her husband, and she told them so repeatedly as they moved towards the lounge. Holly well remembered the heated argument at their previous meeting and, distraught though she was, Beth clearly did, too.

'Right, Mrs Harper,' Holly said, ignoring the woman's sour look. 'Is there anywhere he's likely to have gone?'

'I've checked with all our friends, but no one's seen him. He went to the church hall to see if anyone had turned up for the disco, but he rang me from there over two hours ago to say he was on his way home.'

Holly cleared her throat and leant forward, her expression solemn. 'I don't know how to put this, Mrs Harper, but could there be someone you probably don't know about? A friend he might be visiting?'

Beth bristled immediately. 'Another woman, you mean? No, Sergeant, I assure you I'm quite capable of holding on to my man. Anyway, he's hardly likely to tell me he's on his way home if he's planning to meet another woman, is he?'

'Sorry, Mrs Harper,' Josh cut in, 'but we do have to ask.'

'Have you found his car yet?'

'No,' Holly said, 'but we've established it's not in the car park at the church hall.'

'He wouldn't have left it there. Since all the rumours and tittle-tattle started flying about he's been parking away from the church. He reckons there's less chance of it getting damaged if he does that.'

Annoyance welled up inside Holly. 'I see. It would have been helpful if you'd told us that before,' she said shortly. 'Anyway, never mind, we know now.' She stopped to scribble on her notepad. 'The fact is, Mrs Harper, your husband won't be listed as missing for twenty-four hours, and even then there's little we can do about it.'

She turned on them then, her face distorted by rage. 'It's all your fault,' she hissed. 'Those awful rumours flying about, and all because of your investigation. Somebody's harmed Noel because they think he's some sort of pervert, you mark my words, and I lay the blame for that firmly at your door.'

Josh stepped forward, his manner conciliatory. 'Mrs Harper, I think that in the circumstances we could look into the matter now,' he said, ignoring Holly's reproachful glance.

'Yes, you do that,' she flared back. 'And while you're at it, why don't you go and see that lunatic who attacked my husband and who's been stalking him ever since?'

'Larry Byron's daughter is missing,' Holly said. 'He's obviously in a highly emotional state.'

'Maybe, but that doesn't give him the right to attack and terrorise innocent people.'

'We'll look into it,' Holly said stiffly.

She grabbed her shoulder bag and hurried from the room, eager to be gone. Beth at least had the good manners to show them out, but the door was shut in their faces even as Josh was saying goodbye.

'That bitch is getting right up my nose,' Holly muttered.

'You can't blame her for having a go at us,' Josh said, reaching for his radio. 'She's worried about her husband.'

'What now then, Josh?'

'I'll get on to control and see if uniformed can locate Harper's car in the vicinity of the church hall.'

Holly glanced at her watch. 'Okay, and then I think we'd better find out whether Larry Byron's at home. If he's not, I'm afraid we'll have to bring the guv'nor in on this.'

'Huh, he will be pleased.'

'He can join our little club, then, can't he?' she retorted, as she stomped off to the car.

* * *

Noel Harper made no attempt to move, but he knew it was important to keep talking, to flood Byron's mind with words.

'Okay, listen, I know you're upset, I can understand that,' he said, 'but I want you to consider what you're doing here.'

'I'm getting my daughter back,' Byron said, his voice strangely calm. 'You took her, and I want you to tell me where she is. I know why I'm here — I'm here to beat it out of you.'

'But I haven't got her, Larry. You must understand, I could never harm a child, it's not in me.'

'You've got her . . . you and the rest of the church scum.'

'They're just groundless rumours,' Harper said quietly. 'And if you're honest with yourself, Larry, you'll admit that you know they are.'

The room was in darkness now, and only the white of their faces showed. With the temperature dropping and the heating turned off their breath began to fog the air. Harper could sense a wavering in Byron's rigid stance.

'You're getting yourself into a lot of trouble, Larry. Think about your wife. The police will go to her first; after all, you attacked me, you've been following me. As soon as they realise I'm missing they'll go to your wife and then they'll be looking for you. And how long do you think it'll take them to find us?'

'Shut up,' Byron spat.

'What are you going to do, Larry? Are you really going to beat me up? Could you really injure me? I don't think so. It wouldn't make any difference if you did because I don't know where Amy is. You'll be hurting your wife, Larry, not me. She's probably at the police station now, and they'll go on and on at her until she tells them where you are.'

Byron lunged forward a step, the iron bar brandished above his head. 'Shut up,' he screamed. 'I promised Jilly I'd find Amy.'

'And I'll help you.' Harper slowly climbed to his feet.

'Keep away from me, you bastard, just keep away from me.'

'Okay, okay,' Harper said, his eyes on the iron bar. 'I'm not moving. I'm not going anywhere near you.'

* * *

When Jilly Byron opened the door Holly was struck by the glassy look in her eyes, and by the fact that she made no comment as to why they were there.

'Yes?' was all she said.

'Can we come in?' Holly asked gently.

'I suppose so.' She ushered them into the hall, her movements strangely mechanical.

'Is your husband at home?' Josh asked.

'No,' she said, suddenly agitated. 'He's gone out. He says he can't just sit in the house, it's driving him mad.'

'Mrs Byron, do you know where your husband is?' Holly quizzed.

She shook her head, her expression quite adamant.

'It's really important that we find out where he is, Noel Harper's gone missing—'

'Our daughter's gone missing as well,' she countered in a toneless voice.

'I know,' Holly said with a sigh. 'Mrs Byron . . . Jilly . . . your husband hasn't done something stupid, has he?'

'Larry doesn't do stupid things,' she said, running fingers through her uncombed hair. 'Will you leave now, please?'

'Okay.' She reached for the door handle. 'If you want to tell us anything, just pick up the phone.'

Jilly made no reply and, with a distant look in her eyes, she let them out.

'I'd better have a word with the guv'nor, Josh. I'm certain they've got Harper.'

'But that's ridiculous, they're a respectable couple.'

'Yes, and under a lot of pressure. Come on, let's get back to the nick.'

* * *

Ashworth was equally sceptical.

'The Byrons wouldn't kidnap Harper,' he exclaimed. 'What would be the point?'

'Guv, if they think he's got Amy they might be trying to get her back,' Holly said. 'They've already let on they don't think we can do anything. What if they've decided to take the law into their own hands?'

He cast her a doubtful look.

'Believe me, guv, when we saw Jilly Byron this morning, she was right on the edge.'

'Of course she is, her daughter's missing.'

'Yes, and that's the point. She didn't even ask if we'd got any news about Amy. She's right on the edge, guv.'

'Josh?' Ashworth said.

He turned from the computer screen, his manner thoughtful. 'I've got to agree with Holly. The woman's really churned up—'

'And if her husband's the same . . .' Holly cut in.

'All right, all right, you've convinced me,' he said, holding up his hands. 'Go and pay her another visit.'

* * *

Holly rang the bell three times, but there was no answer. She took a step back and caught sight of the net curtains twitching at the lounge window.

'Mrs Byron? Jilly, open the door, please. Please, Jilly, I have to talk to you.'

She went back to the door and banged hard with her fist, not letting up until it was opened. Jilly stood in the hall, her eyes red from crying.

'What do you want now?'

'I want to help,' Holly said. 'Let me come in.'

'No. I don't know why you can't just leave me alone.' She moved to close the door, but Holly jammed her foot on the threshold.

'I want to help you, Jilly. Do you understand? Just let me talk to you.'

What little spirit the woman had left seemed to drain away. She turned from the open door and wandered into the lounge.

Holly was quick to follow and found her sprawled in an armchair. The room looked as if it hadn't been tidied for days. On the hearth were two teacups, their dregs turning green. The ashtray was overflowing, and two spirit glasses lay on their sides on the carpet. Holly squatted down in front of the chair.

'Jilly, I want you to listen to me. Now, I believe your husband has got Noel Harper. Am I right?'

'I'm not going to say anything,' she said, her face a blank.

'You're going to get yourselves into a lot of trouble.'

Jilly gave a hollow laugh. 'Trouble? Do you think we could be in any more trouble than we are now? There's nothing you could do to us that would make things worse.'

'But can't you see what you're doing?' Holly implored. 'By doing this, you're taking valuable police resources away from looking for Amy.'

There was a note of acceptance in Jilly's voice, when she said, 'You won't find Amy. Larry and I both know that. You haven't found any of the others.'

'I promise you we're doing everything we can.'

'But it isn't enough, is it? You haven't the powers to do what needs to be done.' She gazed into the middle distance. 'It's far worse for a man. I've been watching Larry fall apart. He feels he has to do something, and I want you to know that I'm proud of my husband, Sergeant, bloody proud.' She broke down, then, her tears coming fast.

'Jilly, I'll do everything in my power to find Amy, I promise.'

'Huh, that's just the way you people talk,' she sobbed. 'You won't do anything, because there's nothing you can do.'

'If Harper's got your daughter, then we'll find her,' Holly said. 'But you've got to help us. Let us concentrate all our efforts on that, instead of having to look for him.'

There was a knock on the front door. Alarm filled Jilly's eyes when Holly got to her feet.

'That's probably for me,' she said. 'DC Abraham's waiting outside.'

She opened the door and was confronted by Ashworth's bulk. He was bleary-eyed and irritable.

'The station phoned me,' he told her, his voice gruff. 'Harper's car's turned up two streets away from the church hall. Has Mrs Byron said anything?'

Holly shook her head. 'She's on an emotional tightrope, guv. She's pretty close to snapping altogether.'

'Right, let me have a word with her.'

When he stepped into the lounge, Jilly shot him a look of utter despair. 'I'm not going to say anything . . .' Her voice broke. 'Larry's doing what he thinks is right.'

'I'm sure he is,' Ashworth said kindly. 'And I can understand why you're one hundred per cent behind him.' He crouched in front of her chair. 'You know, Mrs Byron, all of us here understand totally what you're both going through.'

'No, you don't,' she sobbed. 'You couldn't.'

'If it's any consolation, I'd probably be doing the same if it was my child. I'd be doing exactly what your husband is doing now. But that wouldn't make it right, because we don't know if Harper had anything to do with Amy's abduction.'

She stared at him with unseeing eyes. 'It's our only chance, Chief Inspector. Larry said he couldn't spend the rest of his life knowing he hadn't tried.'

'Tell us where he is,' Ashworth coaxed. 'He's not in any real trouble yet, and I'll do everything in my power to see that he's not punished in any way.'

Jilly gave a violent shake of her head, causing tears to scatter across her cheeks. 'No, no, I won't let you take Larry's manhood away from him. You can't do anything to stop those people, but at least my husband's trying.'

'Jilly, I've told you we're doing all we can,' Holly said from the doorway.

'And I've told you it's not enough,' she fired back. 'You'll just wait for Amy's body to turn up, and then you'll pursue your investigation. That's the jargon you use, isn't it?'

Very slowly and very gently Ashworth grasped her shoulders. 'Listen to me, Jilly . . .'

She tried to pull away, but his huge hands held her firm, and Holly watched as strong emotion, brought on by his understanding of the woman's suffering, broke through that hard, outer shell that her guv'nor showed to the world.

'Listen to me,' he said firmly. 'I promise you that I will move heaven and earth to get Amy back to you. But you must help us, you must trust us. Jilly, you must stop seeing us as the enemy.'

CHAPTER 32

Harper backed away across the cold dark hall, and as he stood resting his back against the wall, he could almost feel Larry Byron's resolve weakening. The iron bar was still held at a threatening angle and every time he moved Byron jumped, but nevertheless the likelihood of an attack seemed to be quickly receding. If he could only stay calm, if he could only keep the man talking, he might just win Byron over.

'I've suffered as well,' he said lightly. 'My wife has, too. Oh, not like you and Mrs Byron, I'll grant you that.'

'How have you suffered?' Byron asked bitterly.

'We've had the police searching our cottage. I've had people staring and pointing fingers at me in the street. I could tell by their eyes what they were thinking, what they were whispering behind their hands. They've got me down as some sort of pervert who goes around murdering kids.'

Byron tensed, the words reminding him of Amy's desperate plight. Harper went on hurriedly, 'I love those kids, Larry, I love them as if they were my own. And the thought of someone harming them fills me with an anger I find hard to control.'

'You don't fool me, Harper. I still believe you know where Amy is.' Byron took tentative steps towards him, the bar raised. 'I was going to get you in here tonight, and I was going to hit you and keep on hitting you until you told me.'

'But now we're here you can't do it, can you, Larry?'

Byron's desolate groan rang out loudly in the gloom. He lowered the iron bar. 'No,' he said quietly. 'No, I can't.'

'Of course you can't, because you're a decent human being.' He ventured to the centre of the room. 'I blame myself for this, Larry . . . You've made me question my faith, my commitment as a Christian. All I've been concerned about is the effect this has had on me, when I should have been trying to help you.'

* * *

After much coaxing Ashworth finally prised the truth from Jilly Byron. Although fearful of leaving the woman alone he needed Holly and Josh with him. So, as they rushed to his car, Ashworth radioed for a WPC to be sent to the house immediately, and soon they were on their way to the church hall.

They travelled in silence, each pondering the implications of Byron's wild actions, and each ready to find Noel Harper badly injured, or worse. After a twenty-minute drive through fast deepening snow, the car skidded to a halt in the car park.

'Do we need back-up, guv?' Holly asked, her gaze fixed on the doors to the hall.

'No, not yet,' he grunted. 'We need to establish that they're actually in there before we press the panic button. Josh, I want you to cover the back, while I try the main door. Holly, you come with me.'

* * *

The car's headlights lit up the interior of the church hall as it swerved to a stop, and Larry Byron whimpered.

'That could be the police,' Harper whispered. 'I said it wouldn't be long before they found us.'

Byron looked like a soul possessed, his face a deathly white. Harper approached him, his steps cautious.

'Larry, I'm willing to say none of this ever happened. I'll say we came in here for a chat . . .'

The iron bar fell from Byron's grip and landed with a clatter on the wooden floor.

'There's some information I've got for them. It may help, it may not. And I could start an appeal. I'll put my own money into it and try to get others to do the same. In a couple of days we could build up such a huge reward for information leading to Amy's rescue that we're bound to get some response. Money jogs memories, Larry.'

Byron's hostility resurfaced, the change in him so sudden that Harper recoiled. 'You're trying to trick me, you bastard.' He was watching the door, expecting sounds of heavy knocking at any moment.

'But, I'm not,' was Harper's fervent reply. 'Larry, let me open the window and see if it's the police. I'll tell them everything's okay . . . yes?'

Byron nodded dully. Straight away Harper rushed to the window and threw the catch. The snowy blanket illuminated the exterior perfectly and, gazing across the car park, Harper could see the formidable shape of Ashworth standing by the vehicle with Holly at his side.

'Chief Inspector,' he called. 'It's Noel Harper. I'm in here with Larry Byron. There's no problem, we've just been talking. We're coming out, now.'

Ashworth waved a relieved acknowledgement and Harper exhaled sharply as he turned back to Byron.

There,' he said. 'Are you convinced, now?'

'I suppose so.' He hesitated. 'I've made a first-class idiot of myself, haven't I?'

Glistening beads of sweat stood out on Harper's forehead, despite the bitter temperature, and with a hand that trembled slightly he took a handkerchief from his pocket to mop his brow. But, along with it, Harper pulled out a small object that hit the floor with a slight metallic ping.

The silence was ear-splitting as both men stared down at the small silver cross.

* * *

'Come on, come on,' Ashworth muttered, as he waited for the doors to open.

'There's something up, guv,' Holly said. 'They should be out by now. Let's—'

She was interrupted by a howl of pain from within the hall, followed by sounds of crashing furniture.

And then Harper was screaming, 'No, please don't hit me again, please . . .'

'Jesus Christ.' She quickly activated her radio. 'All mobiles, we're at St Giles's Church Hall. Back-up needed urgently.'

'Help Josh cover the rear,' Ashworth ordered. 'There're two fire exits, plus a back door. As soon as uniformed get here, we're going in.'

Back-up arrived in the form of four patrol cars within three minutes. Ashworth had eight uniformed officers at his disposal and promptly sent four around the back and stationed the remaining four a few yards from the main doors. Crisp snow crunched beneath his size twelve shoes as he made his way to Holly and Josh waiting at the rear.

'Right, I'm going in.'

'I'm coming with you,' Holly said.

'No, you're not, I want you and Josh to cover this door.'

But she was determined. 'Guv, Byron's in there with an iron bar, and it sounds as if he's gone berserk. You're going to need help.'

'All right, then, but I don't want any heroics. We'll try and talk him out.'

He turned his back on the door and smashed an elbow through the glass panel at the side of the lock.

'Lousy security,' he muttered.

Very carefully he wormed a hand through the gap and found the mortice lock with the key still in it. He turned it swiftly and the door swung open. They crossed the threshold, broken glass grinding beneath their feet, stale kitchen smells assaulting their nostrils. A narrow corridor was before them and they hastened along it squinting into the gloom. A set of double doors loomed ahead.

'That's the hall,' Ashworth whispered. 'Now, remember, no heroics.'

Holly nodded. 'Let's do it, guv.'

Relying heavily on the element of surprise, Ashworth threw open the doors and motioned for Holly to stay close. The sight that met them resembled a strange tableau; its lighting supplied courtesy of the flashing blue beacons on the patrol cars. Noel Harper was lying at the centre of a tangle of overturned chairs, and even in the dimly lit room the blood on his face was all too evident.

Ashworth followed the man's eye-line which told that Byron was behind him. Slowly, his manner utterly controlled, he turned around, his features impassive. Larry Byron was resting his back against the wall, the iron bar poised to strike.

'Drop the bar,' he said softly. 'Drop it, Larry, and step away.'

'He's got Amy,' he said, gesticulating wildly in Harper's direction.

'You don't know that. Listen, you're already in trouble — why get yourself deeper in?'

Byron unclasped his hand and revealed the tiny silver cross. 'This is Amy's. Harper had it in his pocket.'

'But there must be thousands of crosses like that,' Ashworth reasoned. 'How can you tell that one belongs to Amy?'

'I just know,' he screamed.

'All right, son, stay calm.' He was thinking fast. 'Larry, if that cross does belong to Amy, it's the first definite piece of evidence we've got to tie Harper in with her disappearance. Now, think about it — we could be questioning him, uncovering how he came to have the cross—'

'No,' he yelled, wielding the bar, 'I won't be tricked into giving up.'

'You're being stupid, Larry. We're your only chance — you know we are.' Ashworth stepped forward, his hand outstretched. 'Give me the bar.'

But Byron raised it higher and fixed the chief inspector with a demented stare. Ashworth, silently cursing his trembling legs, tried to maintain a calm attitude.

'Give me the bar, Larry.'

'No . . . no, I won't.'

Ashworth reached forward, the movement deliberately casual, until his fingers clasped the cold metal. Byron tightened his grip, his eyes wild, his breathing shallow and laboured. But then, as if realising his impotence, he released the bar and slumped back against the wall, huge sobs racking his body.

Holly darted over to Harper, throwing chairs out of her way to reach him. He was still breathing, but there were several deep cuts on his face. Snatching the radio from her pocket, she pressed the button.

'Control, we're at St Giles's Church Hall. Noel Harper's down — we need an ambulance. Larry Byron's in custody, and we're clear.'

Ashworth motioned to the man. 'Come on, we'd better go outside.'

Byron's nod was almost imperceptible, but was enough to send tears tumbling from his brimming eyes.

'I'm in all sorts of trouble, now, aren't I?'

Ashworth took his arm. 'I'll do all I can to help you, son . . . all I can.'

CHAPTER 33

Back in the CID office Ashworth sat in deep contemplation, all the while holding the small silver cross.

Finally, he said, 'I believe that this once again puts Noel Harper firmly in the frame. Both Larry and Jilly Byron identified it as Amy's.' He turned it over on his huge palm. 'There's a small mark on the back where she tried to scratch her initial.'

'Where are the Byrons?' Holly asked, as she sipped her coffee.

'Mrs Byron's staying with relatives, and her husband's in hospital for observation. I just hope they keep him in there for a few days.'

Josh hurried into the office, a broad beam on his face. 'You've got your wish, guv,' he said. 'Noel Harper's asked to see you. His doctors aren't keen on it, but he's insisting.'

'Well, that's good,' Ashworth said. 'Thank God Byron only used his fists, otherwise we'd be visiting the morgue. We'll go now, shall we, Holly?'

* * *

'You're not to tire Mr Harper unduly,' the doctor lectured. 'And you must leave when instructed by the duty nurse.'

'Of course, doctor,' Ashworth said. 'Now, if you'll kindly tell us where we can find him . . .'

'He's in a private ward on the first floor, go left when you get out of the lift.'

'Thank you, doctor.' He turned to leave. 'Oh, how long will you be keeping Mr Harper in, do you think?'

'He'll be with us for some time yet, Chief Inspector.'

'But his injuries are only slight?'

'Oh yes, cuts and bruises, no broken bones but shock is a strange symptom, Chief Inspector, it could easily take a few days to come out.'

'I see. Thank you, doctor. Come on, Holly.'

The hospital's antiseptic smell was strong in his nostrils as Ashworth guided her along the endless corridors. This was not his favourite place, and he was heartily relieved to find that Harper had been given a private room. The man was sitting up in bed. He looked pale and very tired but managed a smile when the detectives pushed open the door.

'I never thought I'd be glad to see you two,' he said. 'But I definitely was in that hall.'

'You might not be so overjoyed to see us this time,' Ashworth huffed. He sat down and produced the silver cross, now safely packaged in a transparent plastic envelope. 'Mr Byron claims he found this in your possession.'

'That's true, he did.'

'He claims it belongs to his daughter, Amy.'

Harper sank back into the pillows and let out a sigh. 'I found it in the church.'

'In the church?' Ashworth echoed.

'Look, in some ways I feel so responsible for what happened to me, and even for the children that were abducted . . .'

'Do you want to tell us about it?' Holly asked, from her position at the foot of the bed.

'You're expecting a confession, aren't you? Oh, dear . . .' He looked from one to the other. 'I did find the cross in the church. I didn't think anything about it at the time, but now it's all beginning to fit into place.' He hesitated. 'Chief

Inspector, this is something I should have told you a long time ago, but if I had—'

'Just tell us now,' Ashworth urged.

'My vicar, David Thorne, well . . . he had to leave his last parish because of rumours that he was molesting children. Nothing was ever proven, of course, but nevertheless he was moved very quickly and very quietly.'

Holly's jaw dropped. 'Are you saying the vicar's behind the disappearances?'

'No, I'm not saying that . . .' He exhaled loudly. 'Oh dear, this is why I've kept my mouth shut for so long. But now I'm just telling you what I know — okay? I found that cross in the church the day after Amy vanished.' He closed his eyes. 'So many things have been going through my head. You see, it was Thorne who called me out of the car the night that Amy was threatened. He called me out on some lame excuse about having to pay the DJ. I really do want to be wrong, but I don't know.'

'Thank you, Mr Harper,' Ashworth said, standing up. 'You've just given us some vital information.'

'Chief Inspector,' Harper called as they reached the door. 'I won't be making any charges against Larry Byron. I really do feel sorry for the man.'

'Very well, sir,' Ashworth said. 'Take care of yourself.'

'It all fits, guv,' Holly said, hurrying to keep up with his urgent stride. 'Do you remember when Jan Morrison reported those two men in the field? She said one was wearing a dark sweater over a white shirt. Guv, perhaps she was wrong, perhaps—'

'Perhaps he was wearing a dog collar?' Ashworth concluded, as he called for the lift. 'I remember it well, Holly. Interesting, isn't it?'

* * *

'Terrible business . . . terrible,' Reverend Thorne said, hurriedly inviting them into the vicarage. 'Tell me, how is Noel . . . and the Byrons, of course?'

'They're recovering,' Ashworth said.

'That's good. I shall pray for all of them. And for young Amy, too.' He opened the door to the drawing room and gestured for them to sit. 'Can I offer you tea?'

Ashworth declined the offer, and when they were all settled he produced the silver cross.

'Noel Harper claims to have found this in your church.'

The vicar studied it carefully, a frown deepening on his face.

'I can't say I recognise it, Chief Inspector. Is this cross important?'

'It belongs to Amy Byron. Harper says he found it the day after she vanished.'

Thorne shrugged. 'I can't see that it's significant. I mean, what do you expect me to say?'

'This is rather delicate, vicar,' Holly said, 'but we've received reports that you had to leave your former parish very quickly.'

'Oh, my goodness,' he said. 'Noel told you that, no doubt. It's true that rumours had been circulating about me, but they were merely the results of children making mischief. It happens all the time to clergymen, teachers . . . The rumours were completely groundless, but the bishop thought it best to move me and to have someone in my new parish who could deal with all of the youth activities.'

'Would you mind if we take a look around the house?' Ashworth asked.

A look of astonishment fluttered across the vicar's face. 'What?' he blustered. 'You mean you want to search the vicarage? But, Chief Inspector, I'm a man of the cloth, I resent your suspicions, you can't for a minute think that I . . .' He shook his head rapidly. 'No, I'm sorry, but you have no grounds to request such a thing, and I shall strongly resist any moves for you to do so.'

'A little girl is missing,' Holly said. 'Doesn't that concern you, vicar?'

'What a question — of course it does. But you people, you don't care about personal rights at all, do you? Look what you did to Noel. There wasn't one shred of evidence against him, but you kept hounding him until everyone in Bridgetown assumed he was guilty. I refuse to let the same thing happen to me.'

Ashworth rose from the chair and looked down at what he regarded as a pompous little man.

'That's not quite the way I see things, Reverend, but I think it's better if we leave it there.'

At the car he stood looking back at the house. 'Well, what did you make of that?'

'Righteous indignation, guv? Or do you think he's got something to hide? It's difficult to tell, really.'

Ashworth drummed his fingers on the roof of the car. 'I favour the latter, Holly. But he's right, we haven't got enough to ask for a search warrant — not through normal channels, at least.'

Holly shot him a puzzled look. 'What do you mean?'

Ashworth gave a chuckle. 'Vicars are like cats, Holly. There's more than one way to skin them.'

CHAPTER 34

At 6.15 p.m. Ashworth's Scorpio was once again cruising along the drive to the vicarage. Holly wrestled out of her seat belt while she watched the vicar scurrying down the front steps, his hair dishevelled, his stoop more pronounced.

'I resent this,' he fumed, as they got out of the car. 'Going to the bishop was unforgivable.'

Ashworth shrugged. 'I did request your permission, but you refused. So I was left with no alternative but to go to the owner of the property . . . the church. The bishop had a word with you, did he? He promised me he would.'

'Bishops don't have words with vicars, Chief Inspector, they issue orders.' He started back towards the house. 'You'd better come in, I suppose.'

'I don't like that man,' Ashworth said to Holly, as they watched the accompanying panda cars pull into the drive.

* * *

A glass of orange juice was hovering at Noel Harper's lips when Josh came into the room.

'Oh no, officer, not more questions?' he said mildly.

'No, we'd like your assistance, actually, sir.' Josh pointed to the chair by the bed. 'Mind if I sit down?'

'Go ahead,' he said with a sigh. 'I really thought you'd leave me alone after what happened.'

'Like I said, sir, we need your assistance, that's all.'

Harper replaced the orange juice on his locker and picked up a Get Well card.

'This is from my wife,' he said. 'She's the only person who's bothered to send one. It's Beth I feel sorry for, officer, because it's still happening to her, the pointing fingers, people hurrying away when they see her coming. But I promise you one thing — we're determined to stay in Bridgetown. Both of us want to make a difference, and that's what we're going to do.'

'We really regret what happened,' Josh said, with obvious sincerity. 'I can see that we made life difficult for you, and for your wife. But if we can clear this up — and we might with your help — then there'll be no reason for people to point fingers at you.' He paused. 'Actually, sir, we're searching the vicarage.'

'You really suspect David?' he asked, his eyes widening.

'There are a number of things pointing in that direction,' Josh confided. 'But perhaps I should ask if you suspect him.'

'I don't want to, I really don't, but if I'm honest I'd have to say yes.' He closed his eyes, as if drained by the dreadful admission. 'So,' he said presently, 'what do you want to ask me, officer?'

* * *

Ashworth made straight for the cellar, and on the way he recalled what the vicar had said to him during his first visit to the vicarage. Harper's house is exactly like this one but smaller, he'd said, and there's supposed to be a priest hole, but no one can find it. He could still hear the words as he made his way down the stone steps.

At the bottom, however, disappointment flooded over him when he considered the supports for the chimney breast overhead. Here, the gap had not been boarded up, and tapping with a small hammer confirmed that the brickwork was solid.

He worked his way along the wall almost in desperation, all the while tapping and hoping to hear a hollow sound that would betray the presence of a hidden space. But there was none and as he climbed the stairs, brushing cobwebs from his suit, Ashworth had to admit that on this occasion he was wrong.

He found Reverend Thorne in the hall with Holly, her eyebrows raised expectantly. Ashworth shook his head in response and listened to sounds coming from above. He had ordered that every piece of furniture be pulled away from the walls in search of hidden rooms or compartments.

'You haven't found anything, then?' Thorne bristled.

'We haven't finished, yet,' Ashworth replied shortly.

* * *

'It's concerning the location of the priest hole in the vicarage,' Josh said. 'Reverend Thorne told my guv'nor that no one knows where it is.'

'He did? Oh, no, this makes it even more difficult,' Harper responded dully. 'The fact is, I've seen it, officer. David showed it to me himself. He was going on about how for centuries priests had taken refuge in it.'

Josh leant forward. 'Where is it, sir?'

* * *

Back at the vicarage a small crowd had gathered opposite, the watchers curious as to the reason for such industrious police activity. Inside, most of the rooms had been searched and nothing had yet come to light.

'It looks like he's clear, guv,' Holly whispered as they waited in the hall.

'Have you heard from Josh?' he growled in response.

She was shaking her head when her radio bleeped.

'DS Bedford,' she snapped.

'Hi, Bedford, it's Josh.'

'I'll take it outside, guv.' She hurried through the front door and on to the steps. 'Okay, Josh.'

'What have you got?' he asked.

'Absolutely sod all, so far. What have you come up with?'

'A cellar behind a cellar,' was his cryptic reply.

* * *

The uniformed officers were about to file out of the vicarage when an exultant Holly bounded back in.

'Don't leave, boys,' she said. 'I think we've got a result.'

She pulled Ashworth into a corner and his face lit up as she whispered rapidly.

'Reverend Thorne,' he said. 'If we could just trouble you by looking in the kitchen again . . .'

'You've already looked in there.' He huffed. 'I promise you, Chief Inspector, I shall be making a complaint to your superintendent.'

Ashworth regarded the man with scorn. 'Your privilege, sir. I can only assure you that everything will be left just as we found it.'

* * *

The chief inspector paced the kitchen with intense concentration, a perplexed expression on his face. He studied the walls closely, feeling the paper until he detected uneven plaster above the sink.

'Is this where the old kitchen flue used to be?' he asked no one in particular.

'I've no idea,' Thorne said from the doorway. 'Would you please tell me what you're doing?'

Disregarding the question, Ashworth opened the cupboard beneath the sink and felt inside.

'I'll tell you what I'm doing, Reverend,' he said with an elated grin. 'I'm looking for the priest hole . . . and I think I've just found it.'

He fingered the floorboards at the base of the cupboard. They were all loose, and he was able to remove them one after the other, placing them in a neat pile on the floor behind him. The vicar became clearly agitated as more boards were taken up to reveal worn stone steps.

'Your torch, Gordon,' Ashworth ordered, as he wormed his shoulders into the cupboard space.

PC Bennett rushed forward with the torch and Ashworth manoeuvred it around until the beam was shining into the hole. Mere seconds later he pulled himself back and stood up, his face ashen.

'Holly, radio for Forensic, and then seal off the house.'

He turned his stern gaze on the vicar. 'Reverend Thorne, it is my duty to tell you that we've found certain items of children's clothing. I must ask you to accompany us to the station and assist with our inquiries.'

CHAPTER 35

It was 9.30 p.m. and the atmosphere in the interview room was tense. The uniformed officer at the door fidgeted constantly and Holly, in dire need of a cigarette, was smoking in full view of the accused. Ashworth, considering the circumstances, let her carry on. He was pacing the room with slow measured steps, his whole demeanour reflecting the abhorrence he felt for the clergyman who sat stiffly at the table, his hands folded neatly in his lap.

'Reverend Thorne,' he began, his voice filled with contempt, 'the pathologist's report states that Nicky Waldon had suffered repeated sexual abuse, she'd been beaten up and her front teeth were missing, and finally, after all of that, she was strangled.' He hesitated, his anger smouldering. 'And as we all know, her clothes were found at the vicarage.'

'But I've already told you, I know nothing about it,' Thorne whined. 'I didn't even know the priest hole was there.'

'Our information tells us otherwise.'

'Oh, dear God,' the vicar whimpered.

'Yes, you'll need His help,' Ashworth said, banging the table with his fist. 'If you don't start giving me some answers, you certainly will need His help.'

Thorne cowered from the attack, and his voice was hardly audible when he said, 'I know nothing about this.'

'Anyway, Reverend, I'm not here to talk about Nicky Waldon, God rest her soul, I've got more than enough to charge you with her murder. But Amy Byron's still out there, possibly alive, so where is she? I want the names of all those in your ring, and I want them now.' Once again his fist came down on the tabletop. 'What about the Perrys? The Scotts? Tell me about them.'

The vicar started to snivel, and with a handkerchief to his face, he said, 'They're all good people, Chief Inspector, they wouldn't be involved in anything like this.'

'Good people?' Ashworth barked. 'Like you, no doubt? Do they like playing with little girls? Do they like hurting them, watching them die? Is that what good people like?'

'I don't know anything about this,' Thorne sobbed into his hands. 'I want you to leave me alone.'

'But I'm not going to leave you alone. You're going to answer my questions, Thorne, or so help me God, I'll—'

'Guv . . .' Holly said, pointing to the tape recorder.

Ashworth pinched the bridge of his nose between thumb and forefinger and tried to slow his breathing. Pulling himself to his full height, he said quietly, 'Charge him with the murder of Nicky Waldon and get him out of my sight.'

* * *

Holly's high heels beat an urgent tattoo along the deserted corridor towards CID. Although the office was in darkness she entered to the sounds of Ashworth's rhythmic breathing. Without switching on the light, she closed the door.

'He's been charged,' she said.

A grunt came from the direction of his desk as she perched on her own and lit a cigarette, her attractive face momentarily illuminated in the glow from her lighter.

'Can I have a word, guv?'

'You're going to give me a telling off, aren't you?'

'That's not quite the phrase I would've used but, yes, I am.'

'I know I lost my temper.'

She chuckled. 'You're always doing that guv, I'm used to it.'

'But I lost my control, as well,' he said heavily. 'I hate those people, Holly. They work their way under my skin.'

The tip of her cigarette glowed in the darkness. 'Me too, guv. I'd like to kick them all the way to next Wednesday and back again. But all I want to say is, if we get other members of the ring and the evidence against them isn't as overwhelming as it is against Thorne, then the interview tapes could go against us in court. Police intimidation . . . that sort of thing.'

'I hear what you're saying, Holly.' He fell silent for a while, and then said, 'Why do they do this? Why harm a child?'

'Who can work out why these bastards do anything, guv?'

'And have they done the same with Amy?' he mused. 'Sorry, Holly, I'm just doing what I would've done if you hadn't come in asking myself questions. I'll still be doing it in bed, tonight.'

'Well, guv,' she said, crushing out her cigarette, 'I won't tell anybody we've been to bed together, if you don't.'

He gave a half-hearted chuckle.

'I'm off home, guv, and it might be a good idea for you to do the same.' She opened the door and let in a swathe of light that cut across the room.

'Holly,' he said softly.

'Yes?'

'Thank you. I do appreciate your concern.'

She grinned. 'All in a day's work for a lowly detective sergeant.'

CHAPTER 36

'I assume you're both aware that Thorne's arrest for the abduction and murder of Nicky Waldon has been picked up by the early morning television news,' Ashworth said to Holly and Josh at the start of their case meeting the next morning.

'Yes, guv,' Josh said.

'My greatest fear now,' he went on, 'is that the whole case will just dry up. As far as the public are concerned we've made an arrest, and it'll be assumed that Thorne committed both murders — end of story. And we all know that isn't so.'

'We know there's a ring out there,' Holly said. 'But we don't have too many leads, do we, guv?'

'Then we'd better get some,' was his brisk reply. 'Don't forget, Amy Byron's still out there.'

'You keep reminding us about that,' Holly flared. 'Do you think we're likely to forget? And what can we do, anyway? We've no grounds to investigate any of the people we suspect.'

Ashworth sat on the edge of his desk and cast her a threatening look. Fearing a confrontation might be developing between the two, Josh jumped in quickly.

'We could make a start with the green Mini that was used to frighten Jan Morrison's daughter,' he said. 'Somebody must have been driving it, and it wasn't Thorne.'

Ashworth glanced at him. 'How do you know that?'

'I've checked it out guv. He hasn't got a driving licence.'

'That doesn't mean he can't drive,' Holly countered.

'Maybe not,' Josh agreed. 'But whoever drove that car needed some degree of skill, at least the amount of someone who drives regularly.'

'Yes . . . good man,' Ashworth said. 'That car, if we can find it, is about the only lead we've got.'

'What did Forensic say?' Holly asked.

'About the Vicarage? Not much.' He reached behind and retrieved a bundle of papers from the desk. 'The only place that had any traces of Nicky was the priest hole. There was no evidence of her having been anywhere else in the house, and no fingerprints of any description in the hole.'

'Which could mean she was never in the hole. Perhaps it was just a convenient place to hide the clothes,' Holly ventured.

'Not necessarily,' Ashworth said. 'There were no prints at the garage where Randall was seen with the car. Remember, Holly, these people are being very careful.' He returned the papers to the desk. 'Anyway, Thorne wants to see me in the cells before he's taken to court, so I'd better get down there.'

* * *

'I'll be waiting at the end of the corridor Jim,' Sergeant Dutton said, as he opened up the cell door.

'All right, Martin.'

Ashworth stepped inside to find the vicar slouched on the edge of the bunk, his cooked breakfast untouched on the table.

'You wanted to see me?' he said with little courtesy, leaving the door slightly ajar.

'Yes, I do.' He considered the chief inspector with puffy eyes. 'You don't like me very much, do you?'

Ashworth let out a scornful laugh. 'What am I supposed to say to that? Of course I do, vicar, you're a man of the cloth, a beacon of good in our crime-ridden society. Is that what you want to hear? Is it? Well, the truth is, I don't like you at all.' He exhaled slowly, his gaze fixed to the man's face. 'Is this why you brought me down here, Reverend, so you could ask stupid self-pitying questions like that?'

'I didn't do it.'

'All the evidence says you did. Now, if you were to give me the names of the others involved, that might well go in your favour.'

'You want me to do a deal?' Thorne gave a wan smile. 'I bet it hurt you to offer me that.'

'The words stuck in my throat,' Ashworth spat. 'But if you were to supply us with information that could save Amy Byron's life . . .'

'I don't have any such information. I really didn't know the priest hole was there. For obvious reasons, it's not on any plans of the house.'

'So, how would you set about finding out?' Ashworth asked.

'I don't know,' he said, shrugging. 'I'd ask someone with a knowledge of history, I suppose. An archaeologist, perhaps.'

Ashworth laughed bitterly. 'I remember you telling me you couldn't find the priest hole, although you'd looked everywhere. Now I find you know exactly who to ask . . . if you'd really been keen to do so, that is.'

'You twist words.'

'I don't think so,' he said, heading for the door. 'I'll make one last plea — tell me everything you know.'

'I've already done that,' Thorne murmured, rubbing at his tired eyes. 'I don't know anything.'

There was a sneer on Ashworth's face, when he said, 'I can see the way your mind's working, Reverend. If you keep your mouth shut you might just get away with fifteen years, but if you tell us who else is involved you'd stand trial for both murders and I doubt if you'd ever set foot outside prison again.'

'I know I won't come out.'

'I hope not,' Ashworth responded hotly. 'And I know you're lying because Noel Harper told us you showed him the priest hole. So, Reverend, you're not half as clever as you think you are.'

CHAPTER 37

The nurse popped her head around the door. 'Noel, are you sure you're up to this?'

'I'm as fit as a fiddle,' Harper replied, pulling on his polo-neck sweater. 'They're not here, yet, are they?'

'No, not yet,' she said, her uniform swishing as she crossed to the bed. 'I've brought you some more Get Well cards.'

He studied the half-dozen envelopes that she placed on the locker, and said, 'Everybody's being so kind.'

'That's because they're genuinely sorry, I suppose. After all, what with the vicar being arrested . . .' She shuddered. 'Who would've thought that someone like him, a man of the church . . .'

'I'm almost a man of the church,' he said, with a trace of bitterness. 'And everybody seemed quite willing to believe I was guilty.'

'Oops, I've put my foot in it, haven't I?' she said, with a look of contrition. 'But you don't wear a dog collar — that's the difference.' She watched him pull on his black leather waistcoat. 'You do dress funny, though — sort of 1970s.'

'This is my uniform,' he said, grinning. 'Young people always go for uniforms. They all like to dress the same; it gives them a sense of belonging, being part of something. So,

I adopt this uniform because it helps them to identify with me, to see me as their leader.'

'You are clever, you know.'

'I do know,' he said with a wink.

Beth came hurrying in then, her arms filled with a huge bunch of flowers.

'Noel,' she said, shocked. 'Should you be out of bed?'

'Don't fuss, Beth.' He planted a kiss on her cheek. 'Nice flowers. Who are they from?'

She grinned widely. 'The Sunday school children.'

'What? Oh, that's great,' he said, punching the air.

'I'll get a vase,' the nurse said.

She paused at the door and glanced back at them. They were sitting on the bed, opening the cards and chatting happily.

'Isn't it nice,' she said to a passing colleague. 'I'm really glad it's worked out for them. He's such a lovely man. And a celebrity, now that the press want him.'

* * *

Most of the morning was spent at the magistrates court, where Reverend Thorne was remanded in custody for seven days. However, as Ashworth and his team left the building they each shared a deep sense of impotency, knowing as they did how rare it was for more than one member of a paedophile ring to stand trial.

'Interview neighbours and fellow church-goers about the Perrys and the Scotts,' he instructed, on the way back to their cars. 'Somebody must know something. Be discreet, but find out as much as you can.'

Holly watched him strut towards his Scorpio, and said, 'We're not going to find out anything though, are we, Josh?'

'Not that way,' he answered, digging his hands into the warm pockets of his overcoat. 'What we could do is keep a watch on the Perrys and the Scotts — tonight, maybe.'

'You could be on to something there.' She stopped to light a cigarette. 'We could even take it further. Think about it — we suspect that those four are involved, and our only other suspect is Gilbert Randall, so if we watch him as well, they might just lead us to Amy.'

'I'll ask Bobby if he's willing to help.'

'Good idea, Josh, we could all do with some unpaid overtime.'

* * *

'Hi, guys,' was Noel Harper's greeting to the reporters now crowding into his room.

'Don't you know the difference between guys and girls?' a busty female from the *Bridgetown Herald* called out.

'I'll pray for your soul,' Harper replied, making the sign of the cross.

Loud laughter exploded in the confined space.

'Seriously, though, I've asked you here for two reasons. Firstly, I want publicity to get the church events back on the rails. But more importantly, I want to try and do something to help find Amy Byron. Somebody out there must know something. Now, I've talked this through with my wife and we're not wealthy people but we've decided to put up a thousand pounds for any information leading to Amy's recovery. I'm just hoping that local companies and businesses will do the same. If the reward is big enough, we might see results.'

'Can we quote you word for word on that, Noel?' someone asked.

'Put it any way you want. The important thing is to get that reward up to say fifteen thousand, more even, because that sort of money jogs memories.'

'How do you feel about Mr and Mrs Byron?' the female reporter asked.

'Obviously I can't say much because of what's happening . . .' He reached across the bed and took Beth's hand. 'But what I will say is that we're both praying for them.'

'How about a photograph, Noel?'

'Why not,' he said, smiling.

The photographer stepped forward and set about studying Harper from different angles.

'What I'd like,' he said, 'is to try and block out all the background, get you just as if you're in a spotlight.'

'Look out, Lichfield,' somebody shouted.

* * *

'Okay, Josh,' Holly whispered into her radio. 'I've got lift-off here. Robin and Marcia Scott are just about to leave home.'

'I hear you, Hol,' he whispered back. 'The Perrys have just come out of the front door, and they're getting into their car.'

'Anything from Bobby?' she inquired.

Josh chortled. 'Randall hasn't left the house, and Bobby keeps moaning about brass monkeys and something that's ready to fall off.'

'Tut, tut, I really must have a serious word with that boy. Anyway, stay in touch, Josh. I'm in pursuit, as they say.'

Keeping the rear lights of the Scotts' Daimler in view she lit a cigarette with the lighter from the dashboard and exhaled gratefully. Then, in the distance, she saw them indicating a left turn. Loath to lose them, she pressed down hard on the accelerator and the Micra leapt forward. At the crossroads she slowed to second gear and took the turn at thirty miles an hour. The Daimler was nowhere in sight.

Cursing loudly, Holly stubbed out the cigarette as her car hurtled along the narrow lane. Suddenly, dipped headlights came around the bend towards her, forcing her to slow down. The car went cruising past. It was the Daimler, and there was now a passenger in the back.

'Shit,' she exclaimed. 'Double bloody shit.'

She carried on, desperate for a place to turn. Fifty yards ahead, she came upon a driveway to a large country house. It was from there, Holly reasoned, that the Scotts must have picked up their passenger. She brought the car to a screeching halt, and gravel flew from beneath the wheels as she reversed into the drive.

For a few moments she stared at the house through the rear window. It was almost a mansion, impressive and foreboding. She debated for a while whether to take a look around the outside, but soon decided against it. She couldn't really afford to be caught snooping around private property, and anyway she would lose the Scotts for sure if she did. The Micra shot out into the lane, and Holly quickly went through the gears before reaching for the radio.

'Josh, I think I may have lost the Scotts. They stopped at a large country house and picked up a passenger.'

'I'm still with the Perrys,' he said. 'They're heading towards town at a steady pace. Randall's still at home, and Bobby says the other one's fallen off, now.'

Holly giggled and carried on to the end of the lane where she turned left on to a long straight stretch of road. There in the distance was the Daimler.

'Josh,' she said excitedly, 'I've found the Scotts.'

Fearful of losing the car again she got within fifteen yards of it and stayed close. Presently the lights of Bridgetown were before them and the open countryside gave way to housing estates.

The Daimler pulled into a large car park, and Holly followed as a set of church bells began to ring. To the strains of 'Onward Christian Soldiers', she brought the car to a stop and watched the Scotts and their passenger cross the road. She reached for the radio.

'Josh, I've followed them to a bloody bell-ringing practice by the looks of it. I'm in the car park opposite St Giles's.'

'What? So am I,' he said. 'I must be on the other side.'

'Oh, and by the way,' she went on, 'the Scotts' passenger turned out to be the Mayor of Bridgetown, would you believe?'

She released the button and listened with exasperation as the bells pealed out: 'O God, our help in ages past'.

'How about some now?' she muttered.

* * *

Holly always claimed that her luck was consistent; once it started to run out, it just kept on going. That observation was doubly underlined the next morning when her car failed to start. Having traced the fault to the starter motor, she telephoned Josh for a lift.

Realising that they would be late getting into work, Holly called to warn the chief inspector but could get no reply from the office. Ashworth was in fact in reception where he had paused for his morning chat with Sergeant Dutton.

'No joy then, Jim?' Dutton was asking.

He shook his head as Bobby Adams sneezed behind the desk.

'Did you catch cold last night, son?' Ashworth asked, with the trace of a smile.

Bobby looked surprised. 'Who told you about that sir?'

'Holly rang me . . .' His smile became a grin. 'It's not every night we chase bell ringers all over the county, is it?'

'She was in a foul mood when we left her,' Bobby confided.

Ashworth chuckled heartily. 'Anyway, Bobby, thanks for offering your help. It's much appreciated.'

'There's a lot of my lads that'll pitch in if you need them,' Dutton said.

'That's good to know, Martin, but what I really need now is some sort of positive lead, and they're a bit thin on the ground at the moment.'

'The vicar's not cooperating, then?'

'Martin, these people are as slippery as a basket full of eels. Thorne's claiming he didn't know where the priest hole was, but I don't believe him. I need to find out how common that knowledge was, because I don't want him to have any escape routes. But the trouble is, I can't think who to ask.'

'Search me,' Dutton shrugged.

* * *

'Drop me by the shop, Josh,' Holly said. 'I need some ciggies.'

'Okay.' He pulled up outside the mini supermarket directly opposite the police station.

'Cheers, lover, I'll catch you up.'

She sauntered into the shop and made for the counter, picking up two packets of cheese and onion crisps on the way.

'Hi, Stew,' she said, placing them on the counter. 'Give me twenty Bensons, as well.'

The man peered accusingly over the top of his glasses as he reached for the cigarettes.

'You're smoking a lot these days, Holly,' he said.

'Oh, given up the shop and gone into medicine, have you, Stewart?' she replied with a sarcastic grin.

He shot her an apologetic look as he opened up the till. 'Sorry, I should mind my own business.'

'No, I'm sorry,' she said, making a face. 'The pressure's getting to me, I suppose.'

'Ah, the missing girl, you mean?'

She nodded. 'And to top it all, my car packed up on me this morning. The starter motor's had it. I'm getting it fixed today, but do you know how much a starter motor costs nowadays — even a reconditioned one?'

'You should go and see old Tom Gardiner.'

'You must be joking.'

'Look, I know Tom doesn't instil confidence, Holly, but last week I picked up two really good tyres for my Mini, for next to nothing.'

'Thanks, Stew, but I'll give old Tom a miss,' she said, on her way to the door.

* * *

'Here you go,' the nurse said to Noel Harper, as she bounded into the room with a large brown envelope. 'Here's the proof copy from the newspaper for your approval.'

Harper was sitting fully clothed on the bed, and an ecstatic grin was on his face when he opened the envelope and withdrew a single sheet of paper.

'This is fantastic,' he enthused. 'Look at it — youth leader and his wife put up a thousand-pound reward for Amy

Byron's return, and challenge local businesses to do the same. Find this girl, is his rallying call. Fantastic.'

'That photo of you is lovely,' the nurse said. 'You look like a pop star.'

He did indeed. The photographer had wholly achieved the effect he was after — Harper was bathed in a pool of light which obscured the background completely.

'Let's hope it does some good.' He glanced at the nurse. 'When do I get out of here?'

'The consultant will come round sometime this evening, and if you're okay he'll discharge you.'

'He'd better,' Harper said ruefully. 'Right I'm going to ring the newspaper straight away and tell them I'll be at their office between ten and twelve tomorrow to take calls from local firms pledging money. That should get things moving.'

CHAPTER 38

Ashworth's highly polished shoes crushed the hard-packed snow as he strode across the field. Andrew Webb, the archaeologist, was staring down into the excavation site as he approached. Sensing another presence, he glanced up quickly.

'Ah, Chief Inspector,' he said, extending a hand. 'This is the first time I've seen a Roman villa in its original form, so I'm gloating a little bit.'

Ashworth looked down and marvelled at the traces of a large sunken bath, its small tiles still perfectly shaped and fitted.

'Two thousand years old,' he murmured. 'It's difficult to believe.'

'Are you interested in history, Chief Inspector?'

'Very, especially at the moment. I want some advice on priest holes and how to find them. If you didn't know where one could be located in a particular house, how would you go about finding it?'

'It depends. How old is the building?'

'It's the vicarage, here in Bridgetown.'

'Hmm, the vicarage,' Webb mused. 'That must date back to the late 1500s. At a guess, I'd say you'd have to look somewhere in the chimney flues.'

'I'm impressed,' Ashworth said. 'You're spot on.'

'Of course, slightly later, when that became common knowledge, they had to change the location.'

'Would it be common knowledge nowadays, Mr Webb? I need to know how accessible the information is.'

'Well . . .' Webb scratched his head, a thoughtful frown on his face. 'If someone was interested in that sort of thing, I'd imagine it would be easy to find out.'

'And how would one go about it?'

'If it was me I'd go to the reference department at the local library. They often carry a good section on local history.'

'Thank you, Mr Webb,' Ashworth said. 'That's very interesting.'

* * *

And it proved to be just that. Ashworth spent a good two hours in the reference section at Bridgetown's small but well-stocked library and soon found that quite a few volumes carried information about priest holes. It would seem that Reverend Thorne needed to journey no further than the high street in order to find the clues necessary for discovering his own particular hidden place.

History was not Ashworth's only passion; he also held a strong liking for good books. And while he pored over some quite wonderful ancient tomes, the hallowed silence was broken only occasionally by the turning of a page or the scraping of a chair on the highly polished and impressive parquet flooring.

But all too soon it was time to return the books to their shelves, and while he did so Ashworth had a thought. He approached the young girl working on an elaborate card index behind the desk.

'Tell me,' he said, his tone hushed. 'Has anyone from St Giles's Church visited here in the past few months to read up on local history?' He was confronted with a blank expression. 'Or perhaps you wouldn't know?'

'I wouldn't, really,' she whispered back. 'I'm only on reference for today because Mr Old has had to go to a conference.' Recognition suddenly showed on her face. 'Oh, you're with the police, aren't you?'

'That's right.'

'Is this information really important?'

'Yes, it might well be.'

'What I could do, then, is give you Mr Old's telephone number. He'll be back later this afternoon.' She took a card from the drawer. 'If he can't tell you, then nobody can — he doesn't miss a thing. He sits here all day looking to see what everybody's studying — there's nothing else to do, really.' She leant forward and added in a confidential whisper, 'When he retires next year the whole department's going to be streamlined.'

'Really? Oh well, thanks for this,' Ashworth said, holding up the card. 'Although I'll probably wait until tomorrow and call in. It's not really urgent.'

He left the quiet sanctuary with much reluctance, and even the swishing of the door sounded loud as it swung shut behind him.

* * *

Holly was at her desk, alone in the CID office. Indeed, that awful feeling of helplessness affecting all three detectives was causing them to avoid each other whenever possible until something concrete came in about Amy Byron. It was dark outside and she critically studied her reflection in the glass wall opposite.

Spread out on her desk was an early copy of the *Bridgetown Post* with the article about Noel Harper prominent on its front page. His offer of a thousand pounds reward was written in huge letters above his picture and that of Amy Byron.

Holly reached for her packet of Benson and Hedges; there were only five left. The cigarettes took her mind back to the corner supermarket and its owner, Stew, who drove a

Mini. A Mini for which Tom Gardiner had supplied spare tyres.

Tom Gardiner linked with a Mini. Of course — why hadn't it registered that morning? Mentally chastising herself she jumped to her feet then, grabbing her shoulder bag from the desk and coat from the rack, she fled from the office.

* * *

It was the first real row Jan and Paul Morrison had had in over twenty years. They often had tiffs, of course; all married couples did. But this was more than a tiff, it was a real screaming match and was not restricted to the matter in hand, either. During it, both poured out built-up resentments, some that had festered for years. Terrible things had been uttered, awful things that were best left unsaid.

She would never forgive him. Never. He had accused her of putting the whole family at risk, and all because of her wretched snooping, as he put it. Her daughter, her grandson — *his* grandson — could so easily have been killed. And all because she couldn't mind her own business and pass by on the other side of the road like most others did.

Now she wanted to start the whole business all over again, just because her memory had been jogged by something she had spotted in the local newspaper. But Paul Morrison was having none of it, not this time. The threats and the violence were not going to start again. This time his foot was going very firmly in one direction, and that was down.

Jan rushed up to their bedroom, all doors *en route* slammed twice. And now, positioned at the dressing table in the darkened room, she knew all too well why the renowned Miss Marple had decided to remain a spinster.

* * *

Holly collected her car, paying with very bad grace, and steered it out of the garage. It was the rush hour and she had little option but to head straight through town, therefore her mood was not helped by the long tailbacks she encountered all the way to Tom Gardiner's cottage.

The dogs were loose when she pulled up and she stayed in the car, leaning on the horn, until Tom appeared in the doorway, muttering and squinting into the dark.

'All right, all right keep your hair on,' he called, as he hobbled towards the gate. 'Oh, it's you, Miss Bedford.'

She opened the window a notch. 'Get those dogs under control, Tom, or I'll nick you.'

'But they're on my property,' he shouted back.

'Just do it.'

Still mumbling, he grabbed the dogs and pulled them two at a time into the house.

'That matter with the videos took all my capital,' he said, on the way back. 'If I was a big company boss, Miss Bedford, I could go bankrupt and live in luxury. You should treat me with more respect, you know.'

'I already give you more respect than you deserve,' she said, climbing out of the car.

'That's not fair,' he grumbled. 'All those things I did were years ago — I didn't know any better in those days. Anyway, the last time I was inside they gave me counselling, so you've got no right to treat me like muck — I am a person, you know.'

'All right, Tom, I won't come on so heavy-handed in future,' she said, softening a little.

'That's good.' He took to flattening his hair. 'Now, what can I do for you?'

'I'm after some information.'

'Is that a fact?' he said, rubbing his hands together. 'Grasses get paid, don't they?'

She gave him a sideways glance. 'You broke a Mini up recently . . .'

'A Mini?' He frowned. 'I'd better consult my records.'

Holly tapped her foot impatiently while he dug a hand into his overcoat pocket and pulled out several crumpled bits of paper.

'You have to keep accurate records now, Miss Bedford, to self-assess your income tax.'

'Hurry up, Tom.'

'Wait a minute,' he said, unfolding the papers. 'Here, can you see the drawing of a Mini on any of these?'

'Oh, come on, Tom,' she said warningly. 'You're not as stupid as you make out.'

Gardiner grinned. 'Nice of you to say so.' He stabbed a grubby fingernail at one of the bits of paper. 'Now, I reckon that's a Mini.'

Holly peered at the drawing. 'I'll have to take your word for it. Okay, for a start what colour was it?'

'Unlucky green, Miss Bedford.'

'And how did you come by it?'

'That uppity schoolmistress sold it to me.'

'Which schoolmistress?'

'Miss Rolands, is it?'

'Tom, are you saying that Miss Rolands sold you a green Mini?'

He nodded, and Holly's thoughts raced. There was no doubt that Amy would have gone to the games mistress if she'd been waiting at the Byrons' garden gate.

'One thing about folk thinking you're stupid,' Gardiner went on, 'they get careless, think you don't notice things.'

'Really? Now, Tom, for the last time — are you sure Miss Rolands sold you that car?'

'On my mother's grave, she did, Miss Bedford.'

'That's convinced me,' she muttered drily.

He stood rubbing together his thumb and forefinger, a sly smile on his face.

'Are you asking me to pay you?' Holly scoffed.

'Just the price of a couple of pints. Eh, Miss Bedford?'

'Jesus Christ.'

She reached into her shoulder bag and put two one pound coins on his outstretched palm.

'How much is beer where you drink?' he asked, eyeing the money.

She took back the coins and replaced them with a crisp five pound note.

'That's all you're getting, Tom. Now, I want to know if the car was damaged when you got it — and you'd better give because I'm running out of patience.'

CHAPTER 39

Noel Harper was pronounced fit and well by the consultant and promptly discharged. Half a dozen nurses walked with him to the main entrance where a taxi was waiting to take him home. The local press were there too, and many flash-bulbs exploded into light as the nurses gathered around and planted kisses on his cheeks.

'Mr Harper,' a reporter shouted, 'the reward money already stands at six thousand.'

'It'll go even higher,' he promised. 'When I'm manning the phone at the *Post* tomorrow, I'll be looking for twenty thousand.'

'Just one last shot, Noel.'

Harper obligingly posed on the steps while they took more photographs.

'I just hope he'll be all right,' a nurse confided to her companion.

'How do you mean?'

'Well, those paedophiles are dangerous, aren't they? Look what they did to that woman's daughter and grand-child. Say they try the same thing with Noel to stop him raising the reward money?'

* * *

The landing light came on and Jan watched as it flooded through the gap below the door, then her whole body tensed when she heard the handle turn.

'Jan?' Paul said, throwing open the door and flooding the bedroom with light. 'I'm sorry, love, I shouldn't have said some of those things.'

She burst into tears. 'No, I'm sorry, Paul. It was my fault.'

'But it wasn't.' He crossed to her quickly and placed a comforting hand on her shoulder. 'I've been sitting downstairs, thinking. You should report it to the police, it's your duty, and if it does help them to find the missing little girl, well . . .'

'Oh, Paul, thank you,' she said, taking the tissue he offered. 'I'll just tell them, though. I won't get involved.'

* * *

Holly swore passionately at the telephone receiver while the engaged signal sounded in her ear. She was at a call box and had been trying to contact Ashworth for the past fifteen minutes, but his line was continually engaged. She slammed down the receiver yet again.

'Are you nearly done, love?' a man asked from behind.

'Yes.'

She scooped up her money and returned to the car, where she waited for him to finish.

'Shit,' she muttered, 'what's the guv'nor doing? I've got something that turns this whole case on its head, and I can't get hold of the man.'

* * *

Harper got out of the taxi.

'Thanks a lot,' he said. 'How much is it?'

'Have it on the house,' the driver said. 'And God bless you.'

'Thanks, that's good of you.'

He waved and watched the cab pull away. There were two cars coming along the usually deserted lane, and he shuffled his feet impatiently while he waited to cross over to the cottage.

* * *

'Cheers,' Holly said, when the man finally left the telephone booth.

She quickly snatched up the receiver and punched out Ashworth's number, half expecting the engaged tone again. But this time she got through. It rang four times and then the connection was made.

'Hello?' Sarah said, the dog barking in the background.

'Mrs Ashworth, it's Holly. Is the guv'nor there?'

'No, I'm sorry, dear, he's not. Actually, he was trying to ring you at home for ages but couldn't get a reply, so he thought you must have gone out.'

Holly let out a mouthed curse. 'Have you any idea where he's gone, Mrs Ashworth? It really is urgent.'

'Yes, he's gone to Jan Morrison's house. She rang and said she'd remembered something else. That's when he tried to get you, and then he went dashing off.'

'Thanks, Mrs Ashworth. When you speak to him, could you say I'll be at the station?' Without waiting for a reply, she dropped the receiver and ran to her car.

* * *

Holly drove straight round to Josh's house and after an urgent discussion he went with her to the police station.

'The guv'nor's going to turn up sooner rather than later,' she assured him, as they hurried along the corridor.

'I still can't see why we couldn't have gone to Jan Morrison's,' Josh said, opening the door to CID.

'Because we could have missed him.' She flicked on the light to find Ashworth sitting behind his desk. 'Hello, guv, I didn't expect you back so soon.'

'We've made a terrible mistake,' he said quietly. 'I just hope it's not too late to rectify it.'

'You've reached the same conclusion as I have,' Holly said, hitching herself up on to his desk. 'Miss Rolands, the games teacher, sold her green Mini to Tom Cardiner. It was a runner but the bodywork was bad, and then somebody borrowed it from Tom—'

'And I bet it was Noel Harper,' Ashworth intoned.

She shot him an amazed look. 'How did you know that?'

'Never mind . . . carry on.'

'Well, as Tom said, everybody thinks he's stupid so they don't feel they have to be careful around him. Harper asked if he could test drive the Mini with a view to buying. Tom jumped at the chance, but Harper brought it back a couple of hours later and said he didn't want it. So the next day Tom went to break it up, and he noticed the bumper was marked and dented, just as if it had been involved in an accident.'

'Presumably the car's been broken down by now,' Ashworth said. 'The chassis and bodywork crushed down for scrap.'

She nodded.

'Very clever — no evidence,' he said. 'But what I've unearthed is even more worrying. Over the last few weeks Harper has been taking a great interest in the history of the vicarage. He's spent hours in the reference library researching it. I believe that's how he found out where the priest hole was. And it was Harper who placed Nicky Waldon's clothes there — he had such easy access to it.'

'Hardly conclusive evidence,' Josh ventured.

'No,' Ashworth said. 'Any more than this is, but it points very much in Harper's direction.'

He took the local paper and spread it on his desk. The large photograph of Harper stared back at them.

'As soon as Jan Morrison saw that picture, she knew it was the man she'd seen about to climb over the gate at Anderson's Farm. For just a few seconds he was illuminated in her headlights. Now, look at his cream polo-neck sweater under that high-buttoned black leather waistcoat. It looks rather like he's wearing a dog collar, doesn't it? Only, not quite. In those few fleeting moments something registered with Jan, but she couldn't place what it was. Whoever took that photograph recreated the exact effect of being caught in car headlights and helped to jog her memory.'

'Is it enough, guv?' an anxious Holly asked.

'In itself, no.' He stood up and headed for the door. 'I'm just hoping that if I can put it well enough to Newton, he'll let us take another look at Harper and his wife.'

'Do you think the vicar was framed?' Josh asked.

'I'm sure he was.' Ashworth opened the door and turned back. 'He was exactly what they needed, you see, Josh. There were even the rumours from his last parish about his behaviour towards children.' He let out a desolate breath. 'These people are very clever. Harper put himself in the frame by making it look so obvious that he was involved in Amy's disappearance. But he took himself out of the frame when we failed to find anything at his house. My guess is, he was going to come back in a couple of days and tell us what he knew about Thorne. But in the meantime, he was held by Larry Byron and was given the perfect opportunity to implicate the vicar and gain public sympathy.'

'What do we do, then, guv?' Holly asked. 'Do you think Amy's still alive?'

'I'm sure she is, but we need to move fast. As for what we do now, I've asked Newton to come into the station. He wasn't too pleased about it but he grudgingly agreed. I'm going to put it to him that we've got enough to warrant another look at Harper.' He glanced at his wristwatch. 'I'd better wait for him in reception.' He left the office.

CHAPTER 40

Holly glanced at the wall clock. Half an hour had passed since Ashworth went down to reception. She lit another cigarette and used it to push around the stubs she had already put out.

Josh was watching her from behind his desk, occasionally coughing when the smoke worked its way around the room, and was about to make a biting remark when Ashworth opened the door. They had no need to ask for the outcome, his expression betrayed all. From the doorway he threw the newspaper on to his desk.

'Turned it down flat,' he growled.

Josh leapt from the chair, his stance indignant. 'But surely he could see some reason for doubt, guv?'

'What he saw, Josh, was evidence collected from a neurotic woman and a scrap metal dealer who wouldn't know the truth if it hit him between the eyes. As far as he can see, there's no need to look into a watertight case against Reverend Thorne. Furthermore, he requested that I produce the relevant legislation that states it's an offence for someone to visit the reference library.'

He came fully into the room and leant heavily on his desk. 'So, unless we get something more concrete, that's it.'

'We just let Amy die,' Holly said quietly.

Ashworth's features were grim. 'That's how it looks, Holly, yes. I partly blame myself — if I was on better terms with Newton things might be different. As it is, if a case hangs in the balance, he comes down against me just for the sake of it.'

Holly stubbed out her cigarette and immediately lit another. 'I'm going to Harper's house, tomorrow,' she stated boldly. 'While he's with his wife at the newspaper office.'

Ashworth gave her a harsh look. 'What are you talking about, Holly?'

'I'm going there to look for Amy, guv. I can't just sit back and wait for her to turn up dead.'

'I don't believe I'm hearing this.'

'Well, you are, guv. Say she is there — if I manage to pull her out it would be very difficult for Newton to take any action against me.'

'Holly, you're a police officer, not some sort of one-woman army.'

'Guv, I'm going in.'

'No, I can't allow it.'

'You can't bloody stop me,' she yelled, getting to her feet. They locked eyes, and then Ashworth took in a deep breath.

'Think about your career,' he said. 'A move like that could ruin it.'

'We're talking about a kid's life here, guv, not a bloody career structure.'

'What about your pension?'

'They can stuff my fucking pension. Can't you understand, I'm talking about me . . . what I am. I couldn't live with myself if I let that kid die without trying to do something to stop it.'

Ashworth stared at her for a long time, his own conscience vying to be heard. Finally, he shook his head.

'Holly, I'm ordering you to stay away from Harper's house.'

She snatched up her bag and rummaged around for her warrant card. Then the plastic holder was thrown onto her desk.

'You've got no right to order me about,' she said. 'I've resigned.'

'Holly . . .'

'No, that's it guv,' she said, on her way to the door. 'End of discussion.'

'It's my duty to report this,' Ashworth told her. 'Do I have to go that far to make you see sense?'

She turned then, and Ashworth fleetingly wondered whether he would ever be able to forget her look of disgust.

'I always thought you had bottle, guv, but you're all talk. Do you remember telling Jilly Byron that you'd move heaven and earth to get Amy back? Well, heaven and earth are out there, between here and Harper's cottage, along with Newton's bullshit. You're just going to stand by while a little kid dies a lingering death — and why? Just because some pompous prick of a superintendent tells you that's how it's going to be. Well, I'm not willing to do that.'

Her words stung him. 'Holly—' he blustered.

'You do anything to stop me,' she said quietly, 'and I'll never forgive you.'

He watched the open door for a long time after she had left.

'She'll do it,' Josh said.

'I know she will. Just as I know she's right.' He turned to Josh, his eyes pleading for understanding. 'But we have to stay within regulations. We can't simply break into someone's house . . . Can't you talk to her? Can't you make her see sense?'

He shrugged. 'If it's any help, guv, I didn't witness what took place just now. That way you're not involved, you didn't know what was happening.'

'Josh, I can't just sit back and let her break into Harper's house.'

But Josh wasn't listening. He strode from the office and quietly closed the door behind him.

* * *

As soon as he walked in, Sarah could see he was troubled. Throughout dinner he was silent, and afterwards he sat in his armchair and stared at the flickering images on the television screen with unseeing eyes. And he had hardly sampled the malt whisky he had been nursing for the past half-hour.

'What's wrong, Jim?' she finally asked.

'Nothing,' he grunted. 'Just the case.'

'I suppose you'll tell me when you're ready, dear,' she said, her tone matter of fact.

'What is this?' he snapped, getting to his feet. 'Why is it that nobody seems to take any notice of me anymore?'

He strode from the room with the little dog barking and growling at his heels.

'Shut up, Peanuts,' Sarah heard him shout.

'Oh dear,' she muttered, sipping her sherry. 'This must be really serious.'

She allowed him ten minutes to calm down and then followed him into the kitchen. He was sitting at the table, his empty whisky tumbler in front of him, the dog asleep across his feet.

'Another scotch, Jim?'

'Yes, please, Sarah.' He pushed the glass towards her.

When she returned with the drink, she sat with him. 'Now, would you like to tell me what this is all about?'

He gave her a feeble smile, took a sip of scotch, and explained what had happened.

'So you're saying David Thorne wasn't involved in this, after all — it was Noel Harper?'

'Yes, that's about it. And now Holly's planning to break into the Harpers' house tomorrow while they're busy at the newspaper office. She's hoping she'll find Amy there. That girl's going to get herself into a lot of trouble.'

'You think she's right, though, don't you, Jim? About Amy being at Harper's house?'

'I'm certain of it and I can understand how she feels. She's such a headstrong girl . . . Believe me, Sarah, I'm almost tempted to let her go.'

'Why don't you, then?'

'Because I'm a police officer. I can't let her go out there and break the law.'

'But you admire what she's about to do,' she said softly.

'That's neither here nor there,' he muttered. 'I'm her superior officer, and it's my duty to stop her.'

'It seems to me,' Sarah began, broaching the subject carefully, 'that you have a difficult dilemma here. On the one hand, you believe the course of action Holly is about to take is the only chance there is of saving Amy's life—'

'But we can't start behaving like vigilantes,' he said, banging his glass on the table. 'If Holly was found out and it came to light that I knew what she was doing but took no measures to stop her, then I'd be in serious trouble.'

Sarah frowned. 'Jim, what is it? I've never seen you like this before.'

He looked at her with hostile eyes. 'You think you know what my dilemma is, do you? Well, you've got no idea, Sarah. Here I have Holly whose action, if it comes off, could save a young child's life. Should I let her go, take the chance, feel at the end of it that I'd done my best?' He gave a derisory snort. 'And then I've got you — I must do what's right for us.'

Sarah jumped to her feet. 'Now, hold on a minute, Jim, that's not fair—'

'But I have to think of our security.'

'Oh, no, Jim. This problem has been forced on you by Superintendent Newton, and you are not going to blame me for it.'

'I'm not doing that. I'm only saying I have to consider you.'

'But I don't want to influence your judgement.'

'Well, you do, we're married.'

'Yes, we are,' she said, leaning heavily on the back of the chair. 'I've never seen you so troubled before, and it worries me. Jim, what's between us has always manifested itself in the way we treat each other, the things we do, rather than, oh, I don't know . . . sloppy talk. But there's something I now feel has to be said.' She sat down again and forced him to meet her gaze. 'I love you, Jim — I always have, I always will, and one of the reasons I do is . . .' Sarah shook her head, her feelings so strong that she had to search for the words. 'Jim, you're the most decent man I've ever met. Whatever you decide to do will be right. It may infringe some rule or regulation, but it will be right. Now, if that means there'll be consequences to be faced, then we'll face them together . . . as man and wife.'

Ashworth was embarrassed to find a lump in his throat. He swallowed loudly and stared into his glass, avoiding her eyes. 'Right then,' he said. 'I . . . I think I'd better take the dog into the garden before I have another drink.'

CHAPTER 41

'Time for another look at the holy man,' the prison warder said to his colleague, on their way up the metal staircase.

'Let's hope he's topped himself,' came the disgruntled reply.

'Huh, we'll be in trouble if he has.' They reached the top landing of the remand wing, their footsteps echoing in the silence. 'I just hope for his sake it's not long before he's sentenced. It's bad enough in here for your ordinary pervert, but a vicar . . .'

They stopped outside a cell door, and the warder pushed back the grille and peered inside. Thorne was kneeling by the side of the bunk, his lips moving in silent prayer.

'God might forgive you, Reverend,' he called out, 'but there's some in here that won't and they'll be kicking your balls every chance they get.' The grille was slammed shut. 'You know, I reckon he's in for a very painful few months.'

His colleague let out a rueful laugh. 'Fine by me. I'll make a point of turning the other cheek . . . so I'm looking in the opposite direction.'

'You, and all the lads.'

* * *

Ashworth was still in a preoccupied mood the next morning, and Sarah was at a loss to know how to help. His *Daily Telegraph* was propped up against the marmalade jar as usual while he ate his cornflakes, but he made no comment about the latest batch of difficulties facing the government, or the forthcoming budget. Normally he would loudly air his views, which were many and varied.

While she was washing up the breakfast things, Ashworth planted a light kiss on Sarah's cheek and told her he would see her that evening. She waited until the front door had closed and then hurried to the lounge window to watch him. He backed the car out of the garage and returned to close the doors, every few seconds staring down at his wedding ring, his face devoid of expression.

Sarah felt something close to despair, and for the first time realised that there were occasions and events in life, during which serious decisions had to be taken, when a marriage partner could be seen as nothing more than an encumbrance.

* * *

He had only been there for a few days, but already Thorne had come to hate the mornings most of all. When his cell door was opened he had to walk out and stand on the balcony, the hostility of the other prisoners, as well as the warders, all around him.

As a remand prisoner he could have worn his own clothes but thought it best not to, for he always wore his dog collar. When he was given the prison garments, however, it was obvious that they were chosen to make him look foolish. The grey trousers were ill-fitting, the sweatshirt too large and a quite unsuitable brilliant red.

Their farcical effect was further compounded by trainers that were two sizes too big. And as a precaution against the vicar hanging himself the laces had been removed which meant that he had great difficulty in keeping them on and had to shuffle along, a practice that did little to help his stoop.

Thorne was aware that all eyes were on him as he stood in line for breakfast, and he silently communicated with God, asked him to forgive his fellow inmates. Close by, a prison officer patrolled the line, making sure that all was orderly, but when Thorne came up to the serving pans, the officer turned his back.

'I heard you didn't do too well at supper, last night,' whispered the prisoner serving the food. 'I heard they didn't give you a full helping.'

Thorne remembered the empty plate and the way in which he was pushed along the line by the other prisoners and then forced to sit at a full table while they ate greedily.

'Well, don't you worry, I'm here to make sure you get plenty today.' He grinned and piled a plate with fried eggs and a mountain of bacon.

'Thank you,' Thorne stammered, his stomach growling as he eyed the breakfast.

'My pleasure.' The man held the plate a little outside the vicar's grasp and spat on the food, then cleared his throat and spat again. Thick phlegm clung to the bacon as it was passed across. 'Enjoy it,' he sneered.

Thorne picked up the plate and flinched when prisoners on either side of him repeatedly added their saliva to his meal. But he said nothing and hobbled to a table where he sat staring down at it.

'Eat it, man.'

The voice made him look up. A giant black prisoner was standing beside the table, with others crowded around him.

'Eat it,' he repeated.

'No, I . . .'

Thorne felt the colour drain from his cheeks as chairs scraped the floor behind him. Then, his arms were held in a vice-like grip and his mouth forced open.

'For what you are about to receive,' said the black prisoner, while he cut up the food, 'may the Lord make you truly thankful.'

* * *

Ashworth set off in the direction of the police station, but changed his mind at the first roundabout and headed instead for the youth leader's cottage. On the way he saw a number of patrol cars and came to the conclusion that his progress was being monitored. This irritated him greatly but, nevertheless, he took a left turn that led to the vicarage, crashing the gears in his haste, and pulled up in the lane where he could observe Harper's cottage without being seen.

After about ten minutes the youth leader appeared with his wife, and the sight of them laughing together caused an intense loathing to well up in Ashworth's chest. Presently they got into their car and sped off in the opposite direction. Ashworth waited, glancing at his watch from time to time.

Josh was the first to arrive. He parked on the grass verge directly outside the cottage and immediately began talking into his radio, while flicking furtive glances in the chief inspector's direction. Ashworth smiled to himself.

A few more minutes elapsed and then Holly pulled up behind his Scorpio. He heard her car door slam and then she appeared at his side window. He wound the window down.

'Well, I suppose I have to thank you for coming yourself, rather than sending Newton,' she said. 'But it's not going to make any difference.'

He pointed to Josh's car. 'You've involved a lot of other officers.'

'He's here because he wants to be.'

'Oh? And what about uniformed? I saw at least six cars on the way here, about ten officers.'

'They're patrolling the area between here and the newspaper office. They'll alert me when Harper and his wife are on the way back.'

'I'm impressed,' he said. 'You've planned it well.'

'Thank you.' She inclined her head. 'But I'm not really involving anybody else in this, guv. Josh's just there as lookout and the lads on patrol are just on patrol. So if it all cocks up, it's just me who gets caught.'

'Beautiful turn of phrase,' he remarked.

'Look, guv, you're not going to talk me out of it,' she said, her eyes on the cottage. 'And your presence here is just going to inhibit everybody — so will you leave me alone?'

'I can't do that.' He opened the car door and climbed out.

'Jesus Christ, guv, why are you doing this? You're not involved, nobody else is involved . . . I'm going in by myself, so—'

'No, you're not.'

Holly pointed a warning finger. 'Just back off, guv.'

'You're not going in by yourself, Holly, because I'm going in with you.'

Her mouth gaped open. 'What?'

He strode off, and then turned back. 'Shall we get on with it, then, or are you just going to stand about?'

* * *

Although he was surrounded by hundreds of prisoners, Reverend Thorne's feelings of isolation finally became so acute that he was forced to put in a request to be locked in his cell, and the warders grudgingly agreed. As soon as the door was clanged shut his heartbeat slowed and a calmness swept over him. He stood looking around, his mind made up.

The window was too high, he reasoned; he couldn't reach it even if he stood on a chair. In desperation he looked towards the bars of the grille fixed in the door. They might just do it.

Feeling in need of contemplation, he lay back on the bunk, took off his wristwatch and placed it on his lap. Just then the cover of the grille was pulled back and a warder's cruel face appeared.

'Enjoy your breakfast?' he mocked.

CHAPTER 42

'Josh, keep in radio contact,' Ashworth barked. 'And if things go wrong, just vanish.'

'Yes, guv,' he replied, surprise widening his eyes.

'How are we going in?' Holly asked, as they headed along the garden path.

He tried the front door. It was locked. 'Let's take a look around,' he said. 'It would be very much to our advantage if we didn't have to break in.'

They checked the back door and every ground-floor window, but all were firmly secured.

'There's only one thing for it, guv. It's either the kitchen door or one of the back windows.'

'The door, I think. It's half-glazed.'

They resembled a pair of fugitives as they wormed their way back to the door. Once inside the porch, Ashworth pressed his considerable bulk against it in an attempt to force the lock, but the door refused to budge.

'It's bolted at the top,' he grunted. 'Give me your shoe.'

Holly stood precariously on one foot and passed it to him. Shielding his eyes, Ashworth hit out at the top of the glass panel with the steel-tipped high heel, but the glass remained intact. He hit it again, harder, and fissures snaked in all directions. Finally, a third tap caused the glass to shatter inwards, breaking into a thousand pieces when it hit the quarry-tiled floor. He reached through the gap and slid back the bolt.

* * *

Although their prisoner was safely installed in his cell, the warders were duty bound to check on him at intervals. Thorne, with his wristwatch at hand, made a mental note of the times between what he saw as intrusions into his privacy, and soon found that their visits were far from regular. Sometimes five minutes would go past at other times, ten. But on each and every occasion, the warder doing the checking would taunt him mercilessly. He began to whisper the Lord's Prayer.

* * *

'I reckon we should have plenty of time,' Ashworth said, as they passed through the kitchen. 'So let's search the house from top to bottom.'

'Okay, where do we start, guv?'

'The cellar. Harper's got a knack of putting himself into the frame and then taking himself out again. He knows we've looked at the cellar, so they may well have put Amy down there, thinking that no one will bother to check it again. I'll go in first.'

He pulled open the door and they crept down the rough stone steps.

'Empty,' he hissed. 'Damn.'

'Hold on, guv.' Holly fell to her knees and examined the floor. 'These are dried bloodstains, and they weren't here before.'

Ashworth studied the tiny dark circles. 'You're right, Holly, it is blood.' He glanced around. 'They could well confirm that Amy's been here. Now, let's take a look at the priest hole.' He hurried across and pulled back the piece of plasterboard.

'Well?' Holly asked.

'Empty.' He turned to her, his face desolate.

'Let's start on the first floor, guv, and work our way down. She's got to be here somewhere.'

'Right,' he said, running up the steps. 'Look in the bedrooms first, especially around the fireplaces for any concealed compartments.'

Holly took the master bedroom. The fireplace was open, the plasterwork around it smooth and undisturbed. She looked under the bed, even riffled through the dressing table drawers, loath to leave an inch of the place untouched. The wardrobe was large and, without thinking twice, she opened the door. Something came hurtling out towards her, and she had to stifle a cry of alarm as a shoe bounced on to the carpet. She stood for a moment her eyes closed, her breath coming in quick gasps.

'Clear in here, guv,' she finally called.

'Likewise with the second bedroom and the bathroom,' he shouted back. 'Let's take a look downstairs.'

* * *

The telephone rang, and Harper reached for the receiver.

'Noel Harper, here,' he announced cheerily, 'at the offices of the *Bridgetown Post*.' He scribbled on a pad, a huge grin on his face. 'Well, that's most generous of you. Thank you very much. And, don't worry, the paper will make sure you get as much publicity as possible.'

He replaced the receiver, beaming at Beth and all of the excited staff crowded into the room. 'That was Arnolds' factory with a pledge of . . . wait for it . . . two thousand pounds.'

A gasp went up and then a cheer while Harper ran his pen down the line of figures on the paper.

'And that's fifteen thousand pounds in total already.' Another cheer exploded as he whispered to Beth, 'At this rate we'll hit twenty thousand within the next half-hour and be on our way home.'

* * *

Their search of the downstairs rooms was taking longer for the lounge was filled with old heavy furniture, and each piece had to be moved so they could be sure nothing was concealed behind it.

While he felt around the fireplace Ashworth realised how ill thought out this whole operation had been. Amy was somewhere in the house, of that he was certain — to his mind, the bloodstains in the cellar confirmed it. But where was she?

'Look in the kitchen,' he ordered, 'while I check the loft.'

There was an urgency in their movements now, an urgency that bordered on panic as recognition of all that they risked careered towards them.

* * *

Noel Harper ushered his wife out on to the front steps of the newspaper office.

'That's the twenty thousand pledged and wasn't it easy?' he remarked to the editor. 'It'll make a good headline for you, tonight.'

'Don't knock it,' he replied. 'It'll make you a local hero. Now, before you go, let's just get one shot of you and Beth.'

They paused on the steps while the camera clicked, and then headed towards the car park.

'Shit,' PC Dickens muttered.

He was parked opposite the newspaper's offices. Hurriedly, he snatched up his radio and pressed the button.

'Bobby, it's John, outside the *Post*. We've got grief, mate.'

* * *

Ashworth had to get a chair from the bedroom in order to reach the hatch of the loft. Pushing it to one side, he eased himself through the gap and glanced around the roof space. It was totally empty, devoid even of those pieces of broken rubbish that usually find their way into a loft.

'Damn,' he spat.

'Guv, the Harpers are on their way back,' Holly called up the stairs. 'Bobby says he'll try to hold them up, but we've got ten minutes at the most.'

Making every effort to remain calm, Ashworth pulled the hatch back into place and jumped down from the chair. Holly was standing on the stairs, watching him.

'What are we going to do?'

'A cellar behind a cellar, Holly. Let's see if this house is the same as the vicarage. It's our last chance.'

* * *

Bobby's panda car fell in behind the Harpers' and followed them across the bridge spanning the river. And all the time he kept an eye on the needle of the speedometer which hovered at a steady thirty. He stayed in close along the high street, and as soon as the traffic began to thin he flashed his headlights to attract their attention.

Beth turned around in her seat and a frown appeared on her face at the sight of the policeman signalling for them to pull over. As they stopped by the kerb the young constable offered up a silent prayer and climbed out of the car. Harper wound down the window as he approached.

'Good morning, sir . . . madam,' he said stiffly.

'What do you want, officer?' Harper demanded to know.

'I've been following you for some time, sir,' Bobby said, his fingers crossed behind his back. 'Are you aware that you were doing thirty-five miles an hour in a thirty zone?'

Harper tut-tutted. 'Have you any idea who we are?'

'None, sir.'

'I'm Noel Harper, and this is my wife, Beth. We're—'

'The names do ring a bell, sir, but I hope you're not suggesting that gives you a right to exceed the speed limit.'

'No, of course I'm not,' he snapped irritably. 'But we had other things on our minds. We've just been raising money at the *Post*'s offices . . .'

Bobby crouched down and adjusted his cap. 'I'm only asking you to keep a check on your speed, sir, that's all.'

'Okay, thank you, officer, of course I will, and I'm sorry. Can we go, now?'

'In a moment, sir,' Bobby said, glancing at his watch. 'If I could just see your documents, driving licence, insurance . . .'

'I don't believe this,' Harper said, reaching into the glove compartment.

* * *

Reverend Thorne heaved his weight off the bunk and stood up, his features set in a determined line. Standing stock still, he waited for the hatch to open and tried to close his mind to the jeering comments tripping scornfully off the warder's tongue.

When the grille clanked shut, he pulled the red sweatshirt up and over his head. His body was thin, his chest flat and scrawny, but his stoop was no longer in evidence as he picked up the solitary chair and positioned it before the door. Climbing on to it, Thorne carefully threaded the sweatshirt through the bars of the grille, then shuffled around on the chair and tied the two sleeves about his neck in the shape of a noose.

'God forgive me,' he murmured.

CHAPTER 43

The shattered pane of glass in the door seemed to stare at him accusingly as they hastened into the kitchen. Hardly able to believe that he was capable of such an offence, Ashworth made straight for the units under the sink.

'Let's hope you're right about this, guv. We're running out of time.'

'We'll soon know, Holly.'

He opened up the doors and found the cupboard jammed full of cleaning equipment and kitchen utensils. With Holly's help everything was removed: bowls, buckets; a whole range of items had been wedged into the space. It looked almost as if they had been put there to hide something — at least, that was what Ashworth hoped.

When the floorboards at the base of the unit finally came into view, they shared a mounting sense of excitement, and Holly took to throwing the last remaining things on to the kitchen floor with a careless abandon.

'At least one of the boards is loose,' Ashworth declared, pulling it free. 'Wait a minute, three or four of them are.'

Holly's radio buzzed. 'Yes?'

'Hol, we're in trouble. They're only minutes away, now. Have you found anything, yet?'

'We might have, Josh. Give us a bit longer.'

'Where's the flashlight?' Ashworth asked, holding out his hand.

She produced a small pencil-thin torch from her pocket and quickly passed it across. 'Hold on, Josh, any minute now.'

Ashworth removed the last of the floorboards and, with shaking hands, switched on the light. With an effort, he managed to wedge his head and broad shoulders into the cupboard and was then able to shine the beam below the floor. But all that showed up were the joists and dusty cobwebs. No hidden cellar. No Amy Byron.

Behind him, Josh's voice sprang from the radio. 'They're here, Hol. They've just turned into the lane. Two minutes and they'll be at the cottage. I've pulled up further along the lane, but I think they've already spotted me, and your cars as well.'

When Ashworth withdrew from the cupboard and shook his head, Holly said hurriedly, 'You'd better get going, Josh, we've drawn a blank.' She gave a nervous laugh. 'If you go straight back to the nick, you'll just be in time to get sent out again to arrest us for burglary.'

* * *

With a racing pulse, Josh stared into the rear-view mirror. The Harpers' car was slowing, and he could see clearly their puzzled expressions as they glanced at all three cars parked along the lane. He reached for the ignition key, but decided not to turn it.

'Oh, what the hell,' he muttered. 'I'm fed up with being a copper, in any case.'

* * *

They sat resignedly on the kitchen floor, the disarray caused by their efforts all around them. Very slowly, Holly got to her feet.

'I'm sorry, guv. I got you into this,' she said, her voice full of remorse. 'I suppose we'd better get ready to face the music.'

From the front of the house came sounds of the Harpers' car pulling up, and as he listened Ashworth's eyes grew steely with determination.

'Hold on, Holly,' he said, standing up, 'don't lose your so-called bottle just yet. Why are we here?'

She shrugged. 'Because we thought Amy Byron was being held here.'

'Not quite. We came because we're sure she's here . . . we're *sure*.'

'Listen, guv, I know you hate to quit,' she said, looking frantically towards the hall, 'but it's over. We've looked everywhere.'

'No, we haven't. Think about it. Harper puts himself in the frame and then takes himself out. He shows us the obvious, so that we miss the obvious.'

The quiet outside was suddenly broken by the slamming of car doors. Holly bit on her lower lip, frowning anxiously.

'Come on,' he said. 'We might still have time.'

Ashworth raced across the kitchen, colliding heavily with a metal bucket that clattered noisily as it was hurtled to the other side of the room.

'Guv . . . ?' she called, chasing after him.

He was already hurrying down the cellar steps, and when Holly got down there she found him at the priest hole, literally tearing the plasterboard away from the opening. He turned to her with a triumphant grin.

'It's here, Holly. Look . . . the bricks are loose. Harper put the plasterboard there to conceal the real entrance.'

Holly cast her doubtful gaze at the brickwork. A good deal of the mortar was missing from the first half a dozen rows up from the floor.

'It's only the mortar that's gone, guv. You're clutching at straws.'

But Ashworth refused to be discouraged. With his breath held fast he drew out the first brick.

* * *

Harper and his wife were standing beside their car, looking to where Josh was parked. His discomfort grew rapidly under their curious eyes, and a guilty flush was burning his cheeks when his radio buzzed on the passenger seat. Soon, Holly's urgent voice was vying with the static.

'Josh, get an ambulance, and call for back-up. We're in the cellar. Follow the Harpers in and get as many bodies in here as you can. Quick, Josh.'

He was already out of the car and running along the lane. 'All units,' he said into the radio. 'We need an ambulance at Harper's cottage. And all officers in the vicinity, get here now. Come on, shift your arses.'

When Noel and Beth Harper saw him speeding towards them, they exchanged a desperate look and hurried into the cottage.

* * *

Holly could feel her heart pounding against her ribcage as Ashworth gently pulled Amy free from the hole. The child's eyes were wild, and her frightened glances darted around the cellar.

'Don't touch me,' she whimpered. 'Please don't touch me anymore.'

Ashworth had to fight to keep his voice steady.

'Everything's all right, now, Amy,' he said softly. 'I'm Jim Ashworth . . . remember me?'

'I . . . I don't know.' Recognition showed for a mere second on the girl's features, and then confusion took its place. 'But you're a grown-up. You're here to hurt me.' She scrambled to the far corner of the cellar and crouched there like a terrified animal.

Ashworth approached the child with care. 'I wouldn't hurt you,' he said, his voice soft and easy. 'We've come to take you home to your mum and dad. Everything's all right, now, Amy. You know I wouldn't hurt you.'

Her brimming eyes searched his kindly face, and she viewed his outstretched hand with suspicion. Nevertheless she reached for it, and Ashworth almost had her within his grasp when the Harpers appeared at the top of the steps.

'What the hell's going on?' Harper yelled.

At the sound of that voice Amy shrank back and clawed at the wall, her slight body cringing with terror. Ashworth was moving to comfort her when Josh could be heard above them in the hall. Soon he was hurrying down the steps, a crowd of uniformed officers close behind, forcing the horrified couple into the cellar. Straight away Harper made for the girl but was forcibly stopped by Holly.

'Don't cry, Amy,' he soothed. 'It's me, Noel, let me make you feel better.'

The child was a pitiful sight as she curled herself up into the foetal position, her feverish cries touching even the most seasoned of the officers present. Ashworth hurried forward and carefully took her into his arms.

'You needn't be frightened anymore,' he whispered tenderly. 'This is Jim Ashworth, and I won't let anybody hurt you.'

She clung to him, wrapped her trembling fingers around his large thumb.

'I . . . I trust you,' she said. 'I trust you.'

'Let me through to her,' Harper shouted. Again he tried to advance, but again Holly pushed him back.

'You filthy bastard,' she snarled.

'Holly,' Ashworth said quickly, 'get Amy upstairs.'

She took the terrified child from his arms and made comforting sounds in her ear as she hurried up the steps.

Ashworth stood for a moment with his back turned against the others, Amy's pathetic cries assaulting his ears. And when the sounds from above began to fade a terrible rage overwhelmed him; he could feel it burning in his chest, restricting his breath. Slowly, he turned towards Harper and his wife.

'Noel and Elizabeth Harper, it is my duty to inform you that you are under arrest—'

'But she loved it,' Harper cried.

Ashworth paused briefly, his fists clenched. 'You are under arrest for the abduction of Amy Byron.'

'She loved it,' he repeated, his crazed eyes skimming across the other officers. 'They all did.'

The chief inspector felt the searing rage tug painfully at his insides, but he clung to his tenuous control.

'I am also arresting you on suspicion that you were involved in the abduction—'

'Oh, Christ, Ashworth, she *loved* it,' he screamed. 'That's what you can't stand.'

An animal roar erupted from Ashworth's mouth and in the space of a second he lunged forward and grabbed Harper by the throat, lifting him from the floor as if he were weightless and smashing him against the wall.

'For God's sake, guv,' Josh shouted.

He grasped Ashworth's hands and tried desperately to free his grip, but he was too strong. Then, three of the uniformed officers seized the chief inspector and between them managed to force his hands open. Harper stood clutching his neck and gagging while Ashworth was wrestled away. Suddenly, he stopped struggling and they let him go. His entire body shook and his face was the colour of chalk.

'Get him out of my sight,' he rasped, 'or so help me God, I'll kill him.'

CHAPTER 44

Superintendent Newton strode into CID and closed the door. He leant back against it, his normally severe expression softened by a troubled frown.

'I've just had word from the governor of the remand prison,' he said heavily, his gaze taking in all three detectives. 'Reverend Thorne tried to hang himself in his cell today.'

'Oh, God,' Ashworth murmured, his head in his hands. 'Is he all right?'

'Apparently, yes. Luckily they found him in time. His throat's badly bruised, but they reckon that a couple of days in hospital should see him fit again.'

His harsh gaze travelled around the room for a second time and Holly and Josh turned away, only Ashworth refused to avert his eyes.

'Officers from Bridgenorton are interviewing Noel Harper and his wife,' he went on, 'and they've already admitted that Reverend Thorne had nothing to do with any of this.' He exhaled sharply. 'I must say, it's highly embarrassing having to call in officers from another division because I can't trust my own.' His eyes settled on Ashworth. 'You seem to inspire such loyalty, Chief Inspector. Ten uniformed officers were present when you attacked Harper, and yet not one of them saw anything. They must all have been looking the other way, perhaps.' He waved his hand dismissively. 'No doubt when I interview your detectives, they will have similar memory lapses. But you can't duck this one. Oh, no—'

'Why don't you ask me straight out?' Ashworth said, getting to his feet. 'I can speak for myself . . . sir.'

'Very well,' Newton said, coming to a halt in front of his desk. 'Now, it seems that half of the officers under my command have deliberately disobeyed my orders. A man brought in for questioning has finger-marks all around his throat and claims that you attempted to kill him . . .' He raised an inquiring eyebrow. 'I shall be very interested to hear your explanation.'

Ashworth cleared his throat. 'I accept full and total responsibility for everything that happened,' he said, staring straight at the superintendent. 'DS Bedford and DC Abraham were merely acting on my orders—'

'No, guv,' Holly said, rushing to her feet.

'Be quiet,' Newton yelled.

'They were unaware that I had been refused permission to go into Harper's house.'

'Bollocks, guv, that's not true.'

'DS Bedford, please refrain from using that sort of language,' Newton said, 'and kindly allow the chief inspector to continue. Apportioning blame can come later.'

'I wanted to save Amy Byron's life, that's all . . .' For the first time Ashworth looked away. He stared down at his desktop.

Newton's features softened a little. 'Let's all be thankful you achieved that. The little girl's all right, I hear.'

'Is she, sir? How do we know? It could take years for the psychological damage to be assessed.'

'Ashworth . . .' Newton paused. 'I've no doubt it must have been hard to check your emotions. I should imagine that something just snapped inside your head. I'm looking for what you'll be telling an inquiry.'

Ashworth glanced up quickly. 'If you want the truth, sir, I attacked Harper because I couldn't see why a bastard like that should be drawing breath. And if he was here now, I'd do it again.'

For a few moments the office was filled with a stunned silence, and then Ashworth exhaled heavily.

'Anyway, there it is, sir, you've got what you came for. But just you remember, Jim Ashworth doesn't duck anything.'

There was a knock on the door and Sergeant Dutton popped his head into the room.

'Excuse me, sir, you asked me to let you know how the interviews are going. Harper's involved the Scotts, the Perrys, and Gilbert Randall—'

'Get out,' Newton bellowed.

'Sir.' A shocked Dutton withdrew.

'So, Chief Inspector, you came to me and asked for a search warrant. I refused because I didn't think the circumstances justified that.'

Ashworth stared at Newton's superior expression and scooped up his car keys from the desk. 'I don't have to listen to this,' he said, walking towards the door.

But the superintendent barred his way. 'You grow on people, Ashworth,' he said quietly. 'I may have refused a search warrant, but I shall tell the inquiry that I cleared you to question Harper at his house. When you arrived with your team you thought you could hear a child crying, so you broke in. Any injuries Harper may have suffered were entirely due to his resisting arrest. In the circumstances, we might just get away with that.'

He opened the door and that tyrannical look was once more on his face when he turned back.

'But if any of you ever do anything like this again . . .'

THE END

ALSO BY BRIAN BATTISON

DETECTIVE JIM ASHWORTH SERIES
Book 1: TIED TO MURDER
Book 2: THE PRICE OF MURDER
Book 3: FLIRTING WITH MURDER
Book 4: MURDER IN THE COTTAGE
Book 5: MURDER IN THE LIBRARY
Book 6: THE TASTE OF MURDER
Book 7: THE MISSING GIRLS

Thank you for reading this book.

If you enjoyed it please leave feedback on Amazon or Goodreads, and if there is anything we missed or you have a question about, then please get in touch. We appreciate you choosing our book.

Founded in 2014 in Shoreditch, London, we at Joffe Books pride ourselves on our history of innovative publishing. We were thrilled to be shortlisted for Independent Publisher of the Year at the British Book Awards.

www.joffebooks.com

We're very grateful to eagle-eyed readers who take the time to contact us. Please send any errors you find to corrections@joffebooks.com. We'll get them fixed ASAP.

Printed in Great Britain
by Amazon

83439308R10161